Once Upon a Time

Marylyle Rogers

St. Martin's Paperbacks

ONCE UPON A TIME

Copyright © 1995 by Marylyle Rogers.

All rights reserved. No part of this book may be used or reproduced in any manner whatsoever without written permission except in the case of brief quotations embodied in critical articles or reviews. For information address St. Martin's Press, 175 Fifth Avenue, New York, N.Y. 10010.

ISBN: 0-312-95758-0

Printed in the United States of America

St. Martin's Paperbacks edition / April 1996

10 9 8 7 6 5 4 3 2 1

Chapter 1

~

Ireland, 1851

" '*T*is sorry you'll be if you provoke the elven-folk's dubious mercies by venturing into their fairy ring." Gentle words were accompanied by a bright twinkle in blue eyes which belied the speaker's advanced years. "Amn't I right, ladies?" As Daffy glanced expectantly about her circle of friends, sunshine amazingly bright for so early in spring drifted through dainty curtains to make her thick white hair seem a halo.

Amy paused in the parlor's doorway while a chorus of voices echoed agreement with Great-aunt Daffy's repeated warning. Smiling fondly, she nodded at her still seated companions, octogenarians all. Though barely more than a quarter their age, she felt like an indulgent mother humoring the fantasies of these elderly women gathered for a luncheon honoring her visit's final day.

Having changed into an older gown both more appropriate for the walk ahead and more comfortable, save for a too tight bodice, Amy was prepared to set off on a small journey to grant her beloved hostess's wish. She hesitated a moment longer, filled with the regret of knowing it would be a long time, if ever, before she again saw most amongst this delightful company. They were all dears, though each as "eccentric" as her great-aunt.

Amy turned to go, grimacing against the half-truth in that description of Great-aunt Daffy. She recognized what few others took the time to see—Daffy merely donned the guise of elderly eccentric to shield amazingly sharp wits from curious eyes. Knowing that, Amy questioned the seeming earnestness of repeated warnings always accompanied by a barely restrained grin.

Holding her packet of drawing supplies near, Amy slipped from the cozy stone house cradled amidst a glade of trees arrayed in their first green sprouts, harbingers of thick foliage to come. She made her way around to the cottage's back and passed through a well-kept garden where various herbs, crocuses and hyacinths were just breaking through rich, dark loam.

From the garden's back Amy began ascending a gentle hill. At its crest an ancient oak towered while a glorious band of flowers grew in a wide circle around the gnarled trunk. Each bloom seemed at its peak of fragrant beauty despite the earliness of the season. It was this, Amy decided, that might lead the gullible to believe these flowers to be cultivated by magic and truly a fairy ring. *But*, Amy reassured herself, *that foolish I am not.*

"Now, you mind, no' a soul in right senses would step into a fairy ring."

2

Amy mimicked an Irish brogue to softly repeat another elderly woman's twittered warning. She was fond of them all but amused that they apparently accepted as fact the superstitions she'd thought only naive children could believe.

It was fortunate, Amy told herself while stepping over the flowers, that she didn't share her luncheon companions' illusions. She moved across a carpet of grass to stand beside the oak's broad trunk. From there she took in an enchanting vision which confirmed her suspicion that this taboo position afforded not merely the only available shade but the best view of her subject.

Crowning the next green hill was the picturesque scene of a crumbling castle, romantic ruins half-covered by a curtain of ivy. From near the first day of her visit Amy had repeatedly promised to sketch it as a farewell gift for Great-aunt Daffy. And this was her last opportunity as tomorrow she must leave, reluctantly, for London and the dreaded opening of the Season.

London, the Season . . . and Orville. With the last of these three unpleasant thoughts in Amy's mind rose a vivid image of the portly, self-important man her parents had chosen as an appropriate husband for her, no matter that he was nearer their age than hers.

Lord Farley Danton, Viscount of Wyfirth, and Lady Cornelia (even in private thoughts Amy called her parents by the titles they so proudly bore) had seen the futures of three older children adequately settled and were anxious to have done with the same chore for her. Never mind that Amy might have ideas on that very personal subject herself. Least of all would they understand that, given the choice, she'd prefer to follow Great-aunt Daffy's initial path into honorable spinsterhood. Anything rather than become a subservient wife shackled to the pompous Orville. Truth be known, she'd rather forsake the Queen's church to enter a Catholic nunnery. Well . . . almost . . .

An invisible cloud of despair darkened Amy's dove gray eyes to charcoal. She was trapped! Trapped and no getting around it. Once back in London—no matter how hard she fought and fight she would—it would be impossible to avoid Orville. Oh, depressing thought!

Frustrated and annoyed by the inevitability of that bleak prospect, Amy abruptly sank to the ground. That action, so lacking in her usual grace, gave reason to be thankful for the hard ground's thick padding of grasses—the dead brown from the past season as well as the fresh blades of the new.

After two decades of training by Beattie, first as her young nanny and now lady's maid, Amy's conscience protested the loosing of stormy responses usually kept locked safely inside. She decorously spread pale rose skirts in an arc before adjusting the drawing pad across her lap. It was a feeble attempt to atone for the further example of her unfortunate and unfeminine temper. Unfortunate not only because Society expected its debutantes to be demure but because it threatened her goal for logic in all things.

The chill in gray eyes melted while gazing across a verdant valley dotted with sheep to the ruins of what must once have been a glorious castle. Amy fervently wished herself able to ignore the parental summons and linger in this peaceful countryside.

During her fortnight's stay she ought to have sought the advice of her favorite relative. After all, Great-aunt Daffy had maintained her single status until well into her middle years. And then, despite either the consternation roused amongst the family or the social scandal, she'd chosen her own spouse—an impoverished Irishman of low birth. More shocking still, Daffy had happily moved to her "vulgar" groom's humble home on this disdained isle. To further confound gossiping snoops, after being widowed Daffy had traveled widely and openly pursued a great many adventures.

In one corner of her mind, Amy guiltily ignored her own avowed wish for cool reasoning and fervently yearned for even a small measure of Daffy's blessed independence, a chance to experience even one of her escapades.

Admiration for Daffy's audaciousness put an impish smile on Amy's lips as she began sketching the castle's outline. While gracefully layering many short, soft lines, she wished Great-uncle Patrick hadn't died before her own birth. From what she'd learned of the good-humored man, Amy suspected that—unlike other family members—she would have approved. Amy was amused by the dismay her snobbish relatives suffered in knowing that the end result of Daffy's unconventional life was a wealth far outstripping their own.

Amy held her drawing at arm's length, glancing between it and the actual scene. Then settling the

Marylyle Rogers

pad again amidst bright skirts spread over grass
like a cheery flower, she adjusted several lines while
musing over the actions of Great-great grandfather
Smythers which had set the scene for family rivalry.
He had amassed a fortune by quietly investing
throughout the expanding British Empire. On his
death it had been equally divided amongst his off-
spring. All of his children, save Daphenia, were burdened with both growing families and overweening
pride demanding they be seen to maintain rich life-
styles. Thus forced by circumstances, they'd steadily
nibbled into their capital while Daffy, with little
reason to touch the principal of her fortune, had
grown only richer. For Daffy's relatives, including
Amy, the carefully hidden prospect of quiet poverty
loomed.

With rueful distaste Amy had watched her cous-
ins and, sadly, even her siblings court Daffy's good
graces in too obvious anxiety to benefit from her
will. Though she couldn't help but love her family,
Amy was shamed by their foolish desire to live an
idle life off the wealth of someone they privately
labeled "Daft Daffy." In Amy's opinion, it was
Great-aunt Daffy's "eccentric" habits, her unique
spirit that made her so special and a favorite rela-
tion. For Amy not even the prospect of severely
reduced circumstances—carefully concealed by
nervous parents—could drive her into so misusing
Daffy. That low she refused to stoop!

Realizing that dark thoughts threatened to undo
the light touch she sought in her drawings and mar
the finished sketch, Amy laid her pencils aside.
Alone on a hilltop it was safe to release the uncom-

6

fortably prim restraints taming dark hair. She threaded slim fingers through the heavy mass before leaning back against the dubious comfort of the oak's massive trunk. Calm. That's what she needed. Calm thoughts on pleasant subjects. Although the sun was riding low, Amy assured herself there was time enough to spare a few minutes for taking pleasure in the verdant peace of her surroundings.

Consciously relaxing, Amy purposefully turned her mind to the innocent faces of her nephews and nieces . . . children who might rationally accept the illogic of fairy rings and magical stories. At their age she, too, had reveled in make-believe dreams. Indeed, she still enjoyed sharing her own favorites with them.

A gentle breeze rustled through leaves above and carried the sweet fragrance of encircling flowers to Amy. As thick lashes drifted to her cheeks she slipped into dreams with the opening to all fairy tales floating through her mind: "Once upon a time . . ."

". . . And after the evil queen cast her dark spell, Snow White lay upon a flower shrouded bier until a handsome, golden prince knelt at her side. Across her lips he brushed the thrilling kiss of life . . ."

Against the sensation nudging her from a safe haven of dreams, Amy firmly squeezed her eyes tight even while slowly lifting fingertips to press against her own mouth. The dream had become too real. Amy could almost swear she'd actually been kissed. . . .

Although a conscience trained to modesty urged

outrage for the liberty taken, it was regret that filled Amy—regret and irritation for being forced from the misty world of fantasy and dropped from sweet slumber into rude wakefulness. Nibbling a full lower lip to squash foolish thoughts, she forced sleep-heavy lashes to lift.

"Beauty awakes."

"I'm not a beauty," Amy instinctively answered the deep voice, despite the jumbled rush of strange emotions assailing her. She was still dreaming. She must be! What else could it be when the stunning, golden-haired prince yet knelt at her side?

"You think to jest with me?" The kneeling man smiled wryly while at the same time visually tracing the delicate oval of her face from wide-spaced eyes down dainty nose to the dusky rose of a tempting mouth. "But I plainly behold a lovely maiden with hair like a midnight sky and a gaze filled with morning's gentle mists. Aye, 'tis a beauty I see."

The mere sound of this husky voice sent an unaccountable shiver through Amy. And yet while remarkable emerald eyes took her measure she studied the man speaking in the cadence of a distant past. Amy's first thought was that the devastating masculine beauty of his face and powerful form were too perfect for him to be anything but a fantasy hero. Yet it couldn't be true! Still, even what he wore seemed to support the unbelievable as fact. He was dressed in the styles of an equally ancient time with hose the shade of a forest covering muscular legs while golden threads were woven into the luminous fabric of the pale green tunic clinging to his broad shoulders.

Amy blinked rapidly, expecting—hoping or was it fearing—that the breathtakingly vivid vision would disappear. It didn't and her confusion deepened. She would swear herself wide-awake. And for proof there was a painful tug on dark strands caught in rough bark as she pulled away from the tree trunk to sit fully upright. But if this wasn't a dream, then for some nonsensical reason he was out here in the hinterlands dressed as if for an elaborate costume ball ... as a fairy-tale prince? Amy didn't realize she'd spoken the last few words aloud until he answered.

"Prince?" Though he feigned affront, amusement glittered in his eyes. "Nay, a prince I am not."

Amy fought against a much despised but all too common hot flood of embarrassment by eyeing him suspiciously while boldly demanding, "Then what are you? And where did you come from?"

"I am Comlan—" Grinning with what even the sheltered Amy recognized as a wicked sensuality, he made an elegant bow to the human damsel more courageous than most he'd met. "King of the Tuatha De Danann."

Inherent pride textured his deep voice but it was the potent smile accompanying this formal answer that threatened to halt the beat of Amy's heart with its near physical impact.

Slight frown puckering delicate brows, Amy struggled to restore composure and make sense of his claim. Tuatha De Danann? Surely here was proof that this truly was a dream. She'd learned enough from tales told by Great-aunt Daffy and her friends to know that Tuatha De Danann was the legendary name of folk inhabiting the Faerie Realm. And she was certain that the elderly ladies' talk was responsible for inspiring this dream. Yes, a dream—nice but definitely a dream.

"As for where I came from," Comlan added once a relieved smile curled the maid's lips, "my home lies there." He waved toward the next hill.

Amy's glance followed his motion to discover the ruins of her drawing replaced by a castle more splendid than any her admittedly active imagination could've conjured. Its towers soared heavenward and even during these daylight hours glowed with the white brilliance of moonlight.

"But I don't believe in the Faerie Realm . . . or its inhabitants," Amy boldly announced, as much to convince herself as him.

Comlan's laughter rumbled out from the hilltop to fill the valley between magical ring of flowers and luminous castle. Humans were a foolish lot who, in the main, were fearful and greedy. Was this dark maid an exception?

"Then how do you explain me?" With the mercurial mood shifts common to beings of his nature, Comlan's eyes abruptly snapped with quick temper. "Or this . . ." He waved his arm and a shimmering mist appeared to hover above lush grass for long moments before resolving into a powerful white stallion.

"You're a dream," Amy flatly stated, squinting against the amazing sight of a magnificent beast that looked as real as the man. And when the powerful figure swung up onto the horse's broad back, she told herself to remember that he was merely a fantasy.

From atop the white horse, Comlan grinned mockingly at the girl plainly struggling to sufficiently bolster her courage to meet him eye to eye. Her bravery was a rare and valued trait. And yet it was her claimed disbelief that piqued his attention as little had in a very long time. Apparently she didn't realize that if truly an unbeliever, she wouldn't be able to see him—not in this, his natural guise.

Amy took exception to his wry amusement, plainly at her expense. "Soon I'll wake up." She fervently hoped he couldn't hear the uncertainty behind her bold statement. "Then—poof—you'll be gone."

"Ah, but till that moment arrives, won't you come with me to my castle?" Comlan leaned down to gallantly extend his hand, offering the dark maid his aid in standing. "Come, enjoy the merry company of my subjects while we sing and dance to enchanting melodies."

Amy froze, suspiciously gazing at his incredible home. It was a daft suggestion and required a decision anything but logical. And for someone who'd claimed a determination to pursue the logical processes of scientific thinking, it was impossible.

"Come." Comlan's potent smile had rarely failed to win whatever he sought, and he was confident it would be enough to melt this human damsel's resistance. "There's a feast of savory delicacies and the finest ambrosia to drink."

For several seemingly endless minutes Amy silently studied this dangerously attractive fantasy hero obviously a figment of her imagination. To her chagrin he, too, remained motionless. His only visible response was the deepening glitter of amusement in the depths of emerald eyes and the open invitation in his waiting hand.

Possessing confidence more than equal to this human maid's visual assault, Comlan permitted his solemn companion to search beneath striking good looks until she recognized an aura of power far beyond his undeniable physical strength or noble position.

Cool logic fought a brave battle with the doubtless despicable wish to yield to the mesmerizing figure reaching for her. But then, Amy self-righteously told herself, this was her chance to experience what she'd so recently claimed to desire—a single page from the book of Daffy's daring adventures. And as a dream, what harm could it cause?

Refusing to admit even the faint possibility that this human maid might pose a threat to his style of living, Comlan's laughter again rolled over the hilltop like warm thunder.

Beneath his devastating smile Amy felt herself almost physically drawn toward him. Her last resistance crumbled. Yes, she would seize the opportunity to enjoy this remarkably real fantasy for as long as it lingered . . . and close her mind to an unsettling suspicion that he'd already cast over her his spell of fascination.

With a bright smile and daring sparkle in her eyes, Amy laid small fingertips across King Com-

Ian's large palm. Certain she'd awaken on the hilltop soon enough, safe but all alone, Amy closed her mind to the conscience screaming warnings about all manner of dire consequences. Gladly she threw long-ingrained caution to the wild winds of impetuosity.

Amy was swept off her feet to lie across the mist-formed horse, cradled by powerful arms. Their journey was remarkably brief, traveling as they did not by riding over the earth but by crossing the sky. It was an action impossible in the world of reality but a thrilling adventure to experience in a dream—and further proof that this truly was no more than an exceptionally vivid fantasy.

Once inside walls seemingly formed of translucent marble Amy was welcomed by an array of golden beings. Charmed by their glowing smiles and joyous laughter, she willfully closed her mind to rational thoughts and, surrendering to the dream, was soon caught up on their tide of good humor. Pipes, harps, timbrels and other instruments she had never seen before produced a chimera of music that carried listeners out on an endless sea. The enticing melody flowed from haunting to sprightly while Amy indulged in her magical escapade.

Amy denied herself only one delight. She remembered enough of Great-aunt Daffy's ardently repeated Faerie Realm lore to know that danger lay in partaking of either their food or their drink, no matter how appealing. Legend held that for a human to consume anything in this enchanted world meant never leaving. Though very nearly convinced this was merely a dream, Amy couldn't be absolutely certain. And while to be daring was one thing, to be foolishly reckless was quite another.

A tiny smile tugged at the corner of Amy's mouth. Happily there was no restriction to keep her from dancing. Thus when Comlan took her into his arms, she eagerly yielded to the strength sweeping her out to join other figures swirling across the floor. He tutored her through intricate steps in a succession of new and delightful dances. Once comfortable with the patterns, she foolishly glanced up.

Nothing in her previous experience had prepared Amy for the shock of closely meeting an intense green fire in the gaze moving over her like a caress, nor the physical impact when it lingered on the too tight bodice.

Comlan willingly met the dark beauty's stare, pleased to see the fascination darkening silvery eyes to charcoal while a faint blush bloomed, emphasizing her exquisite complexion. Never in his long life had he wasted time dreaming of any particular female's company, not when there were a willing number ever near. Thus, he easily dismissed a premonition that this unusual damsel might succeed in holding his interest where many others had failed.

Amy's thick lashes fluttered in a desperate attempt to block the mesmerizing lure in his burning eyes. This fantasy figure was too near, too real. She could feel his heat through the layers of cloth between them while bodies, once barely touching but now pressed tightly together, moved in perfect time. Losing her battle but unable to mourn the defeat, Amy felt a strange awareness wrap her in an exhilaration that carried her deeper into a private world of unfamiliar, thrilling intimacy.

Of a sudden Comlan released Amy. A much deplored but unstoppable tide of rose burned her cheeks more brightly, and she bit her lip against the unpleasant shock of their abrupt parting.

Comlan saw small white teeth nibbling a lower lip to berry brightness. His gaze softened to the hue of a gentle sea mist. Anxious to soothe the self-conscious damsel's unease, he murmured into a small ear the explanation for this separation no more welcome to him than her.

" 'Tis time for tales and songs."

Mortified for having betrayed a too obvious dismay, Amy's gaze dropped. She forced a tight smile and quick nod. However, suspecting herself a likely focus of ridicule, she peeked from beneath demurely lowered lashes and made a welcome discovery. The area around them was clearing, and other dancers were too busy moving toward the walls where seats softened by silken pillows waited to notice her discomfort.

Comlan insisted not only that Amy join him on the dais at one end of the chamber but also that she share his wide, well-padded, *golden* throne. Amy didn't know how to respond. Sharing a single seat, no matter how wide, suggested a closeness that would never be permitted in her world but . . . Uncertain about the customs of this place and unwilling to offend, Amy glanced surreptitiously around.

"Remember," Comlan whispered. "It's only a dream."

All too aware of the mockery behind the words, Amy's chin promptly tilted up. Even without her discovery that shared seats seemed a common practice here, pride would've driven Amy to perch primly beside the annoyingly amused king.

An expectant hush fell before a parade of performers rose one by one. Amy was alternately amused or touched by their well-told tales and lyrical poetry. And, sitting motionless, she surrendered to music of ethereal loveliness.

As Comlan's head rested against the high back of his gilded throne, light that had no identifiable source glowed on bright hair. He intently watched the captivating maiden as enthralled by the entertainments of his realm as he was by her. He ought to have known better. Any traffic with humans was unwise but . . .

The only inflexible rules in his Faerie Realm were those governing contact between it and the human world. That law he had to keep, and it was that law which decreed an invitation to visit his realm must be extended to all of her species who dared trespass on the hallowed ground inside the ring of flowers grown by fairy magic. He'd thought himself far too wily, too experienced for any mere human female to be a temptation to him.

Abruptly aware to her depths of the power in a steady emerald gaze, Amy stared twice as intently at the current performer. The singer's voice soared like liquid silver to fill the very air with a magic able to ease even Amy's tension. She clung to its comfort by focusing on the next performer, an aged man with a long white beard and booming voice.

This performer easily claimed and held everyone's attention with his retelling of an obviously beloved fable. Fast-paced and rollicking, it was the tale of one humorously failed hunt for the gold-horned unicorn. The tale spinner's skill was great. By the end of his adventure, Amy was so thoroughly swept away that when the magical beast eluded its hunters she gave a tiny squeal of delight.

"I see," Comlan murmured with pretended ruefulness. "You sympathize more with the prey than the hunter?"

Beneath Comlan's sardonic smile Amy's cheery, dimple-revealing grin disappeared.

"Your concern is laudable—but unnecessary." Comlan laughed lightly, but his gaze grew more intent. "The gold-horned unicorn can never be caught."

"Then why do you try?" The devastating man was too near and Amy could only hope, however uselessly, that he'd think the color burning her cheeks yet again was a reflection of her heated defense of the unicorn. "Or don't you? Is it only a tale?"

"Oh, no. We hunt," Comlan quickly assured her. "But for the joy of the chase—not its end."

Amy frowned. She'd never heard of such a thing. Still, she had to admit this attitude was a lot easier to understand than was the habit of men in Society who took down great numbers of birds or other animals solely for the thrill of the kill.

When the hot glitter in emerald eyes purposefully dropped to lips that parted on a gasp, Amy glanced quickly away. Anxious to focus her attention anywhere but on the one far too near, she stared toward the center of the vast hall. To her surprise she discovered that dancing had began anew among the others, all seemingly oblivious to the pair on the dais. Initially watching with the blind intent of ignoring the king at her side, eventually she began to see evidence of actions most unlike those practiced amongst members of London Society. A slight, bewildered frown appeared between her delicate brows. Here there were odd, mercurial changes of expression, moods that shifted as quickly as any chameleon changing color.

" 'Tis what I am and they are," Comlan flatly stated, acute senses recognizing the source of her confusion. "Predictability has no value here."

Comlan permitted himself to say no more. In truth, he shouldn't have shared even this much with a human. No member of humankind—whose life spans were so brief—was likely to understand the danger of joy-sapping boredom in things or deeds tediously expected for those who lived a great deal longer. Nothing of fairy nature should ever be revealed to a human. At least, not unless they willingly chose to remain in his realm.

An emerald gaze narrowed on Amy. Truly this dark maid with her solemn eyes was different from most of her kind.

And, as he'd already admitted, her courage in the face of the unexpected piqued his interest. Too bad she chose to believe this visit a dream. . . .

"Amy—" Comlan purred, tilting her dainty chin. She might be determined to view him as some insubstantial fantasy being, but he would give her a memory of something more physical.

Amy's lips formed a soundless "O" as powerful arms swept her up to lie across hard thighs. This was wicked, immodest. She should fight herself free. She should . . . but couldn't force herself to virtuously pull away before his very real lips descended to take possession of hers in a series of short, tormenting kisses that tempted with the promise of unknown delights.

When a tender mouth tasting of innocence welcomed his with unexpected fervor, Comlan accepted the dark beauty's willing gift even knowing he'd likely regret this sampling of a honey-sweet wine he could never drink in full measure.

This was a dream. Only an incredibly vivid dream. With that comforting thought Amy smothered the faint voice of her conscience, leaving her free to revel in the fantasy's pleasures.

Accepting the dark beauty's willing gift, Comlan took her mouth with a warm assault that quickly parted her lips. He deepened the kiss with blatant expertise, built it to a fever of hungry passion.

Amy sank headlong into a fiery whirlwind. Dazed by sparks of hot pleasure, her arms rose to loop about his strong neck as she twisted to press more fully against this source of heady excitement. Blood coursed through her veins like a river of fire, and the heavy pounding of her heart seemed to fill her throat until a strange sound whimpered out.

Comlan instantly lifted his head. Seeing Amy's wild blush, he tucked her face beneath his chin. He knew truths that this plainly confused maid refused to believe, and it would be a contemptible fiend's evil deed to take advantage of her lack of guile.

When her fantasy hero drew back this second time during a surely unreal encounter, the girl who took pride in never weeping felt a prickling of tears born from mingled frustration, anger and embarrassment.

Comlan's strong hand slowly stroked the dark hair flowing unhindered down a slender back. His gentling touch continued until well after tears had dried and she was again at peace.

Amy lay quiescent against a broad, powerful chest, drinking in a strength and masculinity she was never likely to experience again . . . certainly not once wed to Orville. Anxious to banish the image of an unwanted suitor, she peeked up at the hard lines of her unbearably attractive companion's face.

She had endured a wider array of emotions during the course of this dream than in the whole of her previous life, and now faced a singular revelation. Never before had she felt so comfortable nor so secure as she did this moment cradled in the circle of Comlan's embrace. With that pleasant confession spread as a soothing balm over her worries, she drifted into slumber's warm mists.

A ray of bright sunlight pierced thick foliage to disturb Amy's sleep. Slowly, reluctantly, she surfaced in what, by contrast to her dream, was a harsh reality.

Amy frowned. Although positive that sleep had overtaken her while leaning against the oak, she now lay comfortably across shaded grass a little distance from its base. And she could've sworn a great deal of time had passed while she slumbered, but the sun riding just above the horizon as her fantasy began seemed to have barely moved at all. Worried that her grip on the sane and sensible world had grown appallingly weak, Amy chose to accept this trick of the sun as proof her remarkably vivid memories were truly no more than a dream come and gone with the unpredictable haste of such sleep illusions.

However, despite her determined belief that this thought ought to be comforting, Amy was forced to acknowledge an empty ache of disappointment.

Rising fully intent on returning to the prosaic present, Amy attempted to push the whole subject into an unregretted past. She dusted bits of dried sod from a gown far more wrinkled than might reasonably be expected after a brief sojourn on the grass. The unwelcome confusion roused by that small incongruity deepened when Amy lifted her drawing pad. There, in addition to her own sketch of the ruins, was another drawing—a deft rendering of her fantasy castle. Had she drawn it in her sleep?

Its bold lines definitely were not her style but who else could have done it? She was alone, wasn't she? Amy peered into growing shadows, self-conscious about the need to make certain.

No one was there. Of course not!

After tucking the new drawing into the back of her pad and carefully aligning its edges to lie concealed, she started back down to her great-aunt Daffy's cosy cottage.

21

* * *

"Now, Amy-girl, what for gracious sake was it that kept you so long atop yon hill?" Rising from a settee shared with Patience, her only remaining luncheon guest, Daffy moved to meet her returning grand-niece at the parlor door. "Near to sendin' Mr. Meaghan to fetch you back down, I was."

An image of her great-aunt's equally aged gardener hobbling up the hill intent on obeying the command to *force* a young woman's return sent a grin over Amy's lips. It was quickly stifled . . . but not soon enough.

"You ought be shamed, you wicked thing. Shamed—" Though Daffy rightly rebuked Amy's amusement, a betraying sparkle lit her own eyes.

Wise enough to abandon an unworthy cause, Daffy simply took Amy's hand and pulled her into the parlor. She resumed her own position on the settee beside Patience, a friend who always made Daffy think of a small, bright-eyed bird ever flitting about. Then, once the girl settled in a straight-backed chair drawn near, Daffy gently restated the question for which she meant to have an answer.

"Now, me girl, how says you? What reason had you for stayin' so long away on our last afternoon?"

The older woman's penetrating gaze seemed to bore into Amy who blushed guiltily—a revealing contradiction to the blandness of her answer. "After finishing your drawing I was foolish enough to doze and didn't awaken until twilight was falling."

Daffy's lips clamped together against this failure of all her hopes, and despite her near certainty that

... She'd spent a sennight setting the scene and dropping the hints she'd been sure would prick the girl's curiosity. Apparently her actions had been delayed too long, and Amy's parents had already succeeded in crushing a naturally independent spirit beneath the weight of Society's expectations.

Under Great-aunt Daffy's sadly disappointed expression, Amy very nearly confessed the whole of her exciting dream, almost told about the fascinating king who was its hero. But to what good use?

In the next instant Amy wondered why her great-aunt was disappointed? What had she expected?

"Ah, 'tis a sorry fact tha' you must be careful these days." Fretted by the woeful expression so rare to Daffy's lips, the forgotten Patience broke a silence growing between her frowning friend and the young visitor. "For certain true there's danger skulkin' about in th' dark what with prowlers tryin' to break into th' home of a self-respectin' widow."

A gray gaze dark with concern skipped quickly from speaker to hostess. "Someone tried to break into your home, Great-aunt Daffy?"

With a sinking feeling, Amy remembered the elderly woman's distrust of banks and assuredly foolish insistence on keeping the whole sum of her substantial wealth hidden somewhere in this cottage or on its surrounding acres of wild land. Only Daffy knew where.

"Tsk, tsk." Daffy shook her head in mild disgust, irritated with her friend for raising the very subject she'd taken such pains to conceal.

"Faith be, Patience! Like a magpie you clap onto

every stray scrap of gossip to weave a nest out of the most innocent things—here nearer to a hornet's nest."

"But, Daffy," Patience immediately protested. "Some wicked creature did so try to pry open your shutters. I saw th' splintered wood meself!"

As the brogues of the two Irish women intensified with their heated exchange, Amy realized they'd entirely forgotten about her.

"Aye, and sure it be tha' I told you what 'twas all about," Daffy unequivocally stated. "I did, now didn't I?"

"Aye, so as you did," Patience instantly responded. "But you can't rightly think me such a fool as to believe it were no' but a fierce wind wha' done tha' awful deed?"

"Ladies—" Though concern for Daffy hadn't eased, Amy interceded before matters between the other two could worsen. "I would value your opinion on my work."

Remembering how often more respected voices had counseled her great-aunt on dangers courted by the tempting target she made for all manner of thieves and ruffians, Amy bit back a similar useless argument. She reluctantly contented herself by merely pulling her drawing of castle ruins from the folder on her lap.

Chagrined by the rare loss of her temper, Daffy accepted the extended sheet from Amy's hand with a penitent smile.

"I hope it suffices for your intent." Questioning gray eyes met the elderly woman's gaze.

"Ahh . . ." Daffy's prolonged sigh gave Amy more sincere praise than she felt her efforts had earned.

"I thank you with all of my heart," Daffy murmured to Amy, emotion thickening her voice. "Here is proof that the view is even lovelier than my fond memories can restore. But then it's been years since I was equal to the climb." She gave Amy a bright, loving smile. "I'll hang it on my bedroom wall so that it will be both the first and last thing I see each day."

More than touched, Amy leaned forward to hug the beloved woman—but carefully in deference to brittle bones.

Chapter 2

~

*A*my stood primly erect on the dance floor's edge gowned in pale green, a pastel shade acceptable for young women. The first gala ball of the new London Season had barely begun but already the less than sturdy fabric of her patience had started to fray. Its condition was further strained by the invisible yet very real weight of her mother's glaring disapproval. Amy determinedly averted gray eyes darkened by leashed irritation from her parents . . . and their companion.

Hundreds of candles provided a warm, flattering illumination to the whole of the Duchess of Melton's vast ballroom. Their light reflected from highly polished silver and sparkled over the cut edges of crystal vases holding the masses of roses scenting the air. The room was filled by festive women in luxurious gowns and men in equally elegant attire who either danced to music provided by a small band in the gallery above or mingled among the various tables and chairs carefully scattered about the edges. The sounds of soft laughter and social chatter added to the heady atmosphere of the upper class enjoying the company of its peers.

But while most guests were delighting in the festivities, Amy felt like a piece of less than prime meat offered to the highest—or *any*—bidder. This yearly Marriage Mart was disgusting but her mother's deep embarrassment over her youngest daughter's failure to snare a husband during the previous three Seasons was even more disheartening.

And why hadn't she? Why? Amy forced a smile but her eyes remained bleak. According to her mother it was because she'd forgotten that intelligence in a woman was án anathema to men. Forgotten? Hah! Amy was unlikely to ever forget repeated lectures on the need to play a featherbrained fool since any hint of quick wits was a flaw difficult to overcome in the competition to secure a wedding band.

With the cynicism of close exposure to the inner workings of Society, Amy knew what her mother feared most. In an endless pursuit for the approval of the small cadre of elite hostesses who ruled over Society a daughter unwed in her fourth Season was an awkward burden to carry. And even knowing her mother was only one among many anxiously seeking the acceptance of these social arbiters wasn't enough to make it easier.

Amy's eyes narrowed on a figure garbed in rich but matronly purple. When the woman stared back, she nodded at this member of the haughty few who, supported by Queen Victoria's implicit backing, sternly stood guard to ensure that rigid rules of conduct and high moral standards were upheld . . . and socially ostracized those who failed.

Annoyed by the simpering manners expected of unmarried women—in truth of *all* women—Amy fervently wished it were possible to escape. Warm memories of the peaceful Irish countryside beckoned only to be immediately chilled by a bleak truth. It would've been difficult under any circumstances to escape parents anxious to palm responsibility for a daughter near to being termed a hopeless old maid off on some hapless groom. But it was truly impossible now that they had a pigeon in sight. And never mind that Amy couldn't abide the man.

Amy peeked sidelong to where her parents were still listening to the self-important Orville Bennett. The man's muttonchop whiskers trembled with each blustering word but did nothing to compensate for a nearly bald head. The sight was nearly as unpleasant as her parents' willingness, nay, obvious desperation to pair Amy with him. And one that further tightened the knot of cold panic born in her with the first glimpse of her parents fawning over the short, stout man. Their ability to pretend sincere interest in all the windy Orville had to say made it even harder for Amy to hide her growing contempt for the man. Utterly lacking the tact to smoothly insert bald facts into social conversation, Orville too often brashly catalogued his familial bonds with great nobles of the past and bragged of his ancestors' valor. Only Society's discomfort with the grubby world of money forced him to temper his boasts of business successes.

Amy nearly glared at the colorful patterns of

dancers gracefully swirling over the marble floor. She'd never been comfortable during the Season's endless functions and this year would be worse. After this first in the trying round of events she'd be relentlessly thrust into Orville's company. The future was bleak. There would be balls, tea parties, soirees, formal afternoon "at homes," garden parties, dances, the occasional opera, and on and on and on. . . . Then what at the end—a desperately unwanted wedding? Likely so but she meant to fight every step of the way.

Amy's modestly gloved fingers tightened on a fashion-required fan. And at the bleak prospect of that vainglorious little man becoming a permanent part of her life, she nearly snapped the delicate ivory and silk accessory in two.

Couples caught up in the dance whirled past while Amy, anxious to fend off dark thoughts of an unpleasant future and control rising panic, forced herself to take slow, even breaths. She even let herself welcome this scene's reminder of what she'd spent days attempting to forget—similar but much brighter images from her incredibly vivid Irish dream. She'd shared that story only with Beatrice, trusted maid and longtime friend. And Beattie had convinced her that it truly had been a dream, only an unusually tangible dream.

". . . meet Lady Cornelia Danton, Viscountess of Wyfirth. . . ."

The overheard words cast a shadow across Amy's pleasant memories, but Amy valiantly fought the intrusion.

"*Amethyst*, the Duchess of Melton is speaking to you."

The poorly hidden irritation in her mother's voice jerked Amy's attention back to the present.

"My apologies, Your Grace." Amy contritely shifted her full attention to their evening's hostess, a faint blush tinting her smooth cheeks. "I have been enthralled by the beautiful effect you've created by joining this elegant company with the charming background of your gracious home."

Looking only slightly mollified by this praise, the tall and overbearing woman permitted a slight curve to bend her lips with a smile that failed to reach her eyes.

"Yes, well, I interrupted your group's little tête-à-tête to introduce a fresh and welcome arrival to London Society newly come from his Irish estates."

Amy's glance instinctively followed a wave of the duchess's hand. *It can't be!* Her mouth fell open. *It just can't be!*

Amy's unfeminine reaction brought a faint gasp of reproach from her mother even while their hostess continued.

"Comlan, Lord of Doncaully, meet the Honorable Amethyst Danton."

Feeling faint for the first time in her more than two decades, Amy unabashedly stared at the bright green eyes and golden hair of her fantasy king again come to life. Logic, Amy firmly told herself, logic. Yes, that was it. Cool, clear reasoning would see her through this challenge to rational thinking.

Introductions complete, Comlan spoke. "Delighted to meet you, Miss Danton." His gaze slowly moved from the top of dark hair parted down the center and looped back into delicate netting decorated with tiny silk flowers down to the dancing shoes peeking from beneath pale green skirts. He had wondered if his memory were playing tricks on him. But, no. The quiet beauty was here and her eyes truly were solemn gray—a shade unheard of in his realm.

Unwilling to trust her voice, Amy merely nodded with lips clamped tightly together. The given name and even the appearance of his handsome face were the same, but formal words suggested a first meeting which, despite her goal of calm rationality, further flustered Amy. It was an uncomfortable sensation and she didn't like it at all!

When the Irish lord next claimed her abruptly icy fingers to brush a gallant kiss over their tips, Amy was intensely aware of her parents' disapproval and Orville's glower. Comlan's mocking half-smile, hinting amusement over a secret shared, added to her confusion and badly weakened her sorry attempt to find firm footing on the wildly tilting deck of her emotions.

Stifling his contrary nature's instinct to laugh, Lord Comlan courteously extended an invitation to the uneasily frowning damsel. "Would you permit me to lead you in the waltz just forming?"

Before Amy could respond, he swept her out onto the floor. She nearly groaned. The twirling motion could only add to the chaos of her thoughts.

Yet, as the devastating man guided her into the dance's graceful steps, something in Amy's core recognized and yielded to his nearness, to the feel of his strong arms. Her sea-foam gown blended with the other shades floating gracefully around the room while, just as in her dream of the fairy palace, sweet music wrapped the two of them in a lovely, private realm. Knowing she shouldn't but unable to prevent it, Amy gazed upward. With so scant a distance separating them, the whole world faded into obscurity. She saw dangerous emerald fires in his eyes.

When a gray gaze initially darkened by suspicion went cloud-soft with wonder, Comlan once again found himself caught in this mortal woman's thrall. It was more disturbing than he'd willingly admit, proving him not so impervious to the snare at the heart of feminine wiles as he'd long believed. King of a realm where stability was despised while capricious whims and volatile fancies were prized, he'd enjoyed many pleasurable alliances with females amongst his own. But never during the vast length of his days had any succeeded in casting the spell which he feared the mortal Amethyst Danton had all but unknowingly begun to spin the moment he'd discovered her slumbering in the midst of his sister's fairy ring.

Logic, Amy reminded herself again. Logic. Struggling to find the way through a dreamy haze, she forced herself to focus on rational facts. Rational? Hadn't her dream's hero said he and his were by nature unpredictable? If that was so, then this polite gentleman couldn't possibly be him.

Amy bit her lower lip. By thinking of her dream in terms of reality she'd just nullified the whole argument. "Logic ... Sanity ..." She ardently repeated the goal, so anxious to force it on recalcitrant thoughts that she failed to realize she'd murmured the words aloud.

"Traits you admire?" Comlan quietly asked, and then, when the dark beauty in his arms took a misstep, steadied her through the next slow spin.

"And scientific inquiry." Amy nodded, desperately grasping at what seemed a solid anchor to hold her steady in a whirling world utterly lacking such desirable qualities. "It's the future and solid facts based on provable realities are the path to reach that promising day."

Miss Amy Danton's words washed over Comlan like ice water. Their differences, it seemed, went even deeper than the surface ones separating their worlds. Their basic natures were at odds. And yet, he had to fight a near overwhelming compulsion to take her tempting lips and claim again the indescribably sweet ambrosia of her kiss.

Gazing helplessly up, Amy felt as if the mesmerizing lights glittering in emerald eyes were encasing her in a delicate web of dangerous enthrallment which like dandelion fluff effortlessly floated up into an irrational plane of emotions. So thoroughly was Amy lost to her surroundings that when both the music and her partner stopped, she was caught unprepared. The unpleasant shock was a gale that dashed her against harsh reality, and she pulled from the Irishman's hold with a poor demonstration of her usual grace.

His lovely partner's abrupt action restored a sardonic curl to Comlan's lips. Clearly their lengthy and very public visual bond had shaken her. Unfortunately there was little he could do to ease her distress—at least not here and not now. The silver resentment flashing in Amy's eyes deepened his amusement and at the same time inspired sharp regret for all the restrictions placed upon any from his realm venturing into the mortal world.

Amy took exception to the golden man's mocking expression. It seemed a disheartening confirmation that by acting like some lovelorn adolescent she'd made a silly goose of herself. Promptly turning her back on Lord Comlan, she stalked proudly away and paused only on seeing the waiting embodiment of an unwelcome future in the pompous man hovering at the dance floor's edge.

The approaching woman's smile pleased Orville. It held more welcome than Amy had ever shown him before and deepened his confidence in the likely success of the plan to circumvent a foolish foe. And if in the process he got even richer, then so much the better.

As the first strains of a new tune began, Orville stepped forward to meet Amy. "Since the Irish intruder prevented me from claiming the last, surely this waltz is mine."

Thoughts preoccupied by that intruder, Amy permitted the long-despised Orville to escort her back into the dancers midst. She immediately regretted it as a mistake—but too late. Granting even so minor a request was bound to increase the difficulty in refusing more later.

Encouraged by Amethyst's uncharacteristic yielding, Orville led her into the waltz. Having had difficulty mastering the steps, pride for that hard-learned ability partially masked his self-satisfied smirk and prevented him from noticing Amy's faint scowl.

"Doncaully, did the duchess say?" Orville recognized the prudence in an immediate start on discrediting Amy's previous partner. "Never heard of the place, myself. Nor him." Warming to the subject with a sudden inkling of how much a threat the handsome stranger could become, he added, "Egad, who's ever heard of this *Irishman* before?"

Disgust burned in Orville's contemptuous words and Amy felt it radiating out from him. He was a stiff, graceless dancer at the best of times, but now annoyance so intensified his lacks that Amy had to take care in moving her feet swiftly enough to prevent him from tromping on tender toes.

"I'll wager the man is some common lout thinking to work his sort's trickery over us all." Orville glared blindly over the top of his partner's dark hair. "And to what purpose? Not beneficial, not beneficial at all."

The obvious bigotry behind Orville's emphasis on Comlan's Irish heritage made it difficult for Amy to hide her disdain from the man she'd no doubt had only just begun a lengthy diatribe against his target's "sort."

"In truth, we must guard against this barbaric Irishman's mere presence dragging us down into his vulgar mire." Orville was encouraged when Amy's bright smile flashed in response.

Knowing Orville would be certain to misinterpret it as support for his overbearing opinion, Amy quickly stifled her smile. In reality her mirth was inspired by the possibility—though a remote and unlikely fantasy—that the one Orville declared a barbarian might actually be the king of a far richer realm than any Orville was ever likely to see. Absently protecting herself from the bungling moves of an increasingly irate partner and anxious to block the sound of his sour words, Amy turned her attention to their fellow dancers.

Amy focused on the first familiar figure to come into view. Garnet, her only brother, swirled his petite wife around the floor with all the grace Orville lacked. As they passed near, she briefly met her sister-in-law's eyes and caught a glimpse of warm sympathy. Frivolous but loyal, Louvisa had been Amy's best friend since childhood. And Lovey was the only one, besides the faithful Beattie, who knew precisely how Amy really felt about Orville.

"And," Orville pompously announced while leading his dance partner with the unreliable assurance of insufficient experience, "I mean to see that an investigation be done into this Lord of Doncaully's true background."

Harsh words exposed a meanness of spirit that snapped Amy's attention back to Orville.

"If it proves he's as coarse as I've no doubt he is, I'll see his chicanery revealed to all the good people of *our* class!"

Orville's malicious declaration struck Amy with an unaccountably deep fear that he might succeed in destroying the Irish newcomer. She couldn't let that happen! Startled by the fire in her silent vow, Amy rushed to convince herself that she meant to hamper Orville's sorry goal merely for the sake of

causing as much damage to his plans as his courtship threatened to wreak on her life.

But how? Amy's depressingly rational mind
refused to be satisfied with an idle intention to act.
Their stiff dance continued and Orville's harangue
went on and on. Amy heard only the steady whine
of his droning voice while mentally casting about
for some method to upset his aim. The next moment
she was annoyed with herself for not having
instantly known the answer: A simple warning to
Lord Comlan of Doncaully about Orville's plan
would assuredly suffice.

Amy frowned. Simple, yes. But not easily done.
She was an unmarried woman. And the complica-
tions inherent in any unmarried woman boldly pur-
suing private words with a clearly eligible bachelor,
a stranger at that, were many and daunting. Even
to dance with the same man more than twice was
to risk Society's censure. To seek time alone with
this handsome newcomer would be to tempt ruin—
the very thing her parents most assiduously
guarded against.

But, Amy brightened, Lord Comlan might ask her
to dance a second time. . . . She regretfully dismissed
the viability of that possibility, although unable to
smother an irrepressible spark of hope that he
might. Beyond the fact that his nearness seemed to
wipe sane thought from her head, this crowded floor
was hardly the place to bluntly introduce any serious subject.

Amy's gray eyes searched the room and found
an even more troublesome barrier. The sight of the
Irish lord's golden head tilted toward another nearly

as bright seemed proof that he had become yet another devotee among the Reigning Beauty's crowded court of admirers. Amy sternly told herself she didn't care that, under fair-haired Isobel's sway, he was unlikely to waste another glance in the direction of a dark—if not downright dowdy—near spinster, and far less apt to spare her a moment in his company.

But there must be *some way* to manage a few confidential words. Never mind Society's long list of "Don'ts," with cool logic and calm reasoning she would find a strategy to accomplish her goal.

"Did you warn the dark colleen?" demanded the short, wiry man who met the leader returning from a fancy ball at the door of plush lodgings leased for the Season in an affluent area of the City. "Kin we hie ourselves back to where we rightly belong?"

Light spilled through the open portal, laying a bright shape down shallow entry steps and glowing over golden hair ruefully shaken. While stepping inside, Comlan tamed the grin inspired by this irascible companion's refusal to adjust his pattern of speech to match that of those inhabiting their current surroundings. Dooley was a human who, after living more than half his allotted mortal years, had wandered into the Faerie Realm one autumnal eve during the few hours of the annual Samhain festivities when the border between their worlds was fluid. Then, having no family ties to hold him back, Dooley had chosen to remain within King Comlan's bright and cheerful domain.

"Despite all the centuries of mortal time you've

spent in my realm," Comlan softly chided, smile turning wry, "you seem to contemplate violating its rules with remarkable ease."

"Ach, now. Don't you be raggin' on me about them rules again." Having moved very little as the much taller man brushed past, an unrepentant Dooley tilted back a head of carroty hair whose brightness was barely dulled by its liberal sprinkling of gray. He sent his master a baleful glare—albeit one they both knew held only the empty menace of a toothless dragon. "Seems as you forget how rightly I know the glee with which your kind flouts any sech bonds."

"In our own sphere, mayhap." The quietness of Comlan's words lent more impact to the gentle warning that followed. "But never the laws governing contact with the human world."

Comlan would gladly have left humans to handle their own sorry affairs but for the promise given a human friend. And, although those knowing the capricious nature of fairykind might have expected otherwise, the king of the Tuatha De Danann kept his oaths. Indeed, it was precisely because the deed was unexpected that he held his word so dear.

"So what rule is it that I've shattered?" Dooley defensively demanded, bushy brows furrowed.

"'Tis not what *you* have broken but rather the manner of feats you would have *me* perform to hasten our return."

The seemingly older man shifted uncomfortably from foot to foot but held still a tongue he realized ought to have been kept from blathering in the first instance.

"No." Comlan's fondness for Dooley led him to take pity on the man and answer the initial question while motioning him into the smaller of two drawing rooms. "I haven't warned the 'dark colleen,' as you called her."

Comlan had been surprised when Amy firmly claimed herself to be no beauty during their first meeting within his sister's fairy ring, but after a few hours amidst London's Society he'd come to understand why. The value others in her sphere placed on fair coloring and fragile form could only leave the dark and softly curved Amy uncertain of her own attractions. However, he saw her from a completely different point of view. Golden-haired beauties, willow slender and of surpassing loveliness abounded in his realm. For him Amy's ebony hair, solemn gray eyes and alluring curves held a far more powerful appeal.

The sound of Dooley clearing his throat jerked Comlan from an absent reverie utterly foreign to him. Somehow the human maid had crept into his mind as no female of any making had ever before during his lengthy existence.

Aware of his companion's curiosity, Comlan gave a half-smile full of self-derision. He settled into a comfortably overstuffed chair and motioning Dooley to another while picking up where he'd left off.

"The world Amethyst lives in is very different from my realm or even the one in which you were born."

Dooley's eyes skeptically narrowed.

"Truly." Comlan's smile deepened. "They are

Marylyle Rogers

governed by a rigid code of conduct with rules decreed for everything ... even how to properly hold your hands while eating with any of a wide array of different utensils, one for each of many courses—"

Horrified by the prospect of a place burdened with such tight restraints, Dooley interrupted. "But what's that to do with our purpose here?"

"Short of breaking the few rules I *must* uphold by using my powers to unmask lurking dangers and expose a vile plot, there's only one way to rid our old and valued friend of threatening schemes."

Comlan allowed his eyes to briefly close while a remembered scene of sadness flitted through his thoughts—merry Patrick dying at the end of a long, content life. With the mercurial shift in moods natural to him, a further memory sent a flashing grin across his handsome face. That old rogue had weakly offered a final bargain in exchange for Comlan's promise to watch over his "Darlin' Daffy."

"What way?" Never patient, Dooley again demanded an answer.

"We must become a part of the dark maid's world." Well aware of how unwelcome this prospect would be to Dooley, Comlan's grin deepened. "Once that's done I'll try to lead her down a necessary path of discovery."

Although barred from intervening in human affairs unless asked by one of their number, Patrick hadn't needed to strike a bargain to win Comlan's protection for his wife. Daffy was a delightfully unique woman. Comlan enjoyed her company and had gladly agreed to guard her against danger of

42

any making. And during all the mortal years since Patrick's passing, it had been a simple enough chore until . . .

"And then can we be shut of this place?" Dooley asked, not bothering to hide his fervent wish for that moment to arrive as soon as possible.

Comlan slowly nodded but, despite a lingering ache of loss for the sister who'd chosen to shed fairy powers and share a brief human lifetime with her love, other vivid memories weakened his anticipation to share Dooley's goal: The unforgettable feeling of Amy's soft body melting against him as they gracefully spun through a waltz, the gentle touch of beguiling dove gray eyes, the sweet fragrance of her dusky cloud of silken curls. . . . Much as he wished it were not true, these things lingered in his mind and left him more reluctant to leave the mortal world than he'd ever thought possible.

Chapter 3

~

"*What's* put you into such a pet this morning?" Again the softly rounded speaker, Beatrice by name but fondly dubbed Beattie by her charge, smoothed a silver-backed brush through the thick dark hair of a younger woman seated on the backless chair facing her delicate, white dressing table.

"I haven't recovered from the strain of last night," Amy responded, absently staring into a large oval mirror framed by elegant scrollwork and fastened to the table's back.

"Hah! Dancing the night away all togged out in fine silks is a strain?" Falling into their common pattern of teasing give-and-take, Beattie's pleasant face adopted a feigned expression of reproach. "I daresay next you'll be telling me what a troubled life you lead. Well, don't you think it."

Meeting the reflected gaze of her lifelong ally beneath a starched cap riding atop neatly coiled brown hair, Amy's frowning lips curled upward in a reluctant smile. Her maid had a positive loathing for self-pity in any form and never permitted Amy to stay discouraged for long.

While carefully rolling Amy's hair into a tidy snood at her nape Beatrice chided, "I've known you almost since the day you were born and far too well to fall for such humbug. So what is it that's brought on these blue-devils, hmm? Don't tell me you've allowed the buffoonish Mr. Orville Bennett to disturb you. . . ." Beattie paused and moved far enough to the side to meet Amy's eyes directly. "You haven't, have you? Not after we agreed that nary a single one of his actions or opinions are worthy of your concern."

"I, ah . . ." Amy stopped before truly starting, gaze dropping to tightly interlaced fingers folded in her lap. Having shared every secret with Beattie since toddlerhood, Amy struggled for feasible words to explain both a scene she didn't completely understand herself and her resolve to foil Orville's threat no matter what rules might have to be broken.

Sensing Amy's confusion, the last sparks of humor faded from Beatrice's eyes. She moved back to stand behind the one who was once charge, now mistress, and always friend. Hands settling on the slender shoulders below, she silently waited for the young woman to continue.

"The answer is no." Amy looked up and promptly muddied her bold statement by adding, "But yes, too."

Beattie said nothing yet the disgusted expression

Amy could see in the mirror made her response quite clear.

"Beattie, I swear it's true." Amy hurried to defend her claim's contradictory messages with a rational explanation. "I do find Orville's company more than trying but that's only a minor irritation compared to . . ."

When Amy paused again, a rarely impatient Beatrice prodded her onward. "Then, my girl, what is it that has you so upset?"

Knowing her practical maid would find it difficult to believe the answer, Amy took a deep breath and hoped for the best. "Do you remember the dream I told you about after my return from Ireland?"

"Tch." Beatrice was annoyed by this abrupt—and foolish—shift in subject. "A bit of twaddle, if I don't mistake, about a handsome king and a fairy castle . . . or some other such fanciful nonsense."

Amy had expected Beattie's skepticism but still it irritated her. "Wasn't it me who called the dream nonsense in the first place?"

Beatrice slowly nodded, a slight frown wrinkling her forehead. This talk of fairy tales when added to the heat of Amy's quarrelsome responses left her to uncomfortably wonder if this woman who'd grown from a beloved child were unaccountably reverting to immature ways. It was a horrible prospect for someone as sharp-witted as her little lambie!

Twisting around on her chair, Amy faced the

woman taking several steps to the rear and flatly stated, "I met him again last night."

"Met who? Your fantasy king?" Disbelief lent a hollow echo to Beattie's words.

"The Duchess of Melton introduced all of her guests to Comlan, the Lord of Doncaully. But it was *him*."

"Child, you're delirious." Beatrice studied her charge with growing concern. Never in all her born days would she have thought her sweet Amethyst a candidate for Bedlam, but now . . .

"Ask either of my parents," Amy stubbornly insisted. Though Beattie was officially her maid, she'd entered the Danton household as nanny. And as such Beattie had had an important hand in Amy's upbringing. Being fonder of this woman part foster-mother, part friend than almost anyone else in her life made winning Beattie's understanding all the more important. "They'll tell you about the man, the Irish lord we met."

"Man." Beatrice latched onto the word. "A 'man' I don't doubt you met, but a fantasy king . . ." She firmly shook her head.

"But it's true, I tell you," Amy earnestly argued. "The figure in my dream was a golden-haired Comlan with emerald green eyes—just like the one I danced with last evening."

"Come, lambkin," Beatrice urged, voice sinking into the dulcet tones employed in managing a willful child such as Amy had once been—and feared had become again. "Return to your bed. Lie down." Taking the young woman's hand, Beattie gently tugged in an effort to compel obedience. "I'll see that the doctor is summoned. He'll have some nice potion to ease you through this fever."

"You may just as well dose me with laudanum yourself," Amy immediately argued. Eyes flashing, she stubbornly added, "And I don't have a fever."

"Now, lambkin—"

"Don't 'lambkin' me." Amy cut Beattie off, remembering just how long her companion had used that term either to calm an obtuse little girl or comfort wounded feelings. And clearly it was in the former role Beattie spoke now. "It's plain you think that if I'm not ill, then I must have gone mad. I swear that neither is true."

"Of course, lambkin, of course." Beattie's soothing tone perversely sent a warm flash of amusement through Amy.

"Hush, you old fraud." Grinning, Amy stood up and turned her back to Beattie while pointing to a line of still unfastened buttons. "Help me finish dressing or I'll be even later for breakfast and no doubt my parents are already annoyed with me."

Clearly, Amy silently admitted, this wasn't the time to mention her willingness to risk social ruin in order to frustrate pompous Orville's plan. No, not this one morning out of every week when her mother expected the entire family to meet at the breakfast table—punctually.

Beatrice complied though again shaking her head and clicking her tongue in mock disgust.

* * *

The atmosphere surrounding those gathered at the elegant breakfast table of One Ealsingham Court was remarkably stilted for a closely related group. Each having their own secrets and their own objectives—often at cross-purposes with those of the others—a father, mother, son and daughter-in-law uncomfortably waited for one last family member to fill an empty chair.

A dignified Lord Farley sat at the head of the white damask covered table laid with delicate china and gleaming silver, very much the Viscount Wyfirth, but it was his wife who presided from the other end with all the inbred assurance of a spotless pedigree. Lady Cornelia never forgot that her father had been the grandson of a duke; neither did she allow others to forget it. And, of course, no one dared mention that her father had been the youngest of the youngest in a sizeable second generation and reduced to merely serving as the rector of a small village church.

Few knew that under an assiduously preserved shell of pride, Lady Cornelia still privately shivered at the image of what humble circumstances she might have found herself in had she not snared as mate the heir to the local manor. That bleak, too well remembered prospect further reinforced her intention to ensure that her children contract advantageous marital alliances. It was a task almost complete, a task that—pray God—would be finished with Amethyst's marriage at the end of this Season.

When the door from the central hall opened, Lady Cornelia looked up to find the subject of her thoughts entering the informal dining room. As Amethyst settled into a straight-backed chair, Lady Cornelia daintily rang a small crystal bell summoning their maid, Maddy, to bring her tardy daughter fresh tea.

"I truly am sorry to be late, Mother," Amy solemnly assured the older woman while a maid with the beauty required to serve in the front of the house poured amber liquid into a nearly translucent teacup. Anxious to ease a lingering tension, Amy searched for words to fill the awkward silence and fell back on the reserve of small talk every debutante was trained to master. "Your new dress is most becoming. You were right to insist Madame Bertrille use that shade of blue. It suits you perfectly."

A tight smile was Lady Cornelia's response to both the apology and compliment. She questioned the sincerity of Amethyst's regrets—little more than a perfunctory expression and lacking any sort of excuse. As for her morning gown, Lady Cornelia knew perfectly well how flattering this latest style was for her and the appropriateness of its deeper tone for a matron. She took pride in carefully observing all the niceties of Society, intent on impressing the small circle of great hostesses reigning at its peak with hope of one day being accepted as a member of that lofty few. To achieve her goal it was important that her children be seen as shining examples of the finest amongst their class, and she would fight to prevent the tarnishing of that glowing image.

Amy was relieved when Louvisa responded to her wordless plea by shrugging aside the informal dining room's unsettling gloom to cheerfully inquire, "What did you think of Mr. Stanville's shocking actions?"

Grateful for the rescue but having no vague idea what misdeed Lovey meant, Amy smiled and murmured a noncommittal answer.

Lovey's dimples peeked when, despite Lady Cornelia's forbidding frown, she conspiratorially whispered, "I think he had best intend to make a match with the naive Miss DeAmbrough after leading her onto the dance floor *four* times!"

Silent laughter warmed the gray of Amy's eyes as her amiable friend dove deeper into a humorous review of all the previous evening's details. It proved once again that Lovey was a human sponge able to soak up an amazing volume of gossip in a few brief hours. After repeating the Season's first ripple of scandal, Lovey continued with frivolous talk of who'd worn what and talked with whom. Amy's smile widened into a grin while like a merry brook, Lovey effortlessly babbled on and on unconcerned by her table companions lack of participation until . . .

"And didn't Isobel make a perfect cake of herself, fawning all over the Irish lord?" Louvisa blithely allowed idle chatter to flow into a new subject, oblivious to either the frowns earned from two men or her mother-in-law's positive glare. "I thought she might do you some harm, Amy, after he danced with you but no one else."

Despite the others' heavy disapproval, the giggling Lovey's words startled Amy into asking, "Only me?"

"Only you—" Lovey instantly confirmed, setting fair curls to bouncing with an emphatic nod.

That thrilling fact seemed to contain some magic spell for Amy felt as if she'd suddenly been transported back to the ballroom dance floor and into the devastating Irishman's arms. Flustered to discover that even the memory of him could shake her heart and steal her breath, Amy closed her eyes tightly hoping to block unsettling sensations only to find that action increased their potency. Struggling to restore calm, she concentrated on the waiting hard-boiled egg while Lovey's bright chatter continued.

"Only you," Lovey repeated. "Although it's not as if Isobel permitted Lord Comlan to escape her clutches for a single moment after your waltz ended."

Lady Cornelia had heard enough of foolish prattle. Particularly as Louvisa's words clearly had the unfortunate effect of reminding Amethyst of an unsuitable stranger when her attention should be focused to better purpose on a more appropriate potential groom.

"I was pleased to see you dancing so gracefully with Orville, Amethyst." Lady Cornelia adroitly shifted the conversation to this infinitely preferable subject. "He seemed most animated in your company . . . a good sign, don't you think?"

Reluctantly glancing up from the egg carefully perched on its cup in the center of her plate, Amy met her mother's direct gaze. She couldn't possibly mention the threatened injuries to her toes avoided only with great care. Nor would she confess the disgusting gist of Orville's animated words to this woman who would no doubt welcome them, even work to see him succeed. Instead, Amy frustrated her mother by merely nodding while returning her attention to the cracking of an egg.

"Garnet ..." Lady Cornelia's chill gaze moved on to her only son. "Pray tell me you have finished your ... collaboration with the *Lancet*."

Amy surreptitiously watched the sunlight falling through one of this east-facing room's long windows ripple over dark hair as Garnet wryly dipped his head toward his inquisitor. She shared her favorite—not to mention only—brother's amusement over their mother's unwillingness to sully her tongue with the word *work*.

"The tests are complete but I've still a substantial number of reports to write." Garnet's answer was prompt and concise but hardly forthcoming.

"So you really have found more instances of serious tampering with our country's foodstuffs and our health?" As Lord Farley spoke for the first time, keen interest burned in his eyes.

Amy, too, was intrigued by the issue although men, her brother and father included, tended to believe such matters outside a woman's interest and far beyond her ability to understand. But then it was the discounting of feminine presence that months before had allowed Amy to intently listen while her father told his son how, three decades earlier, he'd read Dr. Accun's treatise, *Adulterations of Food and Culinary Poisons*, and been appalled. No doubt that report was responsible for the older man's fascination with Garnet's current role (by social necessity behind the scenes) in further exposing these scandalous wrongs.

"Oh, yes, indeed." Garnet was plainly gratified that his own enthusiasm for the task roused the interest of at least one parent. "In many instances such falsifications act like a slow poison while in a few others they bring the threat of quick death."

Amy smiled. Garnet's fondness for her and longstanding interest in the sciences had prompted him to lead his youngest sister down its path of exciting discoveries. She was as tantalized by the promise of new discoveries as he and as anxious to learn more. However, as a woman—a *wellborn* woman—she was unlikely to have any such opportunity . . . a fact increasing her pleasure in Garnet's unswerving pursuit of scientific knowledge.

While Garnet had been pleased and a little flattered by his former tutor's request for assistance in a massive task, Amy had been thrilled for him. Under the direction of two medical doctors appointed by Thomas Wakely, editor of the medical journal, *Lancet*, her brother and other scientists had begun testing all manner of foodstuffs from around the country. She knew their results were consistently published in that erudite journal read by only the learned few—and certainly no copy had ever appeared in a Wyfirth home. But then recently the magazine *Punch* had taken up the cause, and with its biting wit exposed such wrongs to the masses—even to overprotected Society ladies.

"Milk is routinely whitened with chalk to hide how heavily it's been diluted with water." Galled by these deceptions, Garnet's gray eyes glowed. "We found alum used for whiteness in every loaf of bread we tested from bakeries all over London. And often boiled potatoes were added to increase their weight."

During a pause thick with Garnet's disgust for these actions, Lord Farley met his son's serious gaze in silent accord. Lips firmly pressed together, he nodded encouragement for the younger man to continue.

"All too many sweets are brightly colored by salts of copper and lead—deadly poisons." With the fervor of a revivalist minister, Garnet listed additional wrongs. "Chocolate is enriched with brick dust. And often grocers sell teas containing only a small amount of real tea mixed with roasted leaves of sloe, ash or elder and a dash of verdigris for the right color. Much the same happens with what they call British Coffee which is merely ground beans, peas, grains of sand and—"

"That is quite enough!" Again Lady Cornelia's sharp voice cut across an animated table conversation. Here in Garnet's words lay the second peril endangering her efforts to elevate their family into Britain's highest social level.

"Coarse work for wages is never a proper subject

for people of our class." She paused long enough to be certain her penetrating glare had truly pinned Garnet. "But far less acceptable are the unpleasant details in which you seem to revel. It is improper of you to subject three ladies to this talk of the fraud wickedly perpetrated against all good folk. But it's most unsavory to have this subject discussed while we breakfast!"

"I'm sorry, Mother," Garnet dutifully apologized.

The remorseful words left Amy struggling to restrain a wicked imp urging her to ask for which meal their mother would find the subject more acceptable.

An uncomfortable silence returned, and several unnaturally long minutes passed while the only sounds to be heard were the ting of silver utensils lightly brushing china and crystal.

Lady Cornelia knew she was the cause of renewed strain but refused to repent. Money had tempted Garnet into selling his time and conducting tests. That fact reinforced her firm belief that money was too sordid to bear thinking about let alone lowering oneself to seek. No, it was property which made people who they were and placed them in a privileged position. Clearly it was her husband's lands and her own heritage that placed their family on a higher plane than the common rabble. And that was the all-important fact their son and heir must *not* be allowed to forget.

"Aye, well, at least you had some good news to report, as well, heh?" Lord Farley made a futile attempt to smooth over the awkward lapse in conversation. "Orville tells us you've given his farms a clean report."

Garnet nodded but his already solemn face went cold.

Lovey joined her father-in-law's crusade by leaning nearer to her handsome husband and enthusing, "And your work will see us into our very own home."

"Soon." Smiling into his wife's pretty face, Garnet's tension eased. "Very soon we'll begin looking for a worthy house." Although flighty and an unrepentant coquette, Lovey was the ray of sunshine lighting the long, dull gray parade of his days. And to give her the home she wanted, Garnet would willingly do almost anything.

"I still cannot understand why you, as Wyfirth heir, are so intent on living anywhere but in the Wyfirth town house." It was an objection Lady Cornelia had made often before and yet never hesitated to restate.

Having given their reasons nearly as many times, Garnet and Louvisa merely exchanged a glance of loving amusement.

Amy understood Lovey's wish to escape her in-laws' control and move into a house decorated to her tastes, managed by her own rules. And though Amy loved her parents, despite their foibles, she wished the same could be an option for her without having to pay the price of accepting Orville as mate.

No one risked saying more than a few mundane words through the blessedly short remainder of the meal. At its close, Lord Farley left for the House of Lords while Garnet mumbled something about returning to his lab and tackling unfinished reports. The three women retreated to the back parlor to answer invitations and write the many letters expected of wellborn females.

Chapter 4

~

"*B*ut surely she's more likely to be pleased with ribbons she selects herself?" Beattie hustled to keep pace with her lambie, striving again to convince the girl that this unwelcome task should rightly be left to her sister-in-law.

"Lovey will need them tonight but can't go out for them today." The plume on Amy's bonnet fluttered as she led the way past shops lining London's most fashionable shopping district. "She promised her afternoon to aid in Lady Ophelia's charity work."

"They why, pray tell, didn't you take her place in toiling for charity—freeing Lovey to collect her own ribbons?" Beattie was less than pleased by the morning's duty. "After all, Lovey thrives on traipsing through shops, pawing through mounds of choices to find just exactly what she wants . . . the very thing you least enjoy."

"Ah . . ." Amy sent her maid a grin. "But then I'm not striving to impress Lady Ophelia. Lovey is."

"Tch, tch." Disapproval compressed Beattie's lips.

Before Amy could respond the subdued atmosphere of the refined shopping area was shattered by a desperate, piercing scream.

The well-dressed crowd froze and above the vee formed by the meeting of two ladies' crinoline-widened skirts, Amy had a clear view of the terrified lad who'd tumbled into the roadway just in front of two horses drawing an elegant carriage.

In the next impossibly brief instant a bright haze flashed across the scene, and a golden, devastatingly handsome man lowered the boy safely to his grateful mother's side.

"Comlan—" The name barely squeaked from Amy's throat but drew his immediate attention and earned a brilliant smile no less potent for its wry twist.

"Who?" A frowning Beattie dourly asked.

While the boy's savior climbed immediately through an open door into the still-moving carriage, Amy's gaze remained fixed on him.

"Who was that?" Beattie demanded, shifting her attention from passing carriage to the mistress whose rapt expression showed her too stunned by the incident to answer a simple question.

"That . . ." Amy finally spoke as the carriage rounded a corner and disappeared, "was Lord Comlan of Doncaully—the man I told you about."

"In the carriage?" Beattie had already recognized the name of Amy's Irish lord and the lingering admiration on the girl's face intensified her uneasiness.

"Yes." Amy nodded and gave her lifelong friend

a reassuring smile. "Both in the carriage and rescuing the boy."

"Tch, tch." Beattie's disgruntled frown deepened. She wanted to condemn Amy's foolish claim that the man had been in both places but . . . Much as she'd like to deny it, if forced, she'd have had to admit that the face of the man who'd saved the boy appeared to be the same one she'd glimpsed inside a rapidly departing carriage.

While Amy was both amazed and warmly impressed that her fantasy hero had used his remarkable powers to save a human child, Comlan sat in the coach more than a little annoyed with the whole scene. He didn't regret rescuing the boy but he deeply resented the mess that action had made of his plans.

From farther down Ealsingham Court, unnoticed but with a clear view of Wyfirth House, inside the carriage whose reins Dooley held he'd waited and watched to see the dark colleen depart. She had and he'd followed, intending to arrange an "accidental" meeting where he could open the subject he'd come to see settled. And hopefully with haste enough for him to soon return to his own realm. Yes, escape the human world with sufficient speed to elude the dark beauty's likely unintentional enticements. He'd failed . . . this time.

"So, there you are . . . at long last."

Squinting against bright sunlight, Garnet glanced up to find an irritable Orville impatiently waiting within the shadows beside the door of a small structure housing laboratory facilities leased to the *Lancet*. It was the fact that this was an unfashionable yet respectable area of the City which provided Garnet with hope of keeping his socially unacceptable association with the journal a secret.

Having already settled with the hansom cab which had delivered him here, Garnet took time to wave it off down the cobbled street while gathering his thoughts and pondering his next step. He then leisurely moved to unlock the door and motion his visitor into a room lined with shelves, some crowded with thick leather-bound volumes, others lined with rows of glass jars and bottles. A table in the center of the room held even more bottles along with a complicated arrangement of glass tubing. On either side of the desk against one wall was a variety of notebooks while in the middle was a neat stack of papers covered with tight handwritten lines.

Garnet waited for his uninvited guest to enter and turned to face him before issuing a chill response to the man's initial comment. "Do consider your wait simply a minor part of the price owed."

Expecting Orville's irritation to be greatly aggravated by this statement, Garnet was more than a little disturbed by the wide grin with which the man greeted this reminder of a continuing debt.

"Your price is already too high." The lack of heat in Orville's words made it clear that they offered no more than a perfunctory rebuttal. As recent events provided so much reason to expect future success for his scheme to recoup all losses, Orville was able to hand the other man a flat, tightly packed envelope without the slightest visible twinge of resentment.

"Not as high as it is now." Disgust for the overbearing man deepening each time he saw his face, Garnet took pleasure in announcing this assuredly unwelcome increase.

"What are you saying?" Smile struck from Orville's face by fear of discovery, he glowered at the dark-haired man. "Have we been exposed?"

"Not yet." Garnet's gray eyes hardened to granite while his hands slowly curled into fists. "But *you* soon may be."

Several tense moments of silence passed while Orville steadily returned the gray glare.

At length, although clenched hands tightened, Garnet reluctantly yielded to the demand in this wordless pause by flatly stating, "You can avoid that peril by abandoning the pursuit of my sister."

"Oh, come now, old boy." Orville's lips took on an unsavory upward curl, more sneer than smile. "Betray me and I'll see to it that you've betrayed yourself. And to what purpose?"

Garnet stiffened, glaring at his disagreeable, muttonchopped cohort.

Pleased with the dark man's response, Orville's heavy features resettled into a feigned expression of injured sensibilities while in a too mild voice he added, "So long as—one way or the other—you receive the income you seek, you've no justifiable reason to object."

"But I *do* most heartily object!" Garnet heatedly responded, taking a threatening step forward before reason prevailed and forced him to an abrupt halt.

Orville nonchalantly shrugged. He had no intention of ending his courtship of Amethyst. Indeed, he'd only just taken the first steps to see a possible threat neutralized. Unholy glee deepened the contempt in his smile as he turned to depart.

Chapter 5

❧

*A*my followed her mother's example in accepting their footman's aid in stepping down from the family carriage while Lovey slid to the edge of her seat, preparing to repeat the action. Making room for her sister-in-law's descent by moving aside, Amy peeked up from beneath her primrose bonnet's brim, stylishly short but not shockingly so. The afternoon of Lady's Delwyn's garden party had been blessed with a blue sky marred by only a very few fleecy clouds.

"Amethyst," Lady Cornelia softly remonstrated her daughter in a cold tone at variance with the feigned warmth of her smile. "Use your parasol, if you please."

Amy could see no good use in yet another barrier between her face and the sun, but that fact was not sufficient excuse nor was this the place to defy her mother's dread of a sun-darkened complexion. Obediently unfurling her dainty, lace embellished parasol, she trailed her mother down a laid-brick path marked every few feet with an extravagant satin bow. It led to the back of their hosts' imposing home where they paused at the gathering's outer edge.

Amy scanned gardens amazingly spacious for the grounds of a town house. There were bright beds of daffodils and tulips surrounded by low-growing vegetation. And lined against the deep green wall of the small but famous Delwyn maze's outermost hedge were tubs of summer roses forced into early bloom brought from the conservatory for the afternoon. A large number of guests were already chatting in small groups, selecting refreshments from an abundant array, or relaxing on the few pieces of wicker furniture scattered across immaculately manicured lawns.

Eyes caught by the glow of sunlight reflected by a golden head, Amy silently gasped as its possessor turned toward her.

The shy smile instantly appearing on the dark damsel's winsome, heart-shaped face held such spontaneous warmth that it knocked the self-assured Comlan off stride as little had in a very long time.

"Amy!" Again Lady Cornelia sharply and more firmly demanded her daughter's attention. Her patience was sorely strained by the girl abruptly gone still as if, like Lot's wife, transformed to an inanimate pillar by some unfortunate vision. Her gaze followed the direction of Amethyst's to meet an even more distressing sight: the Irish lord casting his sinfully charming smile at her susceptible daughter. It seemed to confirm Cornelia's many fears and left her determined to caution Amy as soon as possible against the dangers handsome rakes posed to a woman's all-important maidenly virtue.

"Lady Cornelia . . ." A woman of imposing dimensions sailed toward the new arrivals with amazing grace for one of her size. "How kind of you to come and bring your lovely daughters as well."

Amy was both relieved and disappointed when their hostess's welcome smoothly broke her exciting visual bond with the man who for several days she'd hoped to see but hadn't. The Season had begun less than a week past but already Lord Comlan had become its most sought-after bachelor. Thus for any given time he must have a wide variety of events from which to choose, and she'd begun to despair for her plan to talk with him privately.

"Thank you for the invitation, Lady Delwyn." Amy added her greeting to those given by her two companions, careful to show the reticence proper in a debutante—even one entering her fourth Season and near to being labeled "on the shelf." In the next instant, sight of the rapidly approaching Orville intensified her preference for spinsterhood. Yes, she'd rather remain unmarried than wed him despite having been taught, as were all well-bred females, to regard that condition as a heavy cross of humiliating failure to be humbly borne for the rest of one's joyless life.

While her mother and Lovey accompanied Lady

Delwyn to the refreshment table with its huge punch bowl and wide variety of delicacies, Orville blocked the parasol-clutching Amy's path.

"I am so glad to see you here, Amethyst." Orville claimed her free white-gloved fingers with both of his hands. "I was disappointed not to find you at the Wareham's rout last evening."

"Garnet particularly requested that we join him and Louvisa at the Selwyndes' dinner party," Amy politely murmured, careful not to betray either how warmly she'd welcomed the excuse to avoid him or her regret for the lost opportunity to warn Comlan of Orville's threat. A well-trained conscience reproved Amy for the indelicate familiarity in even thinking of the Irish lord by his given name. Hoping Orville wouldn't notice the hint of color caused by her lapse, she continued.

"My father was anxious to hear Sir David's thoughts on the Don Pacifico Affair—a subject to be raised in the House of Lords this week. I believe he is unhappy that the fleet is being recalled from its blockade of the harbor at Perancus." She gave her unappreciated companion a bland smile. "And that's why we were with the Selwyndes while you were at the rout."

Frowning his disapproval of her interest in men's concerns, Orville sought to nudge the conversation down a more useful path. "Ah, yes, Garnet." His intentional pause demanded her full attention and enabled him to watch her closely as he asked, "Will he or your father be joining us here later this afternoon?"

Amy's head dipped in a brief nod. "Father will come if Parliament adjourns in time." Annoyed by Orville's attempt to control her slightest actions, she glanced purposefully away and gave unnecessary attention to a heavily flowered rhododendron. "But I believe Garnet has other commitments to keep."

"His tests?" Orville softly probed, brows arched. Having endured one confrontation earlier today, he hoped to avoid another or at least to be forewarned and prepared.

Amy responded with another noncommittal smile, a little surprised by the question as her brother's work was not commonly known.

"Sir Orville," Lady Delwyn called. "An unexpected gift has been bestowed on our gathering. Do bring Miss Danton to see the fine portrait Lord Comlan has done of Lady Isobel." Exercising her talents as hostess, she presided carefully over the ebb and flow of mingling guests.

As a polite guest Orville could hardly ignore this summons although if he could, he would've refused or at least avoided escorting Amy to where Lady Delwyn stood beside the Irish newcomer.

Too aware of Comlan already, Amy kept eyes downcast while being led toward the fascinating man seated at one of several small tables. Once there, she focused on the sketch pad beneath his hands. On the top sheet there was a perfect likeness of Isobel. Yet it was more than the artist's undoubted skill which held Amy's full attention. She'd seen similar sure and steady pencil strokes before—in the mysterious drawing of her Irish dream castle. Was this further proof that her fantasy hero and the Lord of Doncaully were one? This confirmation sharpened Amy's determination to win private words with the man.

"Sir Orville . . ." A still hovering hostess again intruded, intent on ensuring a true mixing of guests by rearranging their combinations. "May I impose on you to take Lady Isobel to view the arched gateway to the west gardens?"

Orville saw that Lady Delwyn, believing her request anything but an unpleasant duty, clearly expected his compliance. Nonetheless, he obeyed and offered his arm with an ill grace almost as poorly concealed as the distaste with which Lady Isobel accepted.

Vision blurred by a rosy mist of satisfaction with the success of her party, their hostess happily assured them, "It makes a lovely sight now that I've had my gardeners train flowering vines to cover the structure."

Amy saw the irritation tightening Lady Cornelia's lips. Though sympathizing with her mother's frustration over this unwelcome twist given to her plans by their hostess, Amy couldn't stifle a smile. Both ladies hosted the same social aspirations and each year vied for the chance of stepping up to a higher rung on the upper class ladder. And Amy had long suspected that Lady Delwyn took pleasure in frustrating her mother's intentions. Her next, more telling request surely proved it true.

"And, Lord Comlan, I hope that you'll allow Miss Danton to show you my little maze." Smiling benignly, Lady Delwyn waved toward the maze's towering hedges. "It's small but despite the limited size, quite challenging."

White smile flashing, Comlan gladly rose and offered his arm to the damsel whose charcoal eyes danced with sparks of secret laughter. He welcomed the suggestion providing him with an opportunity to move closer to the goal summoning him to this mortal world—a goal proven more difficult than expected what with so many events taking place simultaneously.

While a glowering Orville stalked away with an equally displeased Isobel, Amy lightly tucked her fingers into the crook of Comlan's arm. Even more pleasing, in Amy's view, was Lady Delwyn's action in drawing both her mother and sister-in-law's attention to a completely different matter. She couldn't have concocted a more perfect arrangement if the details had been hers to choose. The pleasure in this unexpected boon made suppressing a decidedly impish grin impossible.

Seeing the young woman's often solemn expression wiped away by a beguilingly bright smile, Comlan gladly allowed her to guide him toward an opening in the wall of greenery. With the confidence of familiarity, she led him down corridors and around corners until even his exceptional senses could no longer identify with any certainty from which direction they'd started.

Muffled by a succession of evergreen barriers,

the sounds of the party became soft and indistinct, increasing the sense of intimacy and flooding Amy with renewed awareness of her companion. She glanced sidelong. Comlan's mocking smile reappeared. Its devastating power caught her breath and drove away any thought of quizzing him about the rescue of a foolish boy. To ward off the danger of making a complete fool of herself by shamelessly throwing herself at this incredibly handsome man, she moved to walk in front of him and lead the way into a narrower corridor.

"Tell me, Miss Danton," Comlan spoke after several minutes of obediently following the dark colleen through an apparently random course. "Is there a goal to our journey or are we meant to simply find enjoyment in the privacy of our meanderings?"

Amy fervently rued her inability to prevent the spreading color warming her cheeks. She'd erred with the very large, very basic mistake of making decisions without prudent consideration. Consequently, the course of action she'd laid out was fraught with pitfalls she ought to have seen before this moment when she hovered unprepared on the precipice.

And only now, after rashly acting with all the impulsiveness of Lovey, did Amy pause to recognize the awful difficulty of launching into the issues she'd intended to raise. Nothing this man had yet done even suggested that they might have met before their introduction at the Melton ball. So, how could she bluntly ask the Season's most sought-after bachelor if he was in reality some kind of fantasy figure? At best, Comlan was apt to think her childish; at worst, a simpleton who actually believed in fairy tales.

"*Is* there a specific destination for our walk?" Comlan patiently asked again.

"Oh, yes." Amy rushed to fill the awkward silence, heartily resenting an unavoidably deepening blush. Upset with herself for permitting thoughts to wander and quiet to fall, she was even more annoyed for letting it seem they were wandering through green corridors without regard to journey's end. "If we follow the right path, we'll reach a lovely fountain surrounded by stone benches."

"And do you know this right path?" Comlan wanted the conversation to continue, giving him the chance to broach matters he feared she'd still refuse to seriously consider, even less accept as fact.

Amy immediately nodded, intent on their route and anxious to prevent further uncomfortable pauses. "Lady Delwyn's oldest daughter was a friend and as children we played in this living puzzle."

Amy directed their way through twists and turns, reassured that her choices were right by the ever-increasing fragrance of Lady Delwyn's prize, imported magnolias. Bushes of fragile white flowers—grown in large pots and tended in the conservatory—were always brought out for parties and lined up along the maze's center square. Turning a last corner Amy paused before an elegant fountain. It was made of marble and shaped like a dolphin riding the crest of a wave while two forever laughing children perched on its back.

"Tibby and I used to pretend that we were the ones boldly riding through the sea on a foam-crested wave." The remembered joys of childhood sang in Amy's voice but a darker note of melancholy also ran through it.

"Tibby?" Bronze brows arched questioningly above a green gaze. "Is she the Delwyn's daughter?"

Amy somberly nodded without glancing his way. "We came out together three years ago, and she married at the end of that Season."

By his secret nature Comlan was able to sense even the slightest emotional nuances. But the dark damsel's regret was so clear his talent was unnecessary, leaving him to wonder only about the cause of her distress. Surely not jealousy for Tibby's success in so quickly winning a husband? No. . . .

"Did Tibby's marriage cost you a friend?" Comlan gently inquired. "Is that why you're sad?"

Amy gave her head a slight shake and, despite the bonnet brim's shadow, Comlan saw her lips curl in a prompt but forlorn smile. It earned a self-derisive smile from him. How could he pride himself on mastery of the Tuatha De's extraordinary perceptiveness while failing to immediately recognize the difference between resentment and lingering grief.

"Last year Tibby was brought to bed with her first baby." Amy took a deep breath. "Neither of them survived the birthing." Fearing he might mis-interpret her sorrow as a craven fear of childbearing, she hurried to correct that impression. "I know enough of nature to realize the end to such events are not always so unhappy." Even knowing she was babbling like some insipid dolt, a mortified Amy couldn't stop. "My two older sisters are mothers of growing families. Indeed, they're not in London now because each is expecting a new addition within the next few months."

Watching a curious assortment of diverse emo-tions chase across the winsome face whose vulnera-bility Amy struggled so hard to hide, Comlan was forced to make a reluctant admission. His keen senses had been tilted badly awry by this intriguing human maid more temptation than in her innocence she could possibly realize, more than he wanted to admit.

Anxious to calm her uneasiness by shifting to an innocuous subject, Comlan asked, "Have you ever seen a real dolphin?"

"No!" Startled, Amy instantly responded. Then, although welcoming the change of topic, she shot her questioner an incredulous glance for asking such a silly thing of a woman born and raised in the chilly British Isles. "But one summer I saw a per-forming seal as part of the entertainment presented at a seaside resort."

"What did this performing seal do to entertain you?" Comlan asked with an honest grin but sar-donic glitter in his dark forest eyes.

Despite the futile wish for an immediate return

to rational thinking, Amy heard herself babbling on inanely. "He played a simple tune on a line of one-note horns." With her hands she mimed pinching bulbs that forced air through the instruments. "And he balanced a ball on his nose." She was going to regret this, her stern conscience warned. Oh, how she was going to regret this foolishness!

A quiet roll of deep laughter, like thunder in the distance, earned a suspicious sidelong glance from cloudy gray eyes. The gentle amusement warming his expression smoothed her ragged tensions even as the golden mesh of his enchantment began wrapping its gossamer strands around her.

"You have an enchanting smile," Comlan murmured, moving to stand very close and gaze down into the piquant face immediately lifted to him. "It brightens the whole world and I fear it able to beguile the very heart from a man."

Perilously near to spinsterhood and unaccustomed to such flowery compliments—or any compliments at all—Amy's wildly erratic heart thumped even louder. Her gaze dropped from the dangerous heat in emerald-flame eyes to blindly study the evenly mowed grass at her feet. Finding herself disgustingly less composed and brave than she'd always wanted to believe herself to be, still Amy was sane enough not to tempt fate by letting him see how fascinated she was with him.

Comlan had entered the maze intending to charm this woman into an amenable mood open to his guidance down an avenue that would lead to discoveries he must help her find for the sake of protecting someone they both cared about. Instead he'd been forced to acknowledge dangers he'd tried to deny.

Reality made it impossible! Their worlds were so completely different, so widely separated that there could never be a shared future for them. Comlan regretfully slid one forefinger down Amy's face from temple to chin, savoring skin like delicate satin. Nudging beneath that softly pointed chin, Comlan titled Amy's face upward again until he could gaze into gray eyes gone nearly black. Dark lashes drifted down to rest on creamy cheeks as with slow, quiet intent he bent to reclaim her delicious mouth and the sweet honey of kisses he remembered all too well.

· Though sensing restrained passion in the long, powerful body looming over hers, Amy lacked the will to protest as Comlan's mouth touched and teased her lips with tender, biting kisses. Instead, her fingers curled into the fine cloth covering his broad chest seeking an anchor in the abruptly shifting tide of pleasure rapidly sweeping her ever further from the safe shores of reality. ·

As the temptation so near yielded against him, Comlan wrapped strong arms about her, slowly gathering the soft body even closer. Amy felt as if her very bones had turned to liquid while beneath the gentle torment of his caresses a tiny moan escaped.

Gladly lost on a wildly tossing sea, surrendering to its tide of shocking excitement, Amy caught a glimpse of a slight, satisfied smile curling the lips that next began an exciting journey down her arched throat.

"Comlan, at last." Against the magnolias' background of shiny leaves and waxy blooms, Isobel stood stiff and almost shaking with poorly suppressed irritation while a glowering Orville hovered a pace behind.

Though certain Comlan's broad back had prevented these two from seeing the extent of their embrace, Amy stepped away so quickly that she'd have lost firm footing had Comlan not placed a steadying hand on her shoulder.

The action drew a positively poisonous glare from Isobel. "Orville and I have come to repair the damage caused by our interfering hostess's ill-conceived arrangements."

"Come, Amy," Orville quickly added, taking several steps forward and extending his hand in wordless demand. "Your mother is worried about your lengthy absence . . . as was I."

An unsmiling Amy permitted the irate little man to escort her from the maze. She recognized the impossibility of rejecting this summons without causing the kind of scene that would see her bundled off to the country and locked in Wyfirth Grange for the foreseeable future. And, since she'd abjectly failed to advance her scheme to see Comlan forewarned of Orville's wretched intents, Amy couldn't permit herself to be exiled from London.

From a tiny corner somewhere behind that virtuous claim her conscience's small inner voice demanded an honest confession: Most importantly she wanted to see her golden, fantasy hero again . . . and again . . . and again. . . .

Chapter 6

~

"*B*ut, lambie," Beatrice wailed, standing just inside a closed door. "It just isn't done!"

Seated at the dainty rosewood escritoire in her own little sitting room, Amy paused with pen poised above a sheet of creamy paper to glance over one shoulder. Though she gave the horrified Beattie a rueful smile, Amy had no intention of abandoning this promising if possibly scandalous tactic.

Amy inwardly acknowledged the disgrace risked by any genteel lady committing such a questionable act as this. But it was also clear that social encounters arrived at in the accepted manner—amid intrusive crowds—were extremely unlikely to afford the privacy necessary for issuing even a delicately phrased warning.

While turning to write a final few words, Amy could feel the older woman's accusing eyes boring a hole in her back. Beattie was right. Were this action to become publicly known, it would badly damage her reputation which, as all self-respecting debutantes knew, must remain unblemished to have hope for making a good match. But then since she'd earlier admitted to having no earnest desire to attain that goal, particularly not if it meant Orville, gray eyes began to glitter with silver sparks of obstinate determination. She wouldn't let unworthy fears keep her from sending this personal invitation requesting Lord Comlan's company the next morning on a carriage ride through Hyde Park.

Because Beattie was her oldest friend, Amy knew very well that the woman was unlikely to accept the rationale of any excuse. Nonetheless, it was important to try. She took a deep, bolstering breath and began.

"At the tea party today I saw a portrait Lord Comlan drew of Lady Isobel."

Beattie went still. They hadn't discussed the Irish lord since the morning after the Season's opening ball. Still, she wasn't the least bit surprised to learn he was the cause of Amy's improper behavior.

"What's a portrait of *Lady Isobel* to do with you?" Brows arched with the question dropped instantly into a disapproving scowl as Beatrice added, "I do hope it's not jealousy that's provoked this indiscretion."

Amy exercised her usual control to restrain an initial urge to snap back a heated denial. Laying her pen down, she pulled out the desk's single drawer to extract her drawing pad. From the very back she slipped a page free and handed it to the suspicious Beattie. Several patience-straining minutes passed while the other woman studied the paper.

"Having watched me sketch for years," Amy broke the uncomfortable silence, "you know it wasn't me who created that powerful image of a mysterious castle."

Beattie nodded but lingering doubts clouded her narrowed eyes.

"It's a picture of the castle in my dream and was lying atop my drawing of the castle's *ruins* when I awoke in the fairy ring." Amy lifted open palms toward her old friend in wordless plea. "Don't you see? The styles are the same. *He* drew both this picture and the portrait of Isobel."

"What I see," Beatrice said, gazing at the younger woman with the same sternness she'd used against arguments of the headstrong child Amy had been, "is that you are still trying to convince me you actually danced with a fairy-tale king and visited his fantasy castle."

"No." Amy shook her head so fervently that thick, dark hair nearly escaped the confining net holding it neatly rolled at her nape. "I'm telling you what truly did happen. It must have been real."

"Whether one way or the other"—as if to mark an end to the matter, Beatrice thrust the drawing back into Amethyst's hold—"it can hardly justify your disgraceful intention."

With growing exasperation, Amy laid the drawing aside, conceding the battle to win even simple acceptance from Beattie. And yet she refused to alter her plan.

"Nothing you say will prevent me from sending this." Amy waved her finished note. "I showed you the picture and tried to explain because I wanted you to understand why doing all I can to thwart Orville is so very important to me."

"Thwart Orville?" Beattie's brown eyes widened. Amy claimed to have given an explanation, but not once had she mentioned the disagreeable man. "What role did that sorry buffoon play in your fantasy?"

"Orville is no part of my dream." Amy almost groaned, annoyed for having lost any thread of rationality in the tangled morass of her ill-prepared attempt to win a friend's support. Taking a deep breath, Amy tried to piece together every scrap of tattered patience she could summon. Only after calmly separating, defining and briefly stating the issues could she start at the beginning and try again.

"Because Lord Comlan of Doncaully's appearance, voice and name are the same I immediately suspected that he was the embodiment of my dream's hero. My suspicions, I believe, are proven true by the similarity between the mysterious picture of my fantasy castle and his drawing of Isobel."

Welcoming the faint encouragement grudgingly provided by the curiosity flickering in Beattie's eyes, Amy went on. "Orville thinks Comlan is a threat to his courtship of me and has sworn to see the Irish lord exposed as a fraud. I am *positive* Orville is wrong."

Beattie looked unconvinced by Amy's fervent defense.

"And yet," Amy tenaciously continued, "how can I refute his accusation? Simply state that Comlan is actually king of the Tuatha De Danann?

"No." Amy grimaced, acknowledging the ridicule such a seemingly absurd statement would earn. "The dilemma I face is how to provide Orville with evidence of—as no doubt you'd say—a fairy-tale king?"

"Tch, tch." These muffled sounds of disapproval were Beatrice's sole comment.

But Amy, familiar with the various inflections Beattie gave this favorite response to anything for which she had no immediate solution, was heartened by their lack of emphasis.

"The answer is, I can't," Amy flatly responded to her own question. "And it's my inability to refute Orville's slanderous charges that leaves me willing to risk shame by sending this invitation which I hope will give me the chance to warn Lord Comlan of a threat he doesn't deserve."

"Aye, well, lambie . . . " Although Beattie nodded in docile resignation, she couldn't hide the dubious gleam in her eyes. "If you insist on meeting that Irishman so publicly in Hyde Park, then you must take me as chaperone to lend some little measure of propriety."

"I wouldn't dream of doing elsewise." Amy grinned. By securing this small measure of support, no matter how unwillingly given, she could claim to have won at least this minor skirmish and that gave hope for success in the greater war.

Amy, anxious to depart unseen, glanced nervously over her shoulder while slipping down an elegant winding staircase and crossing the broad entry hall. To avoid the crush of later hours she'd planned this meeting for the earliest permissible time for rides through Hyde Park—late morning.

When impressive double doors finally closed behind Amy and her maid, the sun was already well on the way to its zenith. The fact that two other genteel residents of the Wyfirth town house were still abed, granting at least a temporary reprieve, gave Amy a heartening sense of relief.

Her mother would be livid when she awoke to discover a daughter absent without approval. Amy had considered leaving a note but, recognizing the effort's futility, had dismissed the idea. She'd failed to convince even Beattie, so how could she possibly compose an explanation acceptable to the sternly disapproving Lady Cornelia?

Yes, there would be a penalty to pay for this *unseemly* behavior. And Amy knew she'd have to pay it . . . but not until after the warning she'd sworn to give had been delivered.

Having succeeded in the day's first challenge by escaping the quiet house, Amy was pleased to see the carriage waiting beyond the front gate. It was an imposing vehicle, well-tended and of a size able to comfortably accommodate the whole family—a necessity as it was the only one they kept in town. She regretted only that the cumbersome vehicle was hardly the thing for a fashionable outing.

James, the tall coachman waiting to open the carriage door and help them inside, looked uncomfortable with his role in this adventure. Knowing she was lucky that he had little choice but to obey a summons from his master's daughter, in wordless thanks Amy gave the uneasy servant a bright smile of uncommon sweetness.

While handing his young mistress up into the vehicle's shadowy interior, the coachman felt sheepish remorse for having initially begrudged this chore for the viscount's daughter—reportedly too independent and unfashionably dark yet undeniably winsome.

Amy tensely perched on a leather seat with Beattie at her side as the carriage lurched into motion. Garbed in her most becoming dress and bonnet, both in her favorite shades of rose trimmed with dark green ribbons, she was filled with an uncomfortable mixture of anticipation and uncertainty.

What if Comlan didn't come? After all, she hadn't received an answer to her invitation. That worry was immediately followed by another question at least as troubling, the same one that had kept her awake most of the night. If Comlan did appear, what specifically should she say to tell him about Orville's intentions? More importantly, what ambiguous phrases could she use so that, were she wrong about his identity, he needn't know her mistake?

The winding trip through city streets brought them, at last, to Hyde Park. Hoping for, yet dreading, a prompt beginning to the task ahead, Amy was disheartened by the length of time that passed while they leisurely moved over Rotten Row's firm gravel surface. She leaned against the door and anxiously peered through a side window at the lane ahead ... to no good purpose. Under growing strain, Amy nibbled her full lower lip. Only nannies pushing prams or guarding small charges could be seen strolling through the patches of sunshine and shadow beneath towering trees.

Her daring plan, it seemed, had failed. Discouraged, Amy started to sit back. But at that moment her attention was caught by four magnificent black horses beginning to pass her vehicle. Admiring gray eyes followed the harness line back to an open carriage of shining ebony and widened on the stunning figure skillfully wielding reins while sunlight gleamed over his golden hair. Though expecting the powerful man to appear, she wasn't prepared to suddenly meet the white flash of his potent smile or the intense heat of his green-fire gaze.

Comlan was equally disconcerted at finding the shield of charm holding his heart impervious to feminine wiles endangered by the welcoming warmth in Amy's sweet smile. Driving four-in-hand, he slowed the beautifully matched stallions to assure his open coach and Amy's massive carriage move forward at the same pace.

"Good morning, Miss Danton." A wicked gleam sparkled in Comlan's eyes while gentle mockery tilted his smile awry. "Fancy seeing you here so early in the day."

With fine disregard for her own conclusions as to Comlan's true nature, Amy was first flustered by the surely too confident man's nearness and the next instant annoyed with herself for that embarrassing response. She proudly lifted her chin as, with none of the composure so long her goal and which she'd intended to maintain today, rushed to snap back.

"As you were invited, it can hardly be a surprise."

Grin widening, an unruffled Comlan purred, "But very much a pleasure all the same." When Amy failed to immediately respond, he smoothly continued as if the brief pause had been intended.

"Will you do me the honor of joining me in this open coach? My man, Dooley"—he tilted his head back toward the groom standing post behind—"can keep your maid company while you and I visit."

Without waiting for an answer, Comlan brought his vehicle to a halt and Dooley jumped to the ground. Once the Wyfirth carriage stopped a short distance ahead, Dooley moved to help down the dark beauty he remembered well from her brief visit in another realm.

Comlan spoke to Amy's coachman while his servant aided her into the open coach. By the time Dooley took her seat in the carriage, James had been instructed to slowly drive his passengers through the park. In two hours time, the two parties would meet at the Marble Arch.

Inside the Wyfirth carriage an indignant Beattie sat stiffly erect, considerably less than pleased by this arrangement. It might be perfectly respectable for a lady to share a gentleman's open coach but she was none too happy about being closed into this carriage with a wiry, rough-looking creature who clearly was no gentleman—an opinion confirmed by the first insolent words to leave his mouth.

"And who might you be, me darlin'?"

Dark eyes gone hard as granite, Beattie frigidly answered her unwelcome companion's impertinent question. "Mrs. Beatrice Milford."

"Puir Mr. Milford." Dooley's bushy brows met

in a feigned show of sympathy that did nothing to tame his teasing grin.

Beattie's eyes snapped with silent rebuke for the man whose flaming hair surely betrayed ill-breeding. She would rather bite her tongue in two than admit to this feckless cur that the *Mrs.* was merely a courtesy title and the only *Mr.* Milford in her life was the father she'd never known.

Faith and begorrah! Dooley grinned. A right banshee was this vinegary creature, and he'd no' waste a moment more tryin' to pierce the wall of ice betwixt them. He made a fine show of gazing with overdone admiration at a lovely view of the Serpentine's calm waters wending through vivid green lawns.

While their servants rode in a chill silence, it was nearly as quiet between the pair in the open coach that soon slowed again to a halt, this time in an area widened for that purpose.

Blind to the beauty of sweeping lawns and bright sky, Amy cudgeled her brain trying to recall her carefully devised speech. But with Comlan so near the feverish effort was to little avail. She instead busied herself opening the seldom appreciated parasol that for once had a useful purpose in providing something for nervous fingers to clutch. His disturbing nearness heightened awareness of him and tossed the fragments of sane reasoning into a chaotic clutter while at the same time summoning vivid memories of each too brief but exciting embrace.

Sweet Heaven! Abruptly realizing the immodest turn of her thoughts, Amy's cheeks burned. No man should be allowed such devastating charms. But then, Amy wryly reminded herself, as king of the

Tuatha De Danann, Comlan could hardly be restrained by the average human male's limitations. The next instant she rediscovered the grave error of glancing up into his mesmerizing gaze. She must look away, truly must but—as she ought to have learned before—couldn't.

Comlan watched rosy heat wash the cheeks of this enchanting damsel who was clearly flustered by their mere proximity. Another wicked grin flashed. Miss Amethyst Danton was the most unique female who'd ever crossed his path. Amy was intelligent enough to be wary of matters she didn't understand and yet brave enough to knowingly risk learning more. He applauded those traits. As one who by nature was most attracted to the contradictory, it was the paradox of her spirit—half dedicated to cool logic and half drawn to the irrational joys of adventure and imagination—which made her both pleasing and intriguing.

Realizing that the maid's reaction to his nearness was also the impediment making it difficult for her to state her purpose for this meeting, Comlan's smile faded. The wordless plea in her charcoal eyes struck a deep chord in him that had never been touched before—one he was quite certain should remain buried. He very nearly broke his realm's first rule for dealing with humankind by giving answers before necessary questions were asked. And, to his shame, it wasn't respect for that principle which prevented the action but the interruption of another human.

"Comlan, old boy," a hearty voice called out. "I heard you'd come to the City but couldn't credit the claim. It hardly seems your milieu."

"Old Pam!" Comlan warmly greeted the speaker, a silver-haired man strolling over to grip the smooth wood railing between walkway and the graveled lane widened to accommodate vehicles pausing for owners to visit. "By what trickery did you escape your duties in the House of Commons?"

Amy was mildly surprised at being hailed by anyone at this hour. Surprise intensified to amazement with the discovery of the speaker's identity and then deepened to shock on seeing how well these two men appeared to know each other. Flustered, she struggled to tame the burning heat of chaotic responses to what seemed a rude revelation. She'd plainly made a complete fool of herself by allowing illogical emotions to cloud rational thinking and convince her that Comlan was a fantasy figure, a fairy-tale hero. It wasn't true, couldn't be if he'd such a close friendship with this famous elder statesman and one time Regency buck, Viscount Palmerston. But, a small inner voice persistently asked, then how had he managed to save the boy?

"We've separated into committees," a shrugging Palmerston explained, first smiling broadly at Amy and then turning curious eyes to her escort. "Mine doesn't meet until this afternoon so I came around first thing this morn to look over what we can only hope are the finishing touches to the Queen's Great Exhibition."

Amy's gaze automatically followed a wave of the statesman's arm to a most amazing structure rising so high it encased even a giant elm and yet was both graceful and delicate.

"Paxton's creation is quite something, ain't it, me

94

girl?" With his famous eye for feminine charms, Palmerston easily shifted admiring attention to the beauty at his seldom glimpsed Irish neighbor's side. "A giant conservatory with more glass in one structure than many a soul might see in a lifetime."

"I, along with a great many others, look forward to the day when our Queen opens her exhibition." Amy's claim was more than mere tact as she really was anticipating the event, despite the hinted concerns of her father and brother. *Hordes of foreigners will descend on London and who knows what dreadful diseases they might bring.*

"That day will soon be here." Palmerston gallantly lifted Amy's fingers to brush his lips over their tips. "And I hope to see you there."

The two gentlemen fell into a brief chat concerning the challenges facing Irish landholders, freeing Amy to more intently study the ingenious pavilion while trying to devise a plausible excuse for requesting this meeting. Her gray gaze moved across impressive expanses of glass glittering in the sunlight until a curious sight caught her eye.

An unkempt figure sporting a ragged eye patch and peeking at them from behind a broad trunk. Strange. What logical reason was there for anyone to hide in a public park free to all? A park beginning to fill with an odd assortment of people from every class? Shabby gawkers met in clusters near the building in progress while various elegantly garbed Society members had embarked on their promenade. Why then should this man skulk about, ineptly hiding behind trees? Had Palmerston an enemy? Or was the peculiar man some dull-witted thief foolish enough to risk striking in bright daylight?

"Miss Danton—"

Comlan's deep voice effectively thrust all thought of their furtive watcher from Amy's mind and lured her into looking his way.

"Lord Palmerston is leaving us and wishes to bid you farewell."

Amy was flustered by her ungracious inattention to the highly respected statesman and immediately gave the man a sweetly earnest smile of apology.

"Yes." Lord Palmerston accepted her regret with easy warmth. "Unfortunately, I must be off to Parliament. There are matters to arrange before my meeting begins." He gave a slight shrug before again taking Amy's hand to kiss her fingertips. "But I do hope to see you again—soon."

Amy nodded, grateful for this gallant response from the older man who tipped his top hat to Comlan before striding across green lawns and away from them. But while Palmerston moved beyond hearing distance, the dilemma posed by his arrival and the friendship it revealed intensified Amy's anxiety. What possible explanation, what purpose could she give to the Irish lord as excuse for her invitation?

Flustered and hoping to keep Comlan's attention diverted, Amy spoke without wise forethought. "Do you know Lord Palmerston well?"

Even as the words fell from her lips Amy wished she could call them back. An open discussion of Lord Palmerston's acquaintanceship with *this* Comlan could only deepen her discomfort with its proof that her Irish dream had been no more than that.

Valiantly attempting to suppress a pang of disappointment, she gave Comlan a brilliant smile.

"His Irish lands and mine share a common border." Comlan nodded, feeling Amy's unaccountable nervousness and wondering if she had some strange idea that he might be a threat to her. After a glimpse of her beguiling smile, he dismissed that plainly absurd notion. However, it underscored an alarming hazard—the ease with which this human damsel could muddle keen senses honed over a length of time she was unlikely to comprehend.

"Government duties keep the viscount thoroughly occupied," Comlan added with a mocking smile whose self-derisive source only he knew. "Leaving little time to spare for visiting."

Amy fidgeted with her parasol. Despite having just wished the words opening this subject unsaid— as if in demonstration of how capable this man was at detouring her once logical, well-ordered thoughts—she was now unhappy that it had been so quickly depleted.

Hating to look like every other vapid debutante playing the weak-wit to flatter a suitor, Amy desperately sought something intelligent to say. However, when the logic behind her carefully planned speech had burst, as might be expected of any fairy tale's insubstantial bubble, it had robbed her of rational words. While an uncomfortable pause lengthened, she sat in doomed isolation . . . featherbrained goose chosen for slow roasting.

"But, yes," Comlan continued at last. "The viscount and I are acquainted."

Amy stared blindly at the sleek black horses held

nearly motionless by the skillful control of the powerful man beside her. She was amazed by how little affected he was by what had seemed to her a wretchedly long, unnatural silence. That thought generated a more pertinent question: Why had he hesitated at all?

"But Lord Palmerston knows your great-aunt Daffy far better than he knows me."

"What?" Thick lashes fluttering in bewilderment, Amy fought to untangle the sudden wealth of conflicting questions his statement inspired. Comlan knew Daffy? He must, how else could he be certain her great-aunt and Lord Palmerston were friends? More disconcerting still, after having accepted that her dream was only a dream, did Comlan's cryptic statement mean that he really . . .

"We're all neighbors." Comlan regretted that this uncushioned declaration of fact was too cryptic to clear Amy's confusion. But, having come hazardously near to shattering the first rule governing the Tuatha De's traffic with the human world by offering answers unasked, his jaw firmed and mouth clenched into a tight line. He dare not risk speaking for fear of saying too much. No matter. With the colleen so close, so clearly fascinated by the beguilement of unfamiliar ways, could the wordless power in a steady, emerald gaze be more effective than simple words?

While the human world settled into its daily routine, birds flitted from tree to tree, and squirrels darted across green lawns, for the couple in an ebony coach reality faded. For uncounted minutes

Comlan gazed steadily down into gentle, dove gray eyes that widened as he willed a question from the dark maid's lips.

"Did we meet in Ireland?" Trembling beneath the intensity of his scrutiny but unaware of its purpose, Amy was pleased to have found this tentative query allowing her to retreat if his response was less than encouraging.

"On a hilltop one sunny afternoon." The soft confirmation was accompanied by a soul-melting smile as powerful as the one which had greeted Amy on awakening amidst a fairy ring.

"Did you summon me to meet you for the sake of asking that question?" The mockery tilting his smile awry did nothing to lessen its impact.

"Yes ... no." Amy bit her lip, disgusted with herself for sounding so uncertain when in dealing with anyone else she was quite the opposite. "I meant to warn you of a danger that apparently is no danger."

"Sounds interesting." Comlan's head tilted inquiringly. "What sort of danger did you think might threaten me?"

"How could I know that with Palmerston's support you're more than able to defend yourself against Orville's wretched scheme?" Amy's eyes began to glitter as temper flared under a renewed jumble of erratic emotions and an accusation slipped from tight lips. "When the Duchess of Melton introduced us, you let it seem it was our first meeting."

Bronze brows arched. "Would you rather I had told the duchess *and* your parents all the details of how I swept you off to my castle in the Faerie Realm where we danced the hours away . . . among other pursuits."

A potent green-flame gaze returned to brush across tender, rose-petal lips with such intensity that it seemed almost a physical caress. It revived heated memories and left Amy helplessly leaning nearer to its source—until doused by the icy water of a sardonic smile.

"I am pleased my concern was unnecessary and that you are in no danger." Amy's cold voice gave lie to the claim while against the humor of this creature so often amused at her expense gray eyes turned to granite.

The too intriguing colleen's distress left Comlan feeling guilty . . . an emotion he had never experienced before and one he found distinctly uncomfortable.

"What, precisely," Comlan solemnly asked, attempting to undo his wrong, "were you concerned about?"

Amy squarely met the gaze now gone a deep forest hue, trying to ignore the unsettling effect of her disconcerting companion's mercurial moods and answer logically. Because he had acknowledged the truth of his nearly unbelievable identity, she owed him an equally frank answer. Taking a deep breath, Amy launched into a concise recounting of Orville's lengthy diatribe at the Meltons' ball.

"You were afraid I might not be able to defend myself against either your suitor's slurs or a possible physical assault?" Reminding himself that this human maid couldn't know how impossible that was, Comlan fought to quash an unjust irritation with her for thinking him so weak.

Feeling foolish, Amy gave a diffident shrug while temper simmered anew. What gap in clear reasoning had allowed her to abandon sanity and attempt to warn him of anything? She glared at the coach's floor. Never mind. She knew the answer. Blame lay with the illogical, despicable imagination she ought to have eradicated years ago—long before it could mislead her into a quagmire like this.

Easily reading Amy's self-recriminations and resentment of him, Comlan wanted to ease both. "It wasn't my intention to slight the valuable gift of your concern."

Amy peeked suspiciously at Comlan from beneath her bonnet's brim.

Exercising exceptional charm, with a penitent smile Comlan enticed Amy further from her shell of doubts. "You didn't know and I couldn't offer you the truths of my making."

Subjected to the full weight of Comlan's potent attention, Amy gave a silent gasp. Unable to resist its lure, she met his smoldering gaze steadily until the unblinking fascination soon filling her own overflowed into a vulnerable smile.

Comlan's eyes warmed to pools of liquid emerald. He was pleased by having won Amethyst's enchanting smile; pleased that by responding to her concern for him one impediment to his pursuit of the goal bringing him to her world had been removed.

"In gratitude . . . " Comlan's deep voice purred with the satisfaction in knowing this payment on the debt owed to a member of humankind justified the day's earlier, isolated breaking of a single rule. "I'll repay the favor, kind for kind, with the gift of a warning about looming dangers clear to the eyes of my kind."

Frowning slightly, Amy nibbled her lower lip. What could he possibly mean? She impatiently waited, curiosity growing.

"Everyone in your world wears a false face."

Amy was disappointed . . . and annoyed. Was he toying with her, rousing her interest for this? Either the king of the Tuatha De Danann had an odd sense of humor or he understood less about her world than she'd assumed. (Likely, she uncharitably decided, both.) Did he seriously think such a blatant fact had gone unnoticed?

"No." Comlan's short burst of laughter was quickly replaced by a frown of exaggerated reproach. Amy's remarkably expressive face had betrayed her reactions. In response he slowly shook his head. "That's not the gift—though I doubt you truly know how deep and widespread the deception goes."

An indignant Amy cast her companion a speaking glance.

"This gift is a warning." The somber depth of Comlan's voice and complete absence of mockery made the serious nature of his words abundantly clear. "Warning of a threat to someone you love which each day grows more ominous."

"Lambie!" Beatrice's disgruntled voice intruded, carrying like a clarion bell.

Glancing over her shoulder, Amy saw the Wyfirth

carriage approaching. Beattie, it seemed, had grown tired of waiting for her mistress at the Marble Arch.

Comlan recognized an imminent end to this private conversation. He shouldn't lose a moment in relating the most important of remaining facts. But, once again this lovely human unknowingly diverted his powerful will, allowing a more personal concern to supersede the duty owed.

"Amy—" Squeezing dainty fingers, Comlan spoke in solemn earnest. "Beware of Orville."

Delicate brows arched. What did he mean? Confused, Amy stared skeptically at the speaker. She already knew what a threat Orville posed in her life. And surely, as Comlan had called Orville her suitor, he also was aware. . . . But it hardly seemed worthy of a warning.

"Truly!" Frustrated by the limits placed on his powers, Comlan gritted out an explanation by necessity succinct. "Where almost everyone here has two faces, Orville has many more."

There was no time for Comlan to argue with the young woman who plainly thought he was being preposterous in attributing a talent for cunning to the pompous man who seemed utterly devoid of either modesty or tact.

Chapter 7

~

$\mathcal{H}$ eart pounding, Amy paused just outside a closed door. Her mother was waiting. She'd been summoned to the formal parlor on the ground level rather than to her mother's private withdrawing room upstairs and that was ominous. Still, it wouldn't ease the situation to further delay this undeniably justified scolding. Social commitments had given a full day's reprieve but, since Amy had spent those hours in growing dread of the looming confrontation with her mother's cold fury, that respite could hardly be seen as a gift. To hesitate now would only add coal to the fires of her mother's displeasure. No. Better to get it over and done.

Amy's solid rap on the door was instantly answered by Lady Cornelia's curt command to enter.

"Close the door behind you." The order was as sharp as its underlying demand of privacy to deliver a serious lecture and stern rebuke.

Amy obeyed. After the door softly clicked into

place, she moved to stand a few paces in front of her seated mother. She wasn't invited to sit. By that Amy realized she was expected to stand as criminal before a judge elegantly but soberly attired in a deep purple gown devoid of softening accessories.

"I have spoken with James about the carriage ride you ordered yestermorn . . . and strictly cautioned him to never again answer your call."

Amy silently nodded, careful to maintain an unemotional expression despite the dismay threatening a guilty frown at the memory of the young coachman's initial uneasiness. She sincerely hoped he hadn't been unfairly punished for her wrong.

"From him I learned that you met Lord Comlan in Hyde Park." Lady Cornelia's thin lips tightened over accusing words. "And on closer questioning, James admitted the encounter was apparently prearranged."

Again Amy nodded but did not speak.

"I was relieved to hear that you at least had the presence of mind to take your maid. However, that solace was short-lived." Lady Cornelia's sharp gaze pierced the girl. "Seems you left James to drive the Wyfirth carriage with only Beatrice and Lord Comlan's servant inside."

A tense silence heavy with recrimination stretched between judge and accused. This, Amy knew, was the moment when charges must be answered; when she must speak in her own defense.

"I rode down Rotten Row in Lord Comlan's *open* coach—an acceptable practice often indulged in by many amongst our circle." By her mother's frown it was clear the argument had accomplished nothing yet she persevered by offering another hopefully mitigating factor.

"The only person of note whom we saw during our ride was my companion's Irish neighbor and friend, Lord Palmerston."

"Lord Palmerston?" Against this unexpected news, the always properly erect Lady Cornelia straightened while her frown became a scowl. "They are friends?"

"By their congenial visit, I believe that's true." Amy hoped this alliance with the famous politician would provide a solid endorsement of Comlan's respectability. Her mother quickly showed her the error of that faulty logic.

"Hah." Deep disapproval hardened the lines of Cornelia's already severe features. "I suppose I shouldn't be surprised that a young rake enjoys the company of an old roué. Whatever the case, it in no way excuses your unsuitable actions."

"I don't ask to be excused!" The temper that had become more unruly under Comlan's disruptive influence momentarily got the better of Amy's sensible intentions but she took prompt action to tame its heat and calmly state, "I accept responsibility for the wrong of going out without first speaking to you."

A wordless condemnation narrowed Lady Cornelia's eyes while she sanctimoniously nodded, signaling her daughter to continue.

"But while I was gone . . ." In proud control of her emotions, Amy willfully ignored her mother's silent caution. "With my maid as chaperone, I did nothing worthy of anyone's censure."

Nothing wrong? Hah! Ice snapped in Lady Cornelia's eyes. Amethyst had lessons to learn. The first of which was that no daughter would ever be justified in speaking to her mother in this manner. No, there could never be an excuse for such disrespect!

"It is for *me* to say when and with whom you may have contact." Each word was colder than the one before. "And as a consequence of your poor choice in this matter, you are not to speak with the Irish lord again. Nor will you be permitted to dance with him in the future."

Amy had expected punishment but found that enduring it was a more difficult matter. Still, after dwelling on every moment spent in her devastating dream hero's company, she'd come to recognize it as what was likely to be the one real adventure in an otherwise mundane life. And she refused to ever regret it.

"Your father and I have enlisted Orville's aid to help us enforce these restrictions," Lady Cornelia announced, fully aware that Amy would view this as another form of punishment. "Furthermore, you may thank Orville's courtship of you for restraining me from immediately exiling you to the country. By rights you ought to spend the rest of the Season at Wyfirth Grange."

Amy fought to exert cool logic over a simmering temper, the better for finding some method to circumvent these restrictions. Although this situation had come about as a result of her determination to warn Comlan, it had ended with the warning given her. Now, prevented from speaking directly with him, how would she learn more about the nebulous peril he claimed was a threat to someone she loved? (A threat, Amy inwardly smiled, whose name could certainly not be Orville.)

"Surely," Amy patiently began, despite any argument's likely failure, "if you are so anxious to see me wed, you must recognize how unwise it is to build a barrier between me and any possible suitor."

"Suitor?" Lady Cornelia's voice rose to a shrill pitch of disbelief. "*Orville* is your suitor and certain to offer you a respectable marriage."

Amy opened her mouth to flatly state how unwelcome that prospect was to her, but she was waved into silence while her mother's implacable voice continued.

"Far too many of our peers seem to have been beguiled by the Irishman, but my vision is not blinded by good looks and surface charm. Lord Comlan is *no one's* suitor. He is a dissolute rake and a threat to your virtue." Lady Cornelia's tone was frigid.

"As with any wolf in the wild, he preys on the weakest and most likely to fall victim to his dangerous wiles. No doubt he believes that a woman in her fourth Season is so desperate for masculine attention that she'll easily succumb . . . but not to an honorable proposal."

Amy wanted to flatly inform her mother Comlan wasn't like that. That, indeed, he wasn't a human male at all. But down in the depths of her uncertain soul, a lack of confidence in her feminine attractions whispered that her mother was right.

"When Lord Comlan marries, it will be with a beauty like Lady Isobel." Cornelia added salt to the wound she'd opened on the daughter whose foolish interest in the Irishman she was determined to end. "Indeed, if Isobel has her way, their wedding will be this Season's grand, culminating event—while you must be grateful for Orville's willingness to forgive your inattention and accept you as wife."

Refusing to let the pain delivered by hurtful words show, Amy stood straight and tilted her chin upward. There was one comforting fact to cradle near. Although Isobel might win every goal she sought throughout the rest of her life, she would lose in her quest to secure Comlan as husband. He had in the past and would in the future have ample opportunity to select a far lovelier and more suitable spouse from amongst the golden folk inhabiting his Faerie Realm.

An instant later, Amy heard that victory's hollow echo in the unpleasant inner voice whispering that its message applied equally to her. Not, Amy told herself in a rush to suppress a betraying ache, that she'd ever considered herself a possible mate for the king of the Tuatha De Danann.

"Amy—" Forced to impatiently demand her distracted daughter's attention, a growing annoyance with this further example of disrespect touched Lady Cornelia's ever pale cheeks with rare color. "It is imperative that you understand and accept these restrictions, Amethyst. Only after I am convinced that you do will I be prepared to see our family join Lord Comlan's group next week for the Great Exhibition's opening."

Silver flashes of unexpected hope sparkled in gray eyes. In mere seconds exhilaration conquered despair, an abrupt emotional shift that left Amy light-headed. And she nearly laughed aloud in welcome of her mother's contradictory plans. She wasn't to talk or dance with Comlan ... and yet they would accompany him to the Hyde Park extravaganza? Plainly her socially ambitious mother found it too difficult to refuse the assuredly coveted social plum of an invitation from the Season's most sought-after bachelor.

And Lord Comlan was that! Not only by debutantes and their scheming mothers but by a good many others who'd been charmed by the handsome gentleman's wit and easy manner. Amy, too, was impressed by those attributes and his admirable rescue of a child. But she was equally impressed by the fact that he showed the same courtesy to people of *all* classes, as witness the fact that the relationship between him and Dooley was more that of friends than master and servant.

And now, with her mother's acceptance of the Irish lord's invitation, endless possibilities beckoned. Though the laughter bubbling up inside was successfully muffled, Amy couldn't quash an irrepressible grin.

"Yes ..." Perturbed by her daughter's sudden, bright smile, Lady Cornelia uneasily attempted to both clarify the circumstances and strengthen the rules surrounding these surprising plans. "We've been invited to join a select company embarking on a daylong excursion which will include the Queen's opening at the Crystal Palace. Trusting that you will accept and obey my restrictions, I accepted on behalf of our family."

Lips tightening into a mirthless smile, Lady Cornelia added a final chill but perversely satisfying fact. "But only after making certain that we'll be joining a large group—including both Orville and Lady Isobel."

Once the interview with Lady Cornelia was concluded, Amy steadily climbed the stairs, intending a return to her own small sitting room. But as she reached the upper landing a door near the end of the long corridor creaked open.

"Amy—" A voice softly called.

In answer, Amy silently nodded and her pace increased as she moved toward her waiting brother. After entering the private suite arranged for the heir and his wife, she was a little surprised when Garnet gently shut the door to lend them a daytime privacy rare inside a large and far from empty house.

"Forgive the foolery of this secretive meeting." Garnet gave his sister a rueful smile.

Amy returned the smile with one warmed by deep affection. Her brother was clearly uncomfortable which left her curious about his purpose.

"I've wanted to talk with you alone for a long time." There was no hint of amusement in his expression now. "And since the beginning of the Season it's become even more important."

Curiosity increasing, Amy chose not to slow his explanation with questions.

Garnet's gray eyes gazed sternly into those belonging to his sister. "No matter what arguments mother uses, or even what our father has to say, *don't* marry Orville Bennett."

"I've already resolved to refuse Orville's suit," Amy promptly said. "But why do *you* feel so strongly about my lone suitor?"

Color darkened Garnet's cheeks. He was determined to see that his sister not be forced to pay the price for his crime but, unable to fully explain, he could only grimly respond, "Because your happiness is important to me, and because I know exactly what kind of bounder Orville Bennett is. He'd make you miserable."

A slight scowl creased Amy's brow. Though agreeing that she'd never be happy with the pompous Orville, surely the term *bounder* was too extreme? Garnet's claim reminded her of Comlan's warning and was likely as inaccurate. The former could be ascribed to brotherly concern but the latter?

Garnet was alarmed by Amy's frown. Anxious to avoid questions impossible to safely answer, he made so hasty an exit that his bemused sister was left standing in the center of the withdrawing room he shared with his wife.

Amy shook her head to free it of the confusion left by her brother's odd actions and took a step forward to follow him out. Again a quiet voice intervened.

"Don't go," Lovey pleaded. "I'm miserable and you're the only person I can talk with."

Seeing the sparkle of unshed tears in her friend's eyes, Amy rushed to the open door connecting Lovey's boudoir to this room and wrapped the now softly weeping woman in comforting arms.

"What has you so upset?" Amy gently asked once the flow of tears slowed to a trickle.

"You heard Garnet," a bewildered Lovey softly wailed. "You heard what he said."

"I heard Garnet urging me not to wed Orville." Amy nodded and then a teasing twinkle appeared in gray eyes. "Knowing how little I think of the man, surely I've not dashed your hopes by rejecting him?"

Despite damp cheeks Lovey responded with a tremulous smile.

"No, I thought not." Although the amusement in Amy's expression faded, warm compassion remained. "But what else did Garnet say? Which of his words have worked you into such a state of distress?"

"Didn't you understand?" Lovey mournfully asked while a fresh bout of tears threatened to over-brim. "Surely it's clear he's so unhappy in our marriage that he doesn't want you to be caught in the same snare."

An immediate burst of laughter broke from Amy's throat—startling both Lovey and herself. Yet, it instantly occurred to her how much more fitting it would've been coming from the purpose-fully contrary Comlan.

Then Amy saw the anguish her reaction had added to Lovey's already pained gaze and remorse rushed an explanation to her lips.

"You're being a silly goose!" Amy gave the other woman another quick hug before leaning back to say, "If anything, it's because Garnet is so *happy* in his marriage that he hates to see me trapped in an unhappy alliance."

"Do you think so?" Lovey pleaded for reassurance, afraid to believe what she so fervently wished was true. "Honestly?"

Amy answered with the promptness of conviction. "I'm certain of it."

"But if he's happy with me—" Tears too close to the surface began to flow again. "What's upsetting my even-tempered Garnet so deeply that he's becoming short-tempered?" Lovey slowly shook her head. "I know it must be due to more than how very little he eats or how much sleep he loses while pacing all night. In fact, I'm certain that whatever is troubling him is what robs him of sleep and appetite."

Having no answer to this question, Amy could only murmur indistinct words of comfort while struggling with guilt for being so preoccupied with her own concerns that she hadn't realized her brother was troubled.

Chapter 8

~

"*A* letter for you, Miss Amethyst," announced an impeccable butler of advanced age.

Polite conversation between the stylish ladies seated in a gracious drawing room was abruptly stilled by this highly unusual interruption. Their attention shifted in a single motion to the erect figure standing in an open doorway.

"Thank you, Bingley." Tight-lipped and holding a highly polished teapot poised above one delicate cup, Lady Cornelia sent her butler a meaningful stare. "Leave it on the credenza, if you please."

The afternoon post, like the morning post, was either left in a neat pile on a small table near the entry or handed directly to Lady Cornelia. But its delivery never interrupted tea, certainly not while company was present. Even less would any part of it be given first to a daughter of the house.

As if he hadn't heard, the elderly servant extended his silver salver toward Amy. On it rested a single creamy envelope.

Amy reached for the letter, torn between an impish urge to wink conspiratorially at Bingley and sympathy for the chagrin her mother was experiencing on a day when already she'd had to deal with a willful daughter. This veiled feud between Lady Cornelia and their butler had been going on for as long as Amy could remember. As a child she'd wondered how their otherwise assiduously correct servant dared brave his mistress's ire in ways even she wouldn't dare. Eventually she'd found an answer in the simple fact that Bingley's family had served the Danton family for generations.

Bingley's lengthy alliance with the viscounts of Wyfirth meant his position was secure enough for him to risk subtly pricking at her mother's patronizing attitude. Indeed, since the old lord's day when the rector's daughter first entered Wyfirth Grange as wife to its heir, anyone living near would be quick to admit that their lady was more than a wee bit haughty. And they'd just as certainly take glee in Bingley's challenge to Lady Cornelia's pride of position.

"It was posted in Ireland," Amy softly stated. Uncomfortably aware that everyone was watching, she concentrated on spidery letters forming the return address. "From Miss Patience."

"Ah, yes, dear Miss Patience." Lady Cornelia hastily followed the welcome lead, anxious to divert attention from a servant's intentional misstep. Close acquaintances might understand Bingley's odd habits but . . . As hostess to one duchess, the wife of an earl, and an additional two of Society's most well regarded matrons, Cornelia deemed it imperative that with the lightest of touches she gloss over the error which had seen a letter delivered directly into her daughter's hand.

"Am I right in recalling her as an elderly, talkative woman?" Not waiting for an answer, Lady Cornelia made a show of casually adding, "Charmingly vague, I believe—not unlike her dear friend, your great-aunt Daphenia."

Quelling the smile tempted by her mother's over-use of a favorite term, *dear*, Amy tried to concentrate on deciphering scrawled words. Toward that goal, she again had reason to appreciate Lovey's talent for social small talk. Her friend smoothly stepped into the conversation and assisted the hostess of Wyfirth House in entertaining important visitors while Amy quickly scanned the rambling letter—stopping to reread several unpleasant points.

"I have most unsettling news of odd events which your aunt Daffy refuses to take seriously . . . a rough-looking *Englishman* asking strange questions of Daffy's gardener, Mr. Meaghan . . . if he'd experience in digging secret vaults . . . inordinately interested in you and your activities. . . .

. . . Do wish you'd return to Ireland and convince Daffy to take sensible measures for her own safety. . . .

. . . Asides, my darling grandson, Paddy, would love to see you again. . . .

Although bright sunlight poured through the drawing room's long windows, clouds of anxiety darkened gray eyes as Amy refolded the letter. How could she have allowed personal matters—even one as exceptional as a mocking, unpredictable otherworldly king—to make her forget the broken shutters of her great-aunt's cottage and all that damage portended?

Here in this letter was undeniable proof that the elderly woman's eccentric insistence on keeping her fortune near had lured greedy knaves to threaten the peaceful Irish countryside. That prospect raised the specter of her great-aunt in physical danger, and Amy fervently wished she could immediately rush to her much loved relative's side.

Memories of the warning Comlan had offered the previous day repeated in Amy's thoughts: *a threat to someone you love which each day grows more ominous.* Daffy!

Guilt added yet another layer to Amy's distress. The unbelievable suggestion of Orville as a danger had distracted her from another infinitely more important. Yet, though certain Comlan overestimated her pompous suitor's abilities, she accepted as unquestioned fact Comlan's mastery of the mystical abilities of his kind. He clearly knew already what she'd just learned from Patience. Yes, he was aware of that and likely a great deal more. She must talk with him . . . a hopeless wish.

Feeling powerless, Amy nearly moaned. Not only was she forbidden to openly talk with the Irish lord, but after her previous day's escapade she'd be carefully guarded to thwart any stealthy attempt at personal contact. It was frustrating to accept a full week's wait for the next opportunity to see Comlan at the Great Exhibition's opening. Amy took small consolation in the fact that at least she'd have time to devise some method for eluding her mother's eagle eye and securing private words with the Lord of Doncaully.

The same sun casting light on the formal group sharing tea and idle conversation in a fine London town house, sent bright rays through the small diamond panes of a tiny Irish cottage's mullioned window.

"Could'a knocked me oer with a feather, I tell you." Despite the number of years weighing heavily on her stooped back, Patience stomped from one side of her cramped parlor to the other. "Says Daffy as how she wants her Amy to wed with an Irish lord. Her next-door neighbor, if you please." She turned to glare at her companion. "As if I don't know every livin' soul in this county and no Lord of Doncaully amongst them!"

Patrick O'Leary casually brushed a lock of bright red hair from his brow and grinned at his great-grandmother. He was amused by his granny's disgust over a plan able to effectively thwart their scheme—but then he found perverse humor in almost everything.

"But faith be, me Paddy-boy, though I sent a letter meant to draw Amy back, 'tis easy seen we must do more to see she returns." Patience sent the handsome young man a meaningful look. "Once done 'tis certain I am that me darlin' boy will charm the maid into givin' all we seek and likely more. For well 'tis known what a rogue you are with the women."

"Ah, but, Granny—" Patrick lifted hands palm-out and motioned as if to hold back her words. "There's a power of difference betwixt seducing either faithless wives or silly milkmaids and wooing a fine lady."

"Don't be a gammonin' me." Patience wagged an admonishing finger at the teasing man. " 'Tis easy seen you'll be havin' no difficulty once given the chance to work your wiles."

Paddy grinned again. His loving granny's view was a mite prejudiced though he liked to think nearer to truth than lie. "Be it powerful pleased I am to give that sweet challenge me best effort." Smile fading to a rueful grimace, he added a serious caution. "But to what good use if the prize is gone afore we've the right to claim it ours?"

"Speak you of lurkin' strangers?" The elderly woman stood squarely facing her seated grandson with gnarled fists firmly planted on bony hips. "Thieves bent on stealin' what is no' theirs?"

Patrick nodded and with that motion sunlight burned over bright red hair in a fine counterpoint to the dark expression of solemnity so rare to his face.

"Aye, we must do our all to guard against their tricks ... yet at the same time 'tis imperative we lose no moment in findin' the lure able to induce Amy's hasty return to Eire."

By the fierce determination in his granny's eyes, Paddy knew better than to even mention further possible pitfalls. Great-grandmother Patience was a tiny, fragile woman and to all appearances of the sweetest nature. But he knew what strong will, what single-mindedness she harbored in that frail form.

More importantly, he had learned long ago the utter futility in attempting to reject any plans she made. And why should he when, if successful, it would see the man of humble origins he was become a wealthy man wed to a wellborn lady.

Chapter 9

~

*A*s the appointed hour neared, Hyde Park teemed with throngs of people from every level of society and all remarkably well-behaved. These gathered masses waited with good-natured patience for the royal party to make its way through streets lined with crowds of onlookers from palace to park. Clouds that earlier darkened this Mayday morning had scattered to leave a sky more blue than gray. It was as if even the heavens were lending approval to the Queen's much anticipated opening of her Great Exhibition.

Though having little choice but to remain obediently positioned between her parents, Amy inwardly chaffed against unwelcome restraints while the man she was anxious to speak with stood just beyond her stern-faced father.

"The papers say the pavilion boasts one *million* square feet of glass!" Lord Farley ponderously announced, turning to glance toward their day's host. "Unbelievable, heh?"

"Indeed," Comlan agreed. "Truly a Crystal Palace." He used the name given by the press, a sardonic smile curling his lips while gazing not at the questioner but at that man's daughter who looked particularly fetching in a lilac gown and bonnet trimmed with white silk roses.

Amy felt the brush of an emerald gaze sliding over her. Though her goal was to speak with him, this was not the time, not while her parents were carefully watching. Fearing she'd betray her fascination with him, she focused on a safe and interesting subject for study, joining the multitude to gaze in awe at the pavilion glittering under bright sunlight. Delicate and airy for all its vast size, the giant glass house seemed to effortlessly soar into an almost cloudless sky.

An unwelcome voice startled Amy from her willful preoccupation.

"Isn't it just too marvelous, Comlan?" Lady Isobel gushed, determined to put a quick end to Amy's feeble challenge. "Like some magical fairy palace."

Accustomed to receiving unstinting admiration from every male who came anywhere near, Lady Isobel was decidedly less than pleased by how often the lucky man she'd honored with her company gazed at the unfashionably dark Amethyst Danton.

Amy's mind filled with remembered images of the far more amazing castle she'd visited in a dream, and she couldn't keep herself from peeking around her solemn father, curious to see the king of the Tuatha De Danann's reaction to Isobel's comparison.

Hiding his impatience with both humankind's rigid conventions and the rules controlling his interaction with them, Comlan responded to a discreet, mist-gray gaze with a faint, mocking smile. Amy wouldn't know its source was as much self-contempt for his inappropriate response to her as amusement over Isobel's inaccurate analogy.

The blond beauty clinging to the Irish lord's arm coyly batted her lashes while flashing smiles of studied allure. Her insincere posturing was distasteful to one with Comlan's acute senses and a telling contrast to Amy's uncontrived allure.

It was just as well that his instincts were curbed by the difficulties posed by the intersection of two very different worlds. The winsome Amy had already fogged his view of this fact too often with her shy smiles but brave deeds—a paradox assuredly unintended and likely regretted yet appealing to him. Against the danger in that fact Comlan again reminded himself that, despite the brief explanation he'd given while she tarried in his realm, Amethyst knew too little of his kind to understand his nature—something an admirer of logic was likely to find distasteful. And this was a further warning to remember that the realities of her present and future were vastly different from his.

Under the devastating man's intense green gaze, Amy's creamy skin took on a faint crimson glow. Apparently inevitable but despised, the regrettable blush deepened under the weight of her mother's scowling disapproval.

Figuratively trapped helplessly between two opposing forces, Amy fought to rid herself of both by staring beyond Comlan . . . only to directly meet the ice blue glare of the woman who had fastened herself to Comlan's side before the Wyfirth family arrived.

Amy's glance skittered away. Not even the scorn she heaped on herself for acting a pigeon-heart was enough to force her attention back to that she-vulture. Instead, Amy was grateful to catch a glimpse of her Beattie standing decorously in the background, the epitome of a proper maid waiting to be of service.

Next to a demure Beattie stood Comlan's manservant, the Irishman her friend had heatedly declared a rude oaf and was earnestly striving to ignore. And it was true that although Dooley also waited unobtrusively to serve, his bold demeanor was far from subservient.

"Ah, at last." Orville puffed as he pushed his way through the crowd to join their party. "Pray forgive my tardiness. I had a devilishly difficult time getting through this mob. Feared I might fail to reach you before the thing's begun."

Amy wished he had failed. She'd have welcomed the reprieve. At the Season's outset she'd sworn to fight Orville's pursuit every step of the way. It was a goal she still meant to keep but one proving more difficult than expected. Particularly now when beneath the scrutiny of her parents' eagle eyes she'd be permitted anywhere near Comlan only by accepting Orville's company.

The clatter of carriage wheels demanded attention. A parade of nine royal carriages swept to a halt before the pavilion's entrance and waited for the Queen, her consort and two oldest children to descend from the last. Then while silver trumpets heralded the way, Queen Victoria led twenty-five thousand guests and season-ticket holders inside. As their monarch, resplendent in pink silk, passed along an impressive nave toward the wonderful fountain and blue-and-silver canopied throne at the far end, one organ after another rang out in homage.

Feeling carried on that thundering wave of music, Amy flowed along with the crowd trailing in the queen's wake. It stopped when Prince Albert stepped forward to begin reading aloud a Report of the Royal Commissioners addressed to his royal wife.

The prince's long, dry monologue and the pious prayer that followed efficiently tempered a growing excitement almost too much to bear. But anticipation rose again when the Hallelujah Chorus soared joyously and a long procession formed to follow the Queen on her tour of this amazing building.

By virtue of aristocratic heritage their group was included in the first quarter of that orderly parade. Before Comlan, as host of their party, moved to follow the Queen's lead Orville maneuvered himself to walk at Amy's side. She felt trapped by the action so clearly supported by her parents and in defiance turned her gaze forward—only to shy away from something infinitely more distasteful.

Amy's gray eyes took on a storm cloud darkness while immediately and pointedly averted from the golden beauty hanging on Comlan's arm. Like a bolt of lightning the piercing heat of jealousy had struck.

Jealousy? No! Amy rejected the mere possibility of

such foolishness. Jealousy was an illogical emotion, diametrically opposed to her long-avowed desire to take a rational view of life, to pursue a sane and well-reasoned approach to everything.

Comlan was to blame. Amy firmly bit her lower lip. He was responsible for knocking her off that safe, carefully supported path. He was the one who'd led her into an utterly unreal and irrational world.

A seldom silent conscience scoffed at Amy's too heated defense with memories of how she'd longed for adventure one spring afternoon while lazing in a ring of flowers.

"Amy, are you not feeling quite the thing?" Orville asked, leaning uncomfortably near. "I could escort you back to Wyfirth House."

"Oh, no." Amy stifled a gasp, annoyed that once again, as too often in recent weeks, she'd allowed herself to become absorbed in reveries of one afternoon's unfortunate lapse of judgment and all its repercussions. Amy gazed at her overly concerned companion, feigning the kind of wide-eyed, vapid admiration she most despised.

"I'm far too curious to miss seeing everything inside this marvelous glass building." Amy forced a bright smile. "Why after breakfast Father read aloud from a newspaper article that said thirteen thousand exhibitors have contributed."

Though mollified by Amethyst's flattering attention, Orville's mouth tightened with disapproval. Her father ought not to encourage such unfeminine interests. Offer of escape refused, he urged Amy to close the gap her inattention had opened in the line.

A fresh flood of glowing color spread flags of embarrassment over Amy's cheeks. Not only had the Queen already moved some distance down one aisle with the column of her subjects trailing after but a space had opened between where Amy stood and the point to which her parents, their host and Lady Isobel had progressed. Garnet and Lovey hovered behind her and others in their group crowded near while the throng waiting farther back impatiently murmured and glared.

Amy hastened forward, sincerely anxious to view the Crystal Palace's innumerable displays. Her first glance inside the pavilion's eighteen glass-enclosed acres had been enough to convince her it held far too much to be seen in a single visit, and she fervently hoped this wouldn't be her last.

Like the two representations standing near the entrance—Courage in the form of an enormous statue of Richard the Lionhearted and Power symbolized by a twenty-four-ton block of coal—the whole exhibition was an amazing mix of art and machines. Things of great beauty vied with others grotesque or just plain gaudy. There were mundane items such as could be seen in any shop but also ingenious mechanical wonders.

The American section included two exhibits that stirred particular interest: a reaping machine designed by an American named McCormick and a new gun called the Colt revolver. While the men in her party fell into a discussion of the various merits of these items, Amy thought it odd that she seemed to be the only one who recognized an obvious paradox: One had the potential to benefit mankind while the other could only destroy.

Unconsciously responding to the call of a steady emerald gaze, Amy glanced sidelong and met Comlan's wry smile. He gave a nod, almost imperceptible but enough to set rays of sunlight rippling over golden hair. She immediately looked away, biting her lip hard. His action suggested that he understood and shared her *unspoken* opinion.

Could he read her thoughts? Surely not! A faint frown marred Amy's smooth forehead. No folklore or fairy tale she had ever heard even hinted that his race possessed such a talent. The mere suggestion that anyone could freely roam through her mind made Amy terribly uncomfortable and left her shifting uneasily at Orville's side.

Comlan saw the fleeting expressions chasing across Amy's face and recognized his mistake. Since humans neither shared nor comprehended the acute perceptiveness of his kind, it was likely that the dark colleen had misunderstood. The viscount and his wife moved on with the procession, but Comlan lingered for a moment longer beside the revolver exhibit. Then, despite either the impatient blond beauty clinging to his arm or the glowering Orville, he gave Amy a quiet explanation couched in an innocuous compliment.

"You have a most expressive face, Miss Danton."

Willing the heat of her cheeks to fade, Amy yielded to Orville's less than gentle hand at her back and followed as Lord Comlan and Lady Isobel moved a few steps forward. When the column of humanity paused again, she studied the exhibit to her left with unmerited intensity although she couldn't later have described it to anyone.

Was it true? Had she shown interest in the reaper but distaste for the gun? Was it that and nothing more which had revealed her opinion to the king of the Tuatha De? But if Comlan could read that in her expressions, what more had he seen? Jealousy? Oh, horrors, no! A renewed flood of color burned.

"Amy—" Orville irritably demanded the return of his companion's attention. After watching the Irishman effortlessly draw Amy's gaze all too often, he'd had quite enough. Certainly enough to confirm his wisdom in arranging to see a permanent end put to such interference.

"Look at that." Orville motioned toward an ornate easy chair made of papier-mâché which, for all its padding, looked woefully uncomfortable. "They call it the Day Dreamer."

Amy murmured a quiet, conventional acknowledgment. It was clear that Orville intended to establish his prior claim on her to Lord Comlan. And she was trapped in his company despite a heartfelt wish to be rid of the pompous man. Again, resentment simmered—resentment of watchful eyes forcing her to welcome Orville to win some small chance of remaining near enough to the devastating Irishman that she could talk with him. . . . Or at least obliquely pass on information gleaned from Patience's letter.

To Amy's growing frustration, that hope proved in vain. By the time the Queen's tour concluded hours later, Amy's feet hurt and her stylishly voluminous skirts felt lead weighted. A whole night's dancing wasn't half so tiring as this slow procession. Yes, the exhibits were as exciting as promised, and she did intend a later return to revisit her favorites. But now she'd be happy to escape this strictly regimented, laggardly walk. She prayed for better fortune at the tea party in winning an opportunity to speak with their host.

As the procession slowly neared the exit, Amy realized that even this tour's sedate pace had been overly trying for Orville. She was tired but the stout man was so weary he wheezed rather than talked. Amy sympathized yet couldn't help being thankful that something had ended or at least slowed the constant droning of his voice.

Thousands of the Queen's guests poured from the pavilion and were absorbed into the tens of thousands still crowding Hyde Park. On leaving the Crystal Palace, Amy's party paused on green lawns to one side. Despite either Lady Cornelia's pointed glare or the deep frown creasing a nearly bald Orville's brow, Amy's dark crystal eyes helplessly shifted to the fascinating man whose hair was burnished a gleaming gold by sunlight.

As if to justify being center of the dark beauty's attention after recognizing himself as inspiration for the condemnation others had turned on her, Comlan graciously reminded his guests. "A hopefully restoring tea awaits in my lodgings."

The masses ebbed and flowed while men busied themselves visually searching the sea of waiting coaches for their own. Their haste betrayed a longing for the welcome ease of the leather seats inside.

"Come, Isobel," a stern voice intruded.

Glancing sidelong, Amy saw Isobel's previously unnoticed older sister. She had been a widow for more than five years but by choice still dressed in severe black and looked impossibly grim while stepping forward to direct Lady Isobel toward their waiting carriage.

Amy's eyes darted to the left and found a tight, satisfied smile on her mother's lips. She was plainly pleased by the vain beauty's departure, even though she'd earlier welcomed Isobel's distraction for the Irish lord. Demonstrating disdain for the retreating pair, Lady Cornelia gave her full attention to dissecting the fashions worn by other women of their class—with Lovey's avid participation. But Amy's gaze returned to Lady Isobel and her sister. She watched until they'd climbed into a plush interior and dealt with the rich cloth of their skirts as well as the multitude of petticoats worn beneath.

Idly glancing again toward the rest of her party, Amy's eye was caught by the silver glitter of a sharp blade.

Despite the lingering crowd, she had an unobstructed view of a burly man dressed in Sunday best plunging his dagger into Comlan's belly.

The Irishman fell back a step, laying one strong hand atop another to press against the wound.

Gasping, Amy started forward but Garnet was closer and reached Comlan first.

"I say, are you all right?" Honest concern filled Garnet's voice while others of their group crowded around. "Damn fool meant to kill you."

"No doubt that's true. But as you can see—" With

a rueful smile of great charm, Comlan spread his hands wide, laying bare the undamaged expanse of his waistcoat. "He did me no harm."

"He missed?" Garnet's dark brows arched in disbelief. "I would have sworn he struck you a mortal blow." Studying the apparently untouched man, he slowly shook a head of hair as ebony-deep as Amy's. "You must lead a charmed life, my friend."

"So it would seem," Comlan agreed. His smile tilted with remarkably gentle mockery as he met solemn gray eyes clouded with concern, confusion ... and sympathy. Sympathy was an emotion seldom necessary in his realm and one he'd almost never received. But now the honesty of it flowed from her to him while the tender warmth in the depths of a charcoal gaze offered a rare and precious gift he fervently wished he could claim as his own.

Calm thoughts knocked askew by the frightening but miraculously inept assault, Amy bit at her lip. She'd seen the weapon and the blow. She had! How could Comlan be unmarked? *Thank God* he was uninjured ... but how? Clearly here was further proof—if she needed it—that strange forces were at work. Forces that had nothing to do with the rationality of science or her safe, sane, predictable world. In that same brief instant she questioned the value of her mundane world when judged against the joys of a life filled with new challenges, adventures ... and love.

"Come, ladies," Lord Farley called to his wife and daughter. "Our transport awaits."

Still numbed by the scene but even more by the staggering revelation of love, Amy automatically obeyed her father's summons, aware to the depths of her soul of an emerald gaze never wavering from her back.

Orville realized Lord Wyfirth and his lady wife were disappointed that he hadn't offered to escort Amethyst to the planned tea in his coach. But, having business to conduct, he climbed alone into his own coach. Not until the vehicle had been maneuvered well away and onto less crowded city streets did he give his attention to the burly figure hunched into one corner of the opposite seat.

"You failed!" Orville's pithy accusation was an ominous hiss.

"Oh, no, I didn't. I swear it. Felt me blade sink in deep, I did." These whined words issued from a man looking distinctly uncomfortable in fancier garb than was his habit to wear. "Only look. 'Tis enow blood on th' blade as to prove it true."

Orville's eyes narrowed on the proffered weapon and its dark, telltale stain.

"Well then, Macraedy," he hissed, "you've skewered the *wrong* man."

"How can you say it?" The sharp arch of sandy brows reflected the speaker's honest consternation. Driven by nervous habit, he reached up to adjust the eye patch missing today in honor of his day's truck with the nobs and plaintively whined, "You saw me!"

"What I saw only minutes ago was the Irishman not dead nor even harmed." Under a growing but impotent anger, Orville's hands curled into fists. "The man looked quite in the pink of health to me.

Why even his clothing revealed not so much as a wrinkle out of place . . . far less a bloody gash."

"Can't be so!" Hair once carefully combed for the part he had played in the Hyde Park charade fell forward in its more usual untidy clumps when Macraedy vehemently shook his head.

"But it *is*. And you'd best make a better job of it next time . . . elsewise I'll call all those loans forfeit and see you carted off to debtor's prison."

The next instant Orville was pleased by his minion's expression, like an animal trapped by a skilled hunter. No, this blundering nitwit wouldn't dare to fail again.

Chapter 10

~

"$\mathcal{F}$arley, I've developed a most vicious headache." Pausing a few brief steps from their waiting carriage, Lady Cornelia pressed fingertips to her temples in affected pain while nearly whimpering a plea. "I beg you to take me directly home . . . please."

"Certainly, my dear." The viscount instantly agreed. "Then after you're settled in your bed at Wyfirth House with a soothing compress and maid to administer a few comforting drops of laudanum, I'll send a footman with our regrets to Lord Comlan. I'm sure the man will understand, considering the long and exciting—but trying—day we shared."

From a mere two steps behind, Amy saw her mother sag helplessly against her much taller father like the delicate flower all well-bred women were taught they ought to appear. Moreover, Amy clearly heard the doleful plea which effectively sabotaged her ill-defined plans for stealing a few private words with their futilely waiting host. She ought to have expected it. Her mother was prone to these headaches ... headaches which conveniently struck at the most opportune moments to ensure a desired result.

Lord Wyfirth settled his wife inside the family carriage, and then turned to help his daughter climb in as well. After hours of alternately standing or creeping slowly forward, Amy was grateful for the comfort of padded leather seats. The coachman skillfully drove their vehicle through lingering crowds while the viscount and his wife rode in silence—her now hatless head resting against his shoulder.

Amy stared blindly through the window at crowds of common people still lining the streets, all dressed in their Sunday best. She was badly disappointed by her lost opportunity for time in the company of the one who'd deflected a deadly blade or healed its wound. That incredible action had simultaneously struck her with the stunning realization that the fantasy hero come to life cradled her heart in the magical power of his hands. Though this day had begun with hopes for a chance to share Patience's letter with Comlan, now she desperately wanted to assure herself that he was truly unharmed.

Thrusting wit-dulling fears for Comlan's safety into a dark recess of her mind, Amy mentally searched for the next logical step. No, more importantly, the next plausible step to take. She couldn't send another message to him and again arrange a morning meeting in Hyde Park, not after her mother had specifically cautioned their servants against playing any role in such a forbidden event. By helping her they'd risk dismissal without character, a punishment certain to see them end quite literally on the street. And that selfish, that heartless, Amy wasn't nor could ever want to be. Yet, if she couldn't rely on the aid of servants, then what?

Of course! The answer was so obvious that Amy was ashamed of herself for not immediately recognizing it. She glared blindly at a guiltless tree daring to rise above the city's rooftops. Any pretension she had to a clear and logical mind was left in question by her failure to see how easy it would be to simply send Patience's letter to Comlan with a note of her own explaining her concerns. After all, during their first meeting in the park hadn't he warned her about such dangers?

Despite its new bruises, Amy's pride in a carefully developed skill for cool reasoning confirmed the wisdom of this cautious plan. However, her long regretted but still untamed spirit of adventure balked. If she merely sent the letter with a note, she wouldn't be able to learn Comlan's thoughts on the matter nor discuss with him actions to foil the blackguard behind Daffy's peril. Worst of all, she'd forfeit one of her likely few remaining opportunities to be near . . .

Even to herself it was hard for Amy to confess that she'd miss most the chance for private time with the stunningly handsome and far too fascinating being from an utterly illogical fantasy realm—far less easily admit an impossible love. Yet, despite her best intents, she couldn't suppress memories of thrilling moments spent in his powerful embrace. Thick lashes drifted down to lie in black crescents on cheeks warming under potent, very private visions.

Amy forced her eyes to open wide and focus on reality. Chasing errant thoughts back into the shadowy corners of her mind, Amy made what she justified as the most rational choice. The only option was to don her long, black, hooded cloak and go to Comlan alone . . . tonight.

She couldn't call for the family carriage nor would a hansom cab be readily available in such finer residential streets as Ealsingham Court. But, though she'd never done it, Amy was certain she wouldn't have to walk too far before reaching busier thoroughfares.

Although as sheltered as most debutantes, Amy wasn't completely unaware of the vague dangers lurking in dark streets. Her courage wavered slightly but she immediately berated herself for the possibility of failing Daffy by virtue of a craven heart.

"Amy—" Lord Farley called his apparently daydreaming daughter—a fault that regrettably seemed to have become her habit of late. "We're home so please join us."

Startled to discover their carriage had not only stopped at the front gate of Wyfirth House but that her parents had already stepped down, Amy hastened to slide across the seat and accept her father's hand to aid in a graceful descent.

Once the trio entered the imposing brick building, several hovering servants solicitously helped Lady Wyfirth up the sweeping staircase to her boudoir while the viscount retired to his study.

Amy trailed up the steps far, far behind her mother's retinue hoping that, after receiving their request to be excused from the tea, someone in Lord Comlan's residence would send Beattie back to her. Beattie and her mother's maid—whose services were shared today with Lovey—had naturally been provided with a hired coach to follow their mistresses. And neither maid could've known in advance about the change Lady Wyfirth had made in their day's plans.

Unfastening her bonnet, Amy stepped into the rose and white bedroom still decorated with dolls, stuffed animals and other mementos of her childhood. She was preoccupied with planning the evening's secret adventure ... leaving her utterly unprepared for what awaited inside.

To Beatrice's disgust, she once again found herself trapped in confines all too close with the Irish lord's impertinent manservant. She fervently wished she could have escaped when Amy had or at least that Mrs. Davis, Lady Wyfirth's maid, was also on her way back to Wyfirth House. But, no, Mrs. Davis was required to remain on the off chance that the future viscountess, Louvisa, might require her services.

"You could've returned to your master after summoning this hansom," Beatrice tartly admonished her unwelcome companion. "I don't need the questionable worth of your company to see me safely home."

"Faith and begorra! A regular tartar you are!" Dooley hooted, plainly not at all offended. "And here I be doin' you a fine favor, Mrs. Milford."

"No heathen Irishman need do me any favors," Beattie huffed, hands clamped tightly around a furled parasol.

"Who be you callin' a heathen? 'Twas the English what turned heretic and broke from the true church." Dooley instinctively defended his countrymen although he'd "no' be admittin' " what an odd quirk of faith his bond with the Tuatha had wrought.

"Tch, tch." Beattie shook her head with feigned regret for his lost soul. "The Irish are a strange lot and as incomprehensible as their way of slaughtering the Queen's English."

"Ah, 'tis an insult you mean." Dooley nodded, mischief dancing in his eyes. "And that's as should be for didn't I say, just as soon as I heard your lady call you Beattie, that 'twas better said Beastie."

Temper heating, Beatrice nearly snorted while turning her burning glare to pierce twilight shadows deepening beyond the window.

"I've no doubt but wha' you drove Mr. Milford to a great likin' for his jar."

The unfamiliar term even more than the mention

of her nonexistent husband startled Beattie into again glancing toward her gleefully grinning companion. And the confusion furrowing her brows brought yet another loud guffaw from Dooley.

"His jar . . . his drink." He cocked one eyebrow, a deeper red than his fiery hair. "You ken?"

"Tch, tch!" Again, Beattie repeated her favorite expression of dismissive contempt and again Dooley laughed louder.

"Surely, since your master is host of this afternoon tea—" Beattie took a different tack, anxious to underscore this incorrigible man's shortcomings. "You should've returned to him as soon as possible."

"Don' you wirra on tha' matter. There's a veritable army seein' to it all. An' I'll no' be wanted." For the first time during their drive, Dooley tamed his nearly irrepressible humor. "Asides, there's things as somat ought be a warnin' your mistress."

"Something *you* would know?" Beattie was clearly dubious.

"Aye." With exaggerated solemnity, Dooley intoned, "There is them as is up to no good."

"Hah! And you think this is some rare occurrence? Something no one else knows?" Beattie thoroughly enjoyed heaping ridicule on the man who'd dared call her *Beastie*. "Why the City is littered with creatures of ill intent. And I hardly like to think what a multitude there are throughout the whole of England."

Though seriously tempted to pretend shock that *her* country was so rife with such villains, he calmly argued. "You silly creature, have you no' under-standin' that I'm a talkin' the safety of your lady's Great-aunt Daffy—no' yours nor even Miss Danton's."

"Ah, hah. And you think I might believe that by some heathen trickery or superstitious nonsense you possess the way to know what's about in a country a good long distance from here?" Beattie's scorn earned the return of Dooley's grin.

"Aye, well, be it you ought for I've learned a fair bit 'bout magical ways durin' me years amongst the good gentry o' Erin."

When his scowling companion looked to have been more thoroughly confused than enlightened by his words, Dooley gleefully cackled, " 'Tis a grand pity that you lack the good sense to be a friend to the sidh dwelling in our blessed Irish raths. Simple fac' it be that the Tuatha De have a great store o' knowledge and talents we puir mortals lack."

Sidh? Tuatha? Beattie had heard quite, quite enough of such drivel from Amethyst. And only for love of her lambie had she listened. But no one could force her to endure so much as a single further insinuation of similar delusional nonsense from this insulting heathen, this coarse . . .

Determined to waste on the man not even the breath required for a further disdainful "tch," Beatrice's fiercely burning glare caught a glimpse of Wyfirth House farther down the street. She demanded that the cab stop immediately and lost no moment in climbing down without the assistance of any useless male.

* * *

"Patrick!" Startled, Amy sagged back against her bedroom's closed door while scores of wild questions chased through her mind. "What are you doing here? And how did you get in? Does anyone know you're here?"

"Climbed in through a window." Paddy boldly winked at his pretty inquisitor.

Despite an inner tremble of unease, Amy forced herself to straighten, control wary suspicions and bravely step farther into a room that should never have contained any unrelated male.

Paddy's eyes danced with irrepressible laughter. But by Amethyst's guarded expression, he saw the right in choosin' to keep some facts to hisself. She was no' likely to appreciate his fine skill and many years experience in getting into and out o' fine houses undetected ... with a few little bobbles o' reward for his trouble.

"And where's the harm?" Like a member of some fine pantomime show, he adopted an exaggerated guise of wounded feelings.

"No one saw you?" This unexpected visit reinforced Amy's long held opinion that Patience's handsome grandson was more irresponsible child than man. And, despite his grandmother's all too obvious hopes, someone whose suit for her hand was no more welcome than was Orville's.

"With all the Society folk at Her Royal Nibs to-do and no callers expected, your servants finished their duties early so as to claim a few blessed moments to themselves."

"But what are you doing here?" Amy whipped initially scattered wits back into order.

147

"Me granny has fussed herself into a fine state over your great-aunt Daffy's peril." The uninvited guest ruefully grimaced.

"Why?" Amy sharply demanded, alarm rising. "What happened? Is she all right?"

Paddy shrugged. "I only know that after the warnin' signs we've seen, granny is sore afraid to think her dear friend alone whilst who knows what wicked rogues have planned for her."

Although hardly a definitive accounting, this single statement seemed to Amy confirmation of all her nebulous fears. Fingers unconsciously folded tightly together, she bit hard on her lip. Trapped in London, what could she possibly do to help Daffy? What, considering how completely she'd failed in today's earnest efforts to discuss the matter with Comlan.

"You must come with me now." Putting the full measure of his vaunted charm into the plea, Paddy gently pulled Amy's hands apart to lightly squeeze them. "Stay with Daffy until the danger passes."

"Now?" Amy was aghast . . . initially. But as Patrick fervently nodded, she made a decision utterly out of character with her claimed admiration for calm and reasoned actions. She would go to Ireland. Go immediately. How could she not? If she chose otherwise and something happened to Daffy that her presence might have prevented, she'd suffer a lifetime of painful regret.

"Amy—" The door swung open under Beatrice's firm hand. Despite well-oiled hinges, it faintly squeaked . . . a sound accompanied by a gasp, equal parts horror and reproach.

Whirling around, Amy gave Beattie a speaking glance effectively warning her to silence.

"Remember," Amy said while softly closing the door, "I told you about the letter I received from my great-aunt's dear friend, Patience?"

Beattie slowly nodded, plainly skeptical of these strange doings on the heels of her unpleasant ride with Dooley.

"This is Patrick O'Leary, her grandson." Suddenly struck by the absurdity of a formal introduction made in the privacy of a debutante's boudoir, Amy couldn't restrain an inappropriate grin.

Attention on the unrepentant intruder, Beattie missed Amy's ill-timed amusement and again nodded. She chose to guard her tongue until some explanation was given for the brazen man's purpose here. And to excuse his presence in her innocent lambie's bedroom it had better be something of importance equal to the Second Coming.

"He has come to escort me back to Daffy's side." With this flatly stated explanation Amy made a valiant attempt for calm.

"Oh, no!" Beatrice firmly rejected the mere notion. "No, no, no! You are not going back to Ireland in the midst of the Season and *not* with that stranger! What could your parents possibly be thinking?"

Now here, Amy ruefully acknowledged, was the biggest challenge to be met.

"They don't know!" Seeing the expressions chasing across her lambie's face, Beattie had read the truth. "Your parents don't know, do they?"

Amy grimaced, no words of hers would ease that uncomfortable truth.

"And how do you think to get away? Just walk out, bold as you please?" After her verbal battle with that daft Irishman in the hansom cab, Beattie's sensitivities had already been sorely chaffed. "What about me? Do you mean to drag me off into the wilds, too? Paying no mind to what your parents are likely to demand of me for helping their scapegrace daughter."

"No." Amy firmly shook a dark head. "I'd never let you risk so much."

"Ah, but you'll risk it? Tch, tch." Beattie solemnly gazed at Amy in wordless rebuke. "As if I'd let my lambie go off alone with any male, least of all some strange Irishman."

"It isn't your choice," Amy firmly stated.

"Ah, well," Beattie responded with equal determination. "We'll see about that."

Watching these two stubborn women, Patrick realized it was time for him to intervene.

"Ladies, ladies. 'Tis a compromise you'll be wantin'." Suddenly the focus of feminine attention, Patrick sensed their hostility. Although they showed no willingness to be convinced, undaunted, he wielded his Irish charm. "Your maid can play mother hen till we reach the train station where me granny waits with earnest hope that you'll be lendin' yourself to this journey. Then you'll never be alone with this strange Irishman." He sent Beattie a teasing grin.

"Already have we secured a private coach on the train," Paddy continued, turning toward Amy. "It'll reach the coast just in time for us to board a ship departin' on the mornin' tide. You'll be at your great-aunt Daffy's cottage in time for tea."

"That's as may be." Beattie was still unconvinced and suspicious of this smooth talking male who sounded all too much like the reprehensible Dooley. Stern expression mitigated by worry, she looked to Amy. "But I don't see how you think it possible to creep away so easily."

" 'Tis the easiest part, me darlin'," Paddy smoothly answered the question not asked of him. "We'll all slip out unseen the same way tha' I came in."

Beattie sent him a brief yet fierce glare.

"But, Beattie," Amy called for the return of her maid's attention. "After I've boarded the train with Patience and before the hansom cab I'll hire brings you home, I've a little chore for you."

Frown becoming a scowl, Beattie turned fully toward Amy. There were too many peculiar things afoot already, and she didn't like to think what more her lambie might request.

"She's done what?" Demanded the tall man silhouetted against light flowing through his home's open front door.

Beatrice was appalled when the Irish lord she'd expected to be horrified by news of her usually stable lambie's escape through a window and flight from the country, threw back his head to laugh uproariously. But then hadn't all three of the Irishmen she'd recently met proven what a peculiar breed they were.

Once again the human maid had done the near

impossible—shock Comlan. He was pleased as Amy's feat also meant her carefully built veneer of unimaginative predictability was beginning to break. Through that crack, however narrow, flowed a weak glimmer of hope that their worlds might yet intersect. As someone who treasured the unexpected and cultivated the unlikely, it was welcome. Furthermore, it afforded at least a slight chance that the dark maid might yet be his alone ... a faint possibility beckoning him with tempting visions of far more than mere welcome.

"I will see to your lady's safety." When Comlan nodded, gleams of light from behind seemed to get caught in his golden hair and glow from within. "Worry on it no more."

"But how?" Beattie demanded, unwilling to be foisted off so easily. "You're here and she's heaven knows where by now."

"I doubt you'd find comfort in my explanation." With a charm that put Patrick's paltry efforts to shame, Comlan smiled at the woman watching him with unveiled suspicion. "The best I can give you is a vow made on all I hold dear that it will be true."

Dooley's claim of years spent with the Tuatha De and their *great store o' knowledge and talents we puir mortals lack* raced through Beattie's mind as clearly as if just spoken. Lord Comlan was right. Beattie slowly shook her head. She wouldn't be comforted by his explanation if it involved such heathen trickery.

"Would you like me to have Dooley accompany you safely home again?" Comlan wryly inquired.

"No!" Beattie gasped, whirling about and

marching back to the waiting hansom. That was the very *last* thing she would ever want. Even less now when she already had before her the daunting prospect of sneaking into Wyfirth House through an unlocked window, just as if she were some common thief.

Chapter 11

~

To fight the strong wind plastering blue-gray skirts down the full length of her legs, Amy aided the purpose of satin ribbons by holding her bonnet in place with one hand. With the other she gripped the ship's rail while watching a distant harbor fade ever farther back into the morning mist.

Amy had grown uneasy after hours in the constant company of Patience and her grandson, first on the train and just now in the cabin below deck. They watched her too steadily and whispered between themselves. No reason they shouldn't, she supposed, but she didn't like it anyway. Giving the weak excuse of a wish for fresh air, she'd slipped their rein to welcome even the bracing cold of morning.

The brisk breeze revived a weary Amy and cleared a mind too long held captive by her companions' useless babble. She was worried about Garnet's trouble and Lovey's fears but even concern for family gave way to images of the golden Irish lord.

These were her first private moments since the revelation of her impossible love for this man from an incredible race so far beyond her own that she could never hope for more than the taste of heaven already experienced in his embrace.

"I hope it's not discomfort caused by the rolling motion of the sea that has you clutching the rail."

The familiar deep but utterly unexpected voice, startled Amy into quickly turning ... too quickly as at that same moment the vessel pitched sharply to one side. She'd have fallen to the deck, if not into the sea, had the subject of her longing thoughts failed to catch her close against his broad chest.

Intensely conscious of their proximity, Amy trembled while Comlan's warm maleness wrapped about her as surely as his strong arms. She gazed up to discover so scant a distance separated them that she could clearly see the hot glitter in emerald eyes. Too, she saw when their burning intensity dropped to her parted lips and trembled. The mere brush of his gaze strengthened heated memories of what had been and inspired wild visions of what could be. . . .

Shocked by the wanton trail her thoughts had so easily followed, Amy allowed her forehead to drop forward and rest against the solid wall he was. That action dislodged a bonnet saved from the playful wind only by deep blue ribbons tied around her throat.

Initially glad to find her alone and unharmed, Comlan's pleasure was increased by her helpless response to him. His green eyes danced with amusement as he tilted a reluctant chin up and again gazed into the dark damsel's winsome face. The charming color warming her cheeks was assuredly due not to the chill breeze but to the intimacy of their innocent embrace. Though well aware of the sweet dangers in such seductive exchanges, he cradled her temptingly soft form even nearer. Potent smile tilting awry, he inwardly mocked himself for the ease with which this *human* beauty swayed the king of the Tuatha de Danann's strong will.

Gaze caught and held by the emerald fire in his, wild sensations throbbed through Amy. It stole her breath, leaving not even enough for a sigh as his firm mouth brushed achingly across hers again and again before settling to nip at her lips until they fell open, welcoming the devastating excitement of a deeper kiss. Hands pressed against his powerful chest felt the mighty pounding of his heart—an echo of her own.

The slam of a distant door intruded with its reminder that they were not truly alone. Amy pulled away. She chided herself for the betraying heat washing her face with vivid rose and fought the craven urge to once more close her eyes and bury her face against his chest. Instead, though it required the mustering of her every shred of courage, she steadily met the melting power of Comlan's gaze while making a calm inquiry.

"Did Beattie give you both my letter from Patience O'Leary and the message I left for you?"

"Indeed, yes." Comlan solemnly nodded, hiding his amused satisfaction with her hard won courage. He was gratified by this further proof that there was much hope for the damsel once determined to follow a safe path through her tedious life in the mortal world—and only wished that he could linger to share it with her.

"But our train was pulling out as Beattie left. You couldn't have caught it. . . ." Eyes darkened to charcoal narrowed on the handsome face so near while Amy tentatively raised a subject her well-trained logic insisted must be addressed. "And as there were no more scheduled last night, how did you get here?"

Comlan regretfully shook his bright hair. It seemed that despite Amy's step forward, she would stubbornly fall back to echo her maid in asking the same question of him. But while the servant had reason to wonder, surely Amethyst should already know that for him any form of physical transport—though possibly amusing—was utterly unnecessary.

More than his negative motion, it was the gentle rebuke lending shadows to an emerald gaze that made Amy feel the fool. How could she have requested a mundane explanation from this incredible being who was anything . . . everything but either predictable or rational?

"Amy, you darlin' girl." Patience's voice was remarkably sharp considering the sweetness of her words. "We feared you'd taken ill or fallen overboard."

"Oh, no." Guiltily stepping farther back from Comlan, Amy turned to face the pair she'd left below but who now stood on the deck at the top of stairs ascending from one lower. "It's only that I met an Irish friend from London on his return for a visit home."

"Oh, really?" After critically looking over the stranger who had moved to wrap an arm around Amy's shoulders, Patience gritted her teeth to muffle the groan of displeasure earned by his stunning good looks. This much competition her darlin' Paddy didn't need.

"I'm sorry, pray forgive me for not immediately introducing you to Comlan, Lord of Doncaully." Embarrassed by the faux pas, in Amy's haste to make amends, she failed to notice the startled look exchanged between the new arrivals. "Comlan, meet friends of my great-aunt Daphenia's— Patience O'Leary and her grandson, Patrick."

"But just call me Paddy." Overly confident, as always, Patrick flashed his most charming smile. "Everyone does."

Comlan nodded but with experience and perceptions beyond human comprehension, he recognized an unpleasant core beneath the young man's facile surface. Something, he sensed, was not as these two purported it to be. Were they a threat to Daffy? Or to Amy? Warily his arm tightened about the damsel for whose safety he abruptly realized he'd even risk shattering the rules of his own realm. That danger doused him with the icy water of reality and reminded him that, despite abilities defying the understanding of humankind, when dealing with their mortal world there were unfortunate limits to what he could foresee and rules governing any action he might wish to take.

"And where is your home?" Patience probed in a voice so honey-sweet it fairly oozed.

"I'm a neighbor of your friend Daffy," Comlan smoothly answered, watching the elderly woman's face intently.

"Hmm . . ." Paddy blandly took up where his granny had stopped. "Only abode I know of thereabouts is a crumblin' castle."

Comlan nodded and with a mocking smile answered, "My ancestral home."

An uncomfortable silence descended while the O'Learys waited in vain for some explanation of where he truly resided. When none was forthcoming from the man whose mocking smile made her uncomfortable, Patience admitted defeat—for the moment.

"Paddy-boy, take your granny below. 'Tis too powerful cold for me ol' bones out here."

Once the pair had descended the steep stairway and closed themselves into their private cabin, the younger turned to the older and let a fearful glimmer of his foul temper flash forth.

"An' what do we do now? What now with the bleedin' giant hoverin' around our prize?"

Patience only shook her head in despair and in a mournful voice uselessly muttered, " 'Tis a grand pity, that. A grand pity."

Paddy could not, would not be so easily thwarted. Hands clenched so tightly his fists were white, in a voice deadly quite he said, "Kill him."

After a very late breakfast in her boudoir, Lady Wyfirth descended her town house's elegant winding stairway perfectly coiffed and modishly dressed for receiving callers as hostess of a planned At Home afternoon.

Bingley solemnly stepped forward to open the hall door into the formal front parlor. A single critical glance proved everything to be in perfect order. Heavy velvet drapes had been pulled back to reveal sheer lace beneath while the scent of spring wafted from fresh-cut flowers arranged in the brass bowls placed on small parquet tables at either end of the massive sofa. Next to her own favorite oval-backed chair, the tea table waited in readiness with delicate cups and saucers of finest Dresden china. At the appropriate moment after guests had begun to arrive, she would ring a tiny bell summoning the parlor maid to bring in a silver teapot gleaming as brightly as the spoons already laid out.

Cornelia was gratified by the servants success in obeying her every demand. Although Farley's presence was, quite naturally, required in the House of Lords, Garnet had promised to remain at home and help entertain. Hearing footsteps and rustling skirts behind, she turned to find her son and his wife approaching.

"You look lovely, Louvisa." Cornelia complimented the daughter-in-law at least as concerned as she with appearances and with all the nuances of proper styles for every event.

"Thank you, Mama-in-law." Lovey smiled sweetly while Garnet gave her shoulders a quick squeeze.

A firm knock on the door sent the three wellborn residents of One Ealsingham Court quickly into the parlor where they prepared to receive their first guests.

Moments later Lady Cornelia, thrilled by the honor, welcomed the Duchess of Aylton.

"How nice of you to call, Your Grace." Once the proud duchess had nodded an acknowledgment, Lady Cornelia's attention shifted to the younger woman hovering demurely a half step behind. "And your daughter, Lady Charlotte, as well."

The two visitors graciously murmured appropriate greetings all around before deigning to settle on the sofa end nearest Lady Cornelia.

Lovey took her role as the future lady of the house seriously and fulfilled her duty by opening conversation with the introduction of a subject surely fresh in everyone's thoughts and likely to evolve into the expected round of unimportant social chatter.

"Did you enjoy the Queen's opening of the exhibition yesterday, Your Grace?"

"Wasn't it thrilling?" The youthful Lady Charlotte, enjoying her first Season as debutante, impulsively answered before her mother could. By that error she earned the duchess's tight, reproving frown.

Well-trained in the niceties of polite company, Garnet smoothed over the momentary unease. "I thought the Hallelujah Chorus sounded particularly inspiring when sung in that vast glass building."

Bingley announced more visitors before anyone could add to that comment.

"Lord Orville Bennett and The Honorables Charles and Eloise Carter-Bourne."

Lady Cornelia welcomed "dear" Orville before

extending the same courtesy to the Baron of Pelleston's son and daughter. She maintained her facade as the epitome of a gracious hostess although after meeting the former's curious gaze, her thoughts were prey to the horrible recognition of a most serious lack in this gathering.

The afternoon was well underway but Amy had yet to be seen. Surely her daughter couldn't still be lazing abed? Lady Cornelia forced a pleasant mask to cover growing irritation. Their past day's promenade through the Crystal Palace hadn't been so tiring as to excuse such sloth. She could only hope Orville had sense enough not to question Amy's absence while other visitors were present.

At the ringing of a tiny bell, the front parlor maid, Alice, promptly appeared with a heavy silver teapot resting atop its matching tray. Her apron was as pristine and well-starched as the cap perched on neatly upswept hair. It crackled when she bent to carefully place her burden on the tea table's appointed open space.

Before Alice could complete her expected chore by unobtrusively withdrawing, her mistress motioned for her to bend closer.

Cornelia turned her face to the side and from behind the shield of an upraised hand issued a soft command. "See that Miss Amethyst joins us here immediately."

While the steaming brew was poured and handed around light conversation flowed with ease . . . yet Amy did not appear. The Carter-Bournes excused themselves shortly after finishing their tea, and soon thereafter the duchess departed with her daughter.

However, with the steady arrival of other guests the parlor remained a busy site of discussion concerning the Great Exhibition.

Concealed by constantly droning voices, Garnet managed a brief statement to Orville. "Amy swears she'll refuse your suit no matter the pressure brought to bear."

Orville responded to these quiet but vehement words with merely a scornful smile before purposefully shifting his attention to matters under current discussion.

The Queen's gown, the demeanors of the two royal children who'd accompanied her, and the report read by Prince Albert were reviewed in detail but the group had only just begun sharing opinions on the various exhibits when Bingley reappeared.

Lady Cornelia glanced up with a smile, expecting the announcement of additional visitors. The smile froze when she saw that he carried a salver bearing a single vellum sheet. This action was no more welcome than when in the middle of an earlier At Home he'd delivered a letter directly to her daughter.

In taking the paper from the silver tray, Lady Cornelia recognized Amy's handwriting. Its message, she was certain, would be unwelcome. Thus she gave only the briefest of glances to the words before deliberately folding and tucking the note into the wide sleeve of her day dress. So skilled a hostess was she that not even a single moment's awkwardness was permitted as she skillfully shifted her guests attention with a question.

"What is your opinion about the overall effect of Paxton's Exhibition Hall."

"Most impressive," an aging dowager responded. "Such a feeling of light and airiness for so vast a structure."

"Indeed," Garnet agreed. "I believe it may be the single most important component of the entire exhibition."

By the time her afternoon responsibilities came to a close and the last guest—save Orville—had departed, the hostess's tightly concealed tension was dangerously taut.

After Alice cleared away the remnants of their tea and Bingley carefully closed the door behind his retreating back, Orville rose. He purposefully turned to face the lady of Wyfirth House with a soft demand.

"Now, Lady Cornelia—" Orville's gaze narrowed on the stiff-backed woman. "Tell me what strange kind of illness can have overtaken Amethyst that it's reported by letter?"

As illness was the expected excuse for anyone's absence, his suggestion was no surprise. But, although Lady Cornelia's hand instinctively moved to cover the spot where her sleeve hid Amy's message, she wasn't so craven as to back away from any direct question. Certainly not when a simple, truthful answer would suffice.

"It's concern for her great-aunt Daphenia's health that's called Amethyst away."

Lips pursed, as always when in deep thought, Orville's gaze moved from Lady Cornelia's haughty expression to her son's unhidden glee. The latter infuriated him the most. Garnet was clearly pleased by the prospect of anything able to complicate his courtship of Amethyst.

"When"—Orville returned his attention to the girl's mother—"does Amethyst propose to return to London and the Season she so abruptly left?"

With years of experience in slighting anyone impertinent enough to challenge her, though seated, Lady Cornelia tilted her head back so far she was able to look down her nose at the short man standing before her. "Not, I daresay, until her great-aunt's health is sufficiently restored."

Orville slowly nodded, reconciling himself to a fact he couldn't change. It was a comfort that at least Amethyst's absence would put her beyond the Irish lord's reach as well. And, by the time she reappeared, his plans to end the man's threat ought to have been successfully concluded.

Chapter 12

~

"*A*my-girl, how wonderful to see you." In the doorway of her ivy-covered cottage, an amazed Daffy leaned her hazel wood cane against the jamb to give this unexpected guest a warm hug. Pulling away with a faint frown she asked, "But whatever brought you back so soon? Has someone fallen ill? Or is there some family difficulty where my help's needed? A loan, perhaps?"

"I came back to help *you*, Daffy." Amy's perplexed frown was a reflection of her great-aunt's confusion. "To help you."

Amy was shamed at an unconscious level by the elderly woman's mention of her family's financial strain in front of Comlan. But it was Daffy's honest surprise that convinced Amy her great-aunt truly didn't believe danger threatened.

"What?" Daffy's head tilted to one side while with a narrowed gaze probing her normally all too practical grandniece's solemn face for some hint of lucid reasoning to support the odd declaration.

"Your friend Patience O'Leary, along with her grandson," Comlan announced to facilitate understanding between the two women, "journeyed to London where they begged Amethyst to come to your aid."

"What errant nonsense," Daffy automatically answered, inwardly pleased by the far more surprising presence of an old but rarely seen friend.

"Then did they lie? Haven't there been further attempts to break into your home? Isn't it true that a number of strange pits have been dug at various places around your property?" Amy purposefully glanced over her shoulder toward one she could hardly have failed to notice as they approached the cottage.

"It's spring you know, with its new batch of moles, hedgehogs, weasels. . . ." Daffy shook her head in a disgust mocked by her poorly restrained smile. "And more's the woe. On top of that there's a whole hutch full of little rabbits that simply will make a mess of my garden."

Amy's frown deepened. The hole she'd seen had clearly been dug by a creature of considerably larger size. More telling still, Daffy had made no attempt to deny recent attempts to stealthily enter her home.

Before Amy could challenge her great-aunt, the elderly woman cheerfully continued in an intentionally thickened brogue.

"But what be I thinkin'?" Daffy's sprightly good humor was a blatant attempt to sweep dark thoughts away. " 'Tis a grand thing, now I've me Amy-girl to stay and to visit a friend haven't clapped me eyes on in donkey's years."

Green gaze soft as sea mist, Comlan returned the frail, white-haired lady's affectionate hug and loudly whispered into her ear, " 'Tis always a delight to see your captivating face, me darlin' "

"Ah, 'tis still the charmin' rogue, you be." Daffy's teasing grin laid a gentle wreath of fine wrinkles around her mouth. The smile remained but the perceptive woman's clear eyes watched the pair carefully while she slipped back into her London accent and asked, "But when and where did you meet my grandniece?"

Comlan answered without hesitation. "It was the Duchess of Melton, wasn't it, Amethyst, who introduced us at the first ball of the Season?"

Nodding immediately, Amy sent Comlan a warm smile of unspoken appreciation for not mentioning their first meeting in the fairy ring. But then had Comlan omitted that on her behalf? Or had he done it because Daffy was unaware of his heritage? She'd returned to Ireland intending to lend her beloved great-aunt support . . . and find answers to who and why. Instead she'd uncovered additional questions. Only ever more questions.

Amy was nudged from her distracted state by a large hand lightly pressing against the small of her back to urge her through the door. Daffy led the pair into her snug parlor where cheery flames flickered in a stone fireplace and old, comfortably overstuffed chairs beckoned.

Once the three were comfortably seated, Daffy asked a perfectly logical question. "If Patience and Paddy went to London to fetch you, where are they now?"

"I'm afraid they were put quite out of countenance by meeting a neighbor of yours—one they'd never met before." Comlan's eyes glittered with amusement although he did his best to temper the cynicism in his smile.

"I see." Daffy slowly nodded. "Yes, that would put Patience in a snit. She prides herself on knowing everything about everyone, so for her the meeting must have been terribly . . . disconcerting."

From this exchange Amy suspected Daffy knew very well all and likely a great deal more than she'd yet learned about the Tuatha De Danann. But sitting here primly correct like Society guests come for a formal At Home afternoon, she couldn't immediately compose the right phrases to ask either, let alone both, for an explanation. And then it was too late.

As if some unspoken signal had been given, Comlan rose to make his farewells.

"Amy, won't you see our visitor out?" Daffy slightly lifted her cane in emphasis of her next claim. "Old bones protest the tiniest hint of damp in the air and we'd a fair torrent of rain last evening."

Amy saw through Daffy's weak, though doubtless well-intentioned, excuse. Yet, never anxious to see her dream hero leave her—as one day and for all time he assuredly would—she gladly obeyed.

Halfway down a narrow, cobblestoned path stretching beyond the front door, Amy paused. She turned to face her companion with hands nervously joined at the waist of a pale blue gown. Twilight's gentle, blue-gray shadows were slowly deepening while ground mists began to rise. And by this mystical light, though Comlan was dressed as any other Society gentleman, she clearly saw him for the fantasy figure come to life that he undeniably was.

"Don't look so forlorn, Amy," Comlan quietly urged, trailing fingertips over her soft cheek. "I'll return in the morning."

"In the morning," Amy agreed but her eyes darkened to the melancholy hue of rain clouds while under his deliberate caress her body went both hot and cold.

"Amy, I must go." Despite the words, Comlan dipped his head and brushed a gentle kiss across petal-soft lips. When his mouth withdrew, her plainly bereft lips instinctively followed. "I must," he repeated. "I haven't returned to my people for far too long. . . ."

Comlan's arguments were as logical as any the once proudly practical Amy could ever have hoped to hear. Yet they did nothing to either ease her distress or prevent him from gently drawing her generous curves against the power of his own body.

A gaze of molten emerald visually traced a path across delicately blushing cheeks and down a straight nose before settling on enticing lips. At the tantalizing sight thoughts of a dangerous temptation echoed through his mind. Might greater joy be found by remaining in this mortal world with Amethyst rather than in retreating to the myriad entertainments easily his in the Faerie Realm?

Again, as so often before, Amy couldn't turn eyes gone smoky with desire away from this fascinating male. Comlan's slow, bone-melting smile held no hint of mockery. Instead its slight curve was both a lure and a promise of wicked delights. It stole Amy's breath even before his mouth returned to brush achingly across hers once, twice, and then once more. Clinging to broad shoulders and trembling beneath the sweet onslaught of wild sensations robbing her of strength, with a hungry sigh she helplessly arched nearer.

Wielding the full power of his charm, Comlan easily held the naive colleen in his thrall while he dispensed with the net restraining her hair. His fingers buried themselves in thick, ebony satin to gently urge Amy's head back and lay her long, elegant throat vulnerable to his lips. Following its tempting path, he savored her skin, drank in the heady spring-fresh fragrance.

"No." Comlan pulled back. Much as he wished it otherwise, Miss Amethyst Danton was not fair game for the experienced hunter he was! The near loss of control blinding him to that fact left Comlan feeling as shamed as if he'd cornered a tame doe. "This must never be!"

Comlan's arms dropped and he fell one step back while his earnest wish to comfort her every woe, protect her from any harm, and ever share the gentle pleasures of her company delivered a deeper, more frightening shock. He wanted above all things to be always with this winsome *human* female. It was impossible! The very nature of his kind urged a flaunting of rules, but a penalty would be demanded for breaking those governing contact with humankind.

"Why?" Hurt replaced passion in Amy's gaze.

She was devastated by his rejection and wondered if in her inexperience she had done something wrong. Or was the problem as basic as her hopeless inadequacy compared to the doubtless exceptional females he'd known among his own kind?

"The cost would be too dear." As Comlan spoke, he recognized the words for an unpleasant truth. Even if he succeeded in proving to Amy that the joys of impulsive adventure were greater than the satisfaction of logical reasoning, it wouldn't be enough to reconcile her to his realm. Her love of family, however unworthy, held her tightly in the human world's web.

In the rough texture of Comlan's voice Amy recognized unspoken facts he plainly found as disturbing as she. As a king Comlan couldn't abandon his people to tarry with her while she couldn't blithely desert her loved ones to live in his realm.

Weighted down by the burden of all the could-have-beens that would-never-be, a mournful Amy turned to literally walk back to her great-aunt's cozy cottage . . . and figuratively toward a bleak future.

"Amy?" Daffy softly called at the sound of an opening door.

"Yes." Amy was prompt to answer, striving to sound cheerful despite a chill freezing her from the inside out. "I'm here."

"Come, join me again in the parlor. We hardly had time for a good natter before you left my cottage last time." After setting the necessities for a simple meal to heat on her old black stove and lighting oil lamps, Daffy resumed a comfortable position atop her favorite chintz-covered chair.

"I would hear all about the Season's festivities. And tell me how are your brother and his sweet Lovey getting along?"

Amy obediently settled at one end of an old-fashioned and well-worn sofa, striving to close her thoughts to the unhappy parting just past by giving the older woman her full attention. But her great-aunt's questions were all too quickly answered. And that fact opened the way for others Amy would far rather have avoided.

"How was Comlan received in London?" Daffy would like to have asked this first but had recognized the need to indirectly approach the matter.

The answer was so obvious that Amy turned it into another question. "A handsome, wealthy, *unwed* lord?"

"An *Irish* lord?" Daffy was just as prompt to return the challenge in Amy's quickly tossed query. In her day, that term would've been a demand for proof of a substantial share of good English blood to balance the taint of the other.

"Lord Comlan almost immediately became the London Season's most sought-after bachelor." At the remembered image of her mother's reluctant concurrence, Amy faintly smiled. "I know of only one man who dared question Comlan's background. But then, when Lord Palmerston greeted Comlan as friend, there was nothing Orville could do."

"Orville?" Daffy leaned forward, head tilting to one side in wordless inquiry. "Isn't he the suitor your parents have chosen for you to wed?"

Amy grimaced but nodded.

"Ah, well ..." Daffy leaned back again. "No doubt he was jealous."

Although Amy said nothing, her skeptical glance spoke volumes

"Now don't you be telling me Orville had no reason." Daffy's penetrating eyes bored into Amy. "It's true that I'm so old I can't walk without my cane—but I'm not blind. I saw the way you looked at Comlan."

Biting her lip hard and staring determinedly down at the random pattern of a home-worked carpet, Amy was furious with herself for having so clearly betrayed her feelings. Had she been that obvious in London, too?

"Tell me, Amy. Tell me truthfully, what do you know of Comlan beyond the fact that he is the hereditary Lord of Doncaully?"

Amy helplessly met her great-aunt's steady gaze and realized that it was time to confess all. At least Daffy was unlikely to be as skeptical as Beattie had been ... and probably still was.

"We met before the ball."

Having suspected this from the first, Daffy nodded but did not speak.

Drawing a deep breath, Amy continued. "Despite your warnings, I drew your picture of the castle ruins from the center of the fairy ring."

"I thought as much." Instead of the rueful rebuke Amy more than half-expected, Daffy grinned. " 'Tis the only place from which you could've captured that particular view."

"Then I fell asleep." Carefully watching the older

woman for the first hint of skepticism, Amy nodded tentatively. "And I thought myself dreaming when I woke to find Comlan kneeling beside me."

"What happened then?" Rather than disbelief, Daffy's eyes glowed with anticipation.

A gentle smile of remembered beauty curled Amy's soft lips. "Comlan offered to take me to his home—the castle standing where had been the ruins I sketched for you."

Daffy's hands came together in a gleeful clap, and she began rapidly asking a great many questions. To these Amy willingly responded, glad—nay, relieved—to share the incredible experience with someone who would believe what she said.

"But tell me, Great-aunt Daffy, how is it that you know Comlan?" Amy felt that after answering so many questions herself, she'd earned the right to ask a few. "And for how long?"

"Seems forever." Daffy's gaze seemed to focus on some invisible point beyond the walls of her cottage. "He was a dear friend of my Patrick's. But when my beloved first told me about his friendship with the king of the Tuatha De Danann, I thought he'd had a dram too many of his favorite whisky." With the confession Daffy sent her grandniece a bright grin. "That's when Patrick insisted on leading me up the hill and into that magical ring of ever-blooming flowers."

Amy's brows furrowed into a slight frown. How could Comlan, who seemed in the prime of life, have been a friend to Daffy and her husband so long ago?

"Amy-girl, I advise you not to focus on the issue

of time." Daffy reached out and took Amy's hand, gently forcing the girl to meet her gaze. "In the Faerie Realm the measure of its passing is vastly different than any method applied in our world. They are magical beings possessing powers beyond our understanding and outside the rigid demands of human logic. For them nothing is either static or predictable."

What Amy had seen and been told during her fairy ring dream and experienced since in Comlan's company supported Daffy's statement. But after the ending to their scene on the cobbled walkway, this further talk of the radical differences between Comlan's realm and her world was disheartening.

Anxious to tutor her beloved grandniece in all the incredible things she'd learned about the Tuatha De, Daffy failed to perceive the girl's distress. "The Tuatha De can move with ease both forward and backward in the parade of human years, although not through their own."

While the logic of Amy's well-trained mind tried to make sense of this seemingly illogical claim, Daffy continued sharing other secret rules governing the Faerie Realm.

"I hope you've learned by now that Comlan cannot reveal to you, or any human, what he knows or senses through his mystical powers—unless specifically asked."

"You mean," Amy asked, meeting Daffy's direct gaze, "if I ask Comlan a question—any question—he'll give me a true response."

Silver hair reflected the oil lamp's mellow light as Daffy solemnly nodded. "If Comlan knows the answer, he'll give it. Far more importantly, it's only if asked that he can help you cross any impasse or solve any riddle to safely reach your goals."

Despite her initial skepticism, Amy accepted this claim without a moment's hesitation. Her only question was why Daffy hadn't already requested Comlan's help to see her protected against threatening danger. And apparently she hadn't. To Amy this fact seemed both an undeniable sign that the elderly woman truly didn't believe herself at risk and crystal clear proof that the guarding of Great-aunt Daphenia was up to her. Beyond a tense nibbling of her lower lip, Amy willingly accepted the responsibility, certain Comlan would lend his aid.

However, seeing no good to be gained by forcing her companion to see danger when clearly she chose to close her mind to the ominous sight, Amy pursued another area of curiosity.

"How did your husband meet Comlan in the first instance?"

"Ah, now thereon lies a fine story." Daffy slid into the comfort of a thick brogue. " 'Tis one which me Patrick was over fond of repeatin' to all who'd listen. And there's a goodly number who'd a grand likin' for his treasure trove of tales 'bout the Tuatha De—though only a pitiful few honestly believed."

Amy leaned forward, impatient to hear every word.

"Unfortunately"—Daffy leaned back with a rueful smile but amusement glittering in her eyes— " 'tis no' mine to tell."

"What?" Amy demanded, "You must tell me. You

can't tease me with that tantalizing prelude and then abruptly stop!''

As if she'd gone conveniently deaf, Daffy rose. Relying heavily on the support of her sturdy hazel wood cane, she hobbled toward her tiny kitchen.

"Come, Amy-girl, me stew has been a'simmerin' too long."

Amy was disconcerted by her great-aunt's ability to change subjects as easily as she slipped into and out of a thick Irish brogue. Almost she could believe that by long acquaintance Daffy had come to share the Tuatha De's unpredictable nature.

Night was full upon them by the time their meal was done. And yet, between its beginning and the moment Daffy suggested that the visitor who'd spent a previous, nearly sleepless night on the train should seek her bed, Daffy deftly saw to it that neither Comlan nor anything pertaining to his realm was mentioned.

Despite her many questions, Amy yielded to her great-aunt's will and followed Daffy to a narrow stairway. There was comfort in remembering that as her stay had only just begun there'd be time enough to later probe for further answers. She climbed to where her small, triangular bedroom was situated at the cottage's top, just under a steeply pitched, thatched roof.

Amy lost little time changing into a thin night rail before gladly stretching out on a goose-down mattress and pulling a thick counterpane up to her chin. Staring up into the gloom where two sharply tilted walls met as the roof over her bed, she feared that either the question of who was behind Daffy's danger or the pain of Comlan's rejection, intensified by the dark, would keep her awake. But once cuddled between cloud-soft mattress and comforter, peaceful sleep too long denied soon drifted gently over Amy.

Hours passed and darkness deepened while only creatures of the night moved stealthily around trees, through hedges or across thick blades of grass . . . the humble vole, hedgehog, fox, badger, and, most fearsome of all, a two-footed predator—man.

Chapter 13

~

Crash! Abrupt, discordant, the loud sound of splintering glass shattered Amy's peaceful dream and rudely thrust her into full, heart-thundering wakefulness. Delayed only by the fight to win free of suddenly unwelcome, entangling covers, Amy rushed down the steep stairway anxious to catch their intruder before further harm was done.

Like a ghost frozen by moonlight, a dazed Daffy stood amidst the shards of her parlor's broken window, desperately clutching the hazelwood cane.

"Are you all right?" With more haste than prudent caution, Amy darted through hazardously scattered pieces of glass to wrap a comforting arm about the thin, trembling woman looking impossibly fragile and every day of her more than eighty years. "What happened?"

When her great-aunt's only response was to gaze back blankly, a worried Amy carefully shepherded the elderly woman safely across the floor perilous to bare feet.

Marylyle Rogers

"Don't sleep as well as once I did." Daffy finally began to speak as Amy eased her down into a favorite chair. "I came downstairs to fetch a drink of water. Then thought I heard my Banshee and came in here to see what mischief she'd gotten into."

Amy smiled. This fond mention of Daffy's big, black and inordinately curious cat briefly eased the moment's stress—but only briefly.

"It wasn't Banshee I saw but an alarming figure hesitating in the shadows right there." Daffy motioned toward a dark corner several steps to one side of the window where no moonlight fell. "He saw me and jumped through the window." She shook her head in confusion. "Just jumped right through as if it had no pane."

"*Who*? Who jumped?" Amy knelt at the frightened woman's side and rubbed her abnormally chilled fingers.

"Couldn't see." Again slowly shaking her head, Daffy mournfully asked, "What could he have wanted of me?"

Startled by the question, Amy rocked back on her heels. Surely her great-aunt was too intelligent not to know its obvious answer.

"Patience, Patrick, me—we've all warned you about this danger." Amy feared Daffy would find her explanation feeble considering how unpersuasive this concern had proven before.

"Hah!" Eyes again snapping with their usual fire, Daffy gave her grandniece a long-suffering look. "You *all* needlessly worry too much about the fools who simply will search for my treasure no matter what I do or say."

Amy would have argued but her great-aunt continued without pause.

"Can't stop them." Making it plain her patience was severely tried, Daffy waved her hands as if these insignificant details were pesky flies to be shooed away. "And see no reason to waste my time trying when I've got the whole safely tucked away where no one will find it."

Amy was relieved to see her great-aunt's bright spirit restored and admired her unwavering confidence in the security of her hiding place. But despite her own genteel upbringing, Amy couldn't help but imagine the fearful depths to which ruffians might descend in their attempts to force the elderly woman into giving it over.

"You told me last night that if I ask Comlan for help, he'll give it . . . if he can."

Quite back to her normal self, Daffy's head tilted curiously to one side as she slowly nodded.

Amy softly posed what seemed an obvious solution, the one she'd intended to take. "Why then don't *you* ask for his help against this danger?"

Impish grin returning, Daffy responded. "No need for me to do that."

"But—" Amy immediately started to argue.

"No need," Daffy overrode her grandniece. "My Patrick already did, and Comlan already gave his word to watch over me for all my days."

"Then how could this—"

"A fine question!"

Still on her knees, Amy glanced over one shoulder to find that the subject of their conversation had suddenly appeared although she'd heard no door, no footsteps, no . . .

"But first," Comlan demanded in a cool tone at odds with the intense heat in green-fire eyes focusing on the beauty in an enticing state of dishabille. "Tell me precisely what *did* happen here?"

Startled by Comlan's inexplicable arrival, Amy was uncomfortably aware of her immodest apparel and awkwardly rose to face him. Feeling vulnerable, she blushed vividly beneath his steady appraisal. Her gaze dropped to the bare toes peeking from a delicately embroidered hem while nervously shoving back a rich mass of free-flowing, dusky curls.

Then Daffy diverted Comlan's attention by succinctly relating the pertinent facts of the scene just past while Amy desperately tugged and pulled in a vain attempt to rearrange her flimsy, nearly transparent night rail into modest folds.

"Your intruder jumped *out* of the cottage from here?" For the sake of a plainly embarrassed Amy, Comlan subdued his natural urge to laugh. Instead he held his face completely devoid of expression and motioned toward the glass-littered floor in front of a shattered window.

Amy misinterpreted her rarely solemn fantasy hero's emotionless face and cold words as an accusation blaming her for Great-aunt Daffy's current trouble. Still, she joined the older woman in nodding to confirm his observation.

"How is it, then . . ." A penetrating emerald gaze moved between one female and the other. ". . . That

the windowpane landed inside this room rather
than in the garden beyond its sill?"

That was an excellent question. One for which
Amy earnestly wished she had a logical answer . . .
or any answer. She didn't. Feeling truly the complete
fool that this man had shown such a talent for
exposing in someone who'd once prided herself on
clever, methodical thinking, Amy instead made an
offer that would also provide a fine excuse for
escaping.

"I'll make tea. Surely we could all do with a bit
of its steadying powers."

Daffy nodded her approval but added a personal
request. "Amy-girl, would you be a darlin' and fetch
the thick lap robe I spent so many hours knitting
last winter? With the fire banked for the night, it's
chilly down here."

While Amy gladly fled up the stairs Comlan bent
to stir glowing coals to renewed life.

Again in the cozy bedroom at the very top of the
cottage, Amy quickly rinsed her face in what tepid
water remained in the basin placed atop a chest at
bedtime each night. She meant to don the first gown
pulled from her hastily packed satchel and was
relieved, even pleased by the one she drew out. This
dress she would happily wear even though it was
several years out of style, made of thin wool in a
deep shade of mulberry, and intended for the
autumn season.

After pulling up warm stockings, tugging on
shoes, and rapidly dragging a silver-backed brush
through sleep-tangled hair then quickly coiled into
the modesty-required net at her nape, Amy rushed

to her great-aunt's room. She gathered up the requested item and hustled downstairs, confident this part of the task had been accomplished with a remarkable speed preventing any undue delay of tea. However, on entering the parlor with blue lap robe folded over one arm, she found her two companions already sharing a pot of that reviving brew.

"Aunt Daffy," Amy gently remonstrated while tucking the wool blanket around the older woman. "You shouldn't have gotten the tea."

"She didn't," Comlan stated with the return of his usual wry smile.

"You did?" Amy was surprised.

"I'm actually quite capable of performing a wide variety of tasks." Comlan's feigned expression of wounded feelings was belied by the amusement sparkling in emerald depths, and his facade almost immediately melted into a bright, mocking grin.

Despite her inexperience, Amy heard these obliquely provocative words as a reference to this dangerously attractive man's undoubted mastery of seductive skills. But was it that, her prudish conscience asked? Or was it her own indelicate preoccupation with him that put such a shameful notion in her head? Renewed color bloomed which in turn prompted yet another vexed frown.

"Now come, have your morning tea." Naming himself a fool for having teased the tender damsel, however lightly, Comlan gently took Amy's hand and tugged her down to sit beside him on the sofa.

"Once the sun crests the horizon, I mean to escort you out for a refreshing walk."

Filled with a curious mixture of anticipation and

uncertainty, Amy glanced sidelong at this unpredictable man. What she found surprised her even more—a rueful expression she'd never before seen.

"We have things to discuss." The cryptic statement was less explanation than gateway to more questions.

Daffy watched the exceptionally handsome Comlan talk with her darlin' Amy of his plans for them. Then she sat back with hands peacefully folded, looking as pleased as a cat presented with a big bowl of rich cream.

"We can't leave Daffy alone," Amy whispered, conscientiously arguing despite a nearly irrepressible longing to spend time alone with the subject of her recently admitted, doomed love.

"Nor will we," Comlan instantly responded, though he refused to answer the silent plea for explanation deepening gray eyes to charcoal until after Amy consumed two cups of tea and the last scone from a batch Daffy had baked early the previous day.

"Now, let's be off." The golden speaker rose, and his powerful figure towered over the dark colleen he effortlessly pulled to her feet.

"You said we wouldn't leave Daffy alone," Amy quietly reminded Comlan while sending a worried glance to the plainly unconcerned older woman.

"She has never been alone since the day Patrick died," Comlan patiently explained before turning to greet the inexplicably appearing figure of a willow-slender female as golden-haired as her king.

"This is Maedra," Comlan introduced the unabashedly curious and brightly smiling newcomer. "She is always here with your great-aunt whenever neither human relations nor friends are visiting."

While Comlan escorted Amy from the cottage, she struggled to sort through tangled reactions to both these new examples of astonishing events and his frank claim of magical abilities. Her nearly life-long suspicion of anything unscientific gave way to a host of other fleeting emotions but all were soon overwhelmed by an awed acceptance that left her with a single bleak and painful certainty. It would be impossible for any ordinary human to attract— even less hold—more than the superficial interest of a devastating being possessing such wondrous mystical powers as did this king of the Tuatha De Danann.

Comlan sensed Amy's confusion and its disconsolate conclusion. However, he made a rare mistake by wrongly assuming its source to be simple uneasiness in his company. And why not? He frowned against the cheerless probability that this human colleen would never comprehend the mercurial nature that urged on him so many rapidly changing moods. It was this, he feared, that clearly defined the differences between them and made too likely an unhappy end for their tale.

Sunlight rippled over hair like sun-bleached wheat as Comlan slowly shook his head, hoping to clear it of unpleasant images. The sky was blue, the air was warm, and despite a laggardly pace the two of them were halfway up the hillside behind Daffy's cottage. Their shared hours were dwindling. And though that time together would account for no more than a brief moment in the long span of his existence, he knew it would remain the most precious for containing this beloved and truly remarkable beauty whose loss he'd mourn forever.

"Maedra and Daffy have become good friends over the years." Again Comlan attempted to banish cloudy thoughts—both his own and his dark maid's. "Each has learned to make allowances for the peculiarities inherent in the other's background."

Maedra? The name caught Amy's immediate attention. Visualizing the lovely fairy woman, she asked a question whose almost certain answer she feared.

"If I hadn't allowed Patience and her grandson to lure me from London and lead me here to Ireland, would Maedra have been with Daffy last night?"

Comlan met apprehensive gray eyes and solemnly nodded.

"And Maedra's presence would've prevented the intruder's success?" That this was less question than statement was just as well since a growing awareness of the golden man's nearness threatened to make forming rational questions difficult.

Again Comlan nodded, wicked smile appearing but in no way hiding the regretful tenderness behind it. These questions indicated his love was learning and accepting what she needed to know about the ways of his realm in order to recognize the impossibility of an alliance between them.

"How?" To lessen her vulnerability to him and clear her mind, Amy avoided meeting her companion's dangerously potent gaze by staring diligently at small bushes, oddly shaped rocks or the occasional wildflower rising above a carpet of grass.

"The mere presence of one individual from among the Tuatha De Danann makes the casting of a protection spell possible."

Although remembering her great-aunt's every word concerning the Faerie Realm's rules, Amy was frustrated by what surely must be an unnecessarily brief answer and glared up at Comlan. In the next moment she realized his curtailed answer had been a ploy to win her attention since, once he had it, Comlan elaborated without a further question from her.

"The spell of protection wraps an invisible shell around any mortal's abode, making it impervious to the ill-intents of other humans."

"But if you can do all that, why did you come to London? And what did you mean when you warned me of a threat to someone I love?" Of a sudden, Amy realized that his less than specific warning hadn't mentioned her great-aunt. "Isn't it Daffy who's in peril?"

Though Comlan ignored Amy's last question it was obliquely answered by his response to the second. "Daffy is in no *physical* danger but there are others less easy to defend against."

After silent minutes spent covering the last few yards of their gentle climb, Amy released a soft lower lip again nibbled berry-bright to pose a question whose answer she hoped wouldn't mean the end to their relationship, such as it was. "What possible use could you have for me—a mere human?"

"There are things to be done that will require a

human's touch." Comlan stopped and waited for Amy to face him before pointedly adding, "Not just any human's touch but *yours*."

Amy wanted to ask what sort of action she was to take, but before she could frame the question, Comlan strode forward into the giant oak's shade. On approaching the golden figure, she found his somber green gaze intently studying the lovely circle of flowers in whose center he stood.

"Do you know what causes a fairy ring?" Comlan asked in an oddly hollow tone and without glancing her way.

Sensing the answer was important to him, Amy hesitated a pace from the ring's outer edge. She temporarily postponed the topic of her curiosity and quietly admitted she'd never thought to question it, let alone learned the answer.

"This one is my sister Lissan's." While staring blindly at the magical circle, memories of his too curious sister put on Comlan's mouth a fond smile tinged with sadness.

Amy watched the brooding man and knew better than to break the aching silence settling around them like cool mists. With love-honed senses, she felt both the depth of his affection for Lissan . . . and an aching loneliness, as if his sister had been lost. She wanted to comfort the hurting man beyond her reach, but a first slight motion broke his preoccupation.

Stunned by a wave of guileless sympathy flowing from the ebony-haired beauty, Comlan turned toward this *human* colleen he hadn't thought capable of such affinity. As he slowly shook his head, bright hair glowed despite the shadows beneath a towering tree.

Comlan offered his amazingly sensitive human companion a strong hand to steady her while stepping carefully into the fragrant circle and rewarded her understanding patience with an explanation.

"A great number of mortal years have passed since Lissan fell in love with a human warrior." Watching a winsome face for even the faintest response, Comlan won a tentative smile of uncommon sweetness and continued. "Killian was a courageous and mighty champion, a member of King Conchobar's elite guard, the Knights of the Red Branch."

Comlan's mention of a romantic alliance bridging their two worlds struck the first spark of hope in Amy's despairing heart. But the next moment she was thunderstruck by a dimly remembered fact from a book of Irish history she'd once read. King Conchobar and his Knights of the Red Branch had existed *more* than a millennium earlier! Amy silently gasped. If Lissan had loved one of those knights, that meant Comlan was . . .

Her nearly inconceivable calculations were interrupted by an oblivious Comlan's continuation of the tale.

"But Killian was also too honorable to desert his king and live in Lissan's realm." Green eyes darkened almost to black with a painful sorrow Amy would have given anything to ease. "Thus it was that my sister chose to surrender her powers, become human, and live in his."

"Surrender her powers?" Amy softly repeated.

Comlan sadly nodded, motioning toward the encompassing ring. "These ever-fresh blossoms sprang up as Lissan's powers drained into the soil and are all that remains of her."

Though his solemn companion didn't speak again, Comlan answered the question clear in the gray-mist eyes beneath a slight frown of concern.

"Lissan lived a human lifetime and shared with her beloved a mortal's death." A sadness from long past swelled anew in Comlan, intensified by the bleak truth that he now faced precisely that same choice: Abandon his kindred and stoop to living a brief mortal life with Amethyst. Or endure a nearly endless lifetime without this dark colleen who'd stolen his heart.

Amy's heart froze. In Comlan's sad tale she'd heard regret and an inability to understand. If he found Lissan's choice to live in the mortal world inexplicable, then he must think love for a human incomprehensible.

The next moment Amy saw in Comlan's expression a battle being waged and pushed her own anguish aside. She also saw its end in a distress greatly at odds with the golden man's bright image. Without the waste of a moment's sane thought Amy instinctively wrapped slender arms about this powerful, mystical being subject to an unhealed wound of the soul she wouldn't have thought possible. Amy allowed the full measure of a bittersweet love previously concealed for fear of ridicule to fill that painful breach with gentle solace.

Shocked again by the tender beauty's unsuspected perceptiveness, Comlan went utterly motionless. Then the experienced ladycharmer seldom surprised in any matter was knocked completely off kilter by the wanton actions of this innocent maiden recklessly pressing her lush form tight against his long, hard body.

Amy was as surprised by her unthinking action as Comlan—yet unrepentant. This might be their last time alone. And, though ill-fated, it was likely her final chance to share the magic of love with this fantasy hero come to life who would forever possess her heart.

Dangerous hungers roused, Comlan desperately wanted to crush Amy's soft body nearer and feed on the aching sweetness of her mouth. But instead he gently pushed her back to hold temptation at arm's length.

"This is impossible!" Though stunned to discover Amy as unpredictable as ever one of his own, still Comlan knew that an intimate relationship would be devastating for them both. For her because it would mean the ruinous loss of a purity prized in her world; he because memories of their love play's sweet delights would deepen the pangs of hurtful loss through all the centuries to follow.

Comlan had denied Amy before and she'd yielded to his arguments. This time she wouldn't! Despite an immediate flood of brilliant color, she stood boldly before him. She was done with the cool reasoning which for all her dedication to its principal had brought her nothing of real value and could do nothing to cure the unhappy truth of a doomed love.

"No!" Misty eyes turned to pools of liquid pain.

"If now is my only chance for happiness—however fleeting—it's too precious to let you deny me."

Desolately aware that her dream hero would soon retreat to his magical world, Amy cast away any thought of wrong. She wielded the weapon of surprise to win free of his restraining hold and rashly dove headlong into the thrilling peril of an unfamiliar sea of fire. Wrapping her arms around his powerful neck and twisting fingers into strands of gold, she clung tightly to this anchor amidst a hungry tempest.

The odd combination of aching plea and determined demand in his unexpected temptress's statement was so perfect an example of the paradox revered in his realm that Comlan looked down suspiciously, fearing it a guise she'd donned to impress him.

Gazing into the beguilingly open face of love, Comlan fell prey to his own desires. His eyes darkened, going so flat they looked to have become emotionless stone. But behind that barrier lay an anguish certain to remain throughout all the centuries to come, an endless ache far more profound than even the sorrow Amy had generously tried to comfort.

Without restraint Amy welcomed the hunger she could feel if not see in a green gaze and willingly surrendered to the golden mesh of his attraction. She yearned upward, inviting the return of his potent kiss. And when his warm, ardent mouth descended, Amy sighed her delight.

Again Comlan impatiently dispensed with a restraining net to tangle his fingers in an ebony cloud of luxuriant hair. He pressed short, teasing kisses against the corners of her enticing mouth before lightly brushing across lips going rosy beneath his ardor.

His caresses tempted but refused to satisfy, and Amy's lips helplessly followed until at last she could bear no more. Then placing hands on firm cheeks, she stilled this torment by boldly initiating the kind of passionate bonding he'd demanded of her in times past.

But soon, very soon Comlan showed her just how inexperienced she truly was by taking control and deepening the kiss to a devastating intimacy that drew a low moan from her tight throat. As his urgent hands swept from nape to the base of her spine, molding her hips against the powerful muscles of his thighs, her hands moved restlessly over him while with eyes closed she savored his strength, his masculinity.

Mouth leaving hers, Comlan leaned back a brief distance. Hooded eyes gazed down into a beguiling face, and the undeniable hunger it revealed won a tense smile of male satisfaction. Amy was more beautiful in her honest passion than any female he'd ever known—a dangerous temptation even to one of his experience.

Comlan knew he should step completely away, end it here but the craving that blazed in his blood was too fierce to be so easily smothered. Instead he claimed her berry-sweet mouth again. This kiss was even hotter, wilder, and filled with such desperate need that he foolishly positioned Amy more intimately against the hardening contours of his body.

Amy arched instinctively and shuddered with

unruly excitement as Comlan curved his hands over a perfectly rounded derriere. Lifting her up, he rubbed her against his throbbing need and groaned under the almost painful pleasure.

Fearing that in desolate futures spent alone they'd both regret this delicious folly, a harsh groan came from Comlan's throat. But it was too late, far too late to control their embrace and see it end before winning sweet satisfaction in their firestorm's explosion.

Thoroughly caught in a spinning world of incredible, wicked sensations, Amy hardly noticed when Comlan swept her off her feet and gently laid her down on a green cushion of lush grass. She was so lost in a burning haze that she couldn't later recall if his fingers had unfastened her mulberry gown's neckline or if he'd parted its edges with magic. But never would she forget how he settled beside her, leaning above on one elbow to lower his mouth against the exposed arch of her throat. She would remember forever the first devastating touch of his lips against the curve of her breast that lit slow, steaming fires in her veins.

Helpless to prevent the action, Amy reached up to tangle her fingers in cool golden strands and tug the shocking pleasure of his intimate caresses nearer. At the same time one masculine hand gradually glided up Amy's side with wordless admiration for the curve of hip and gentle dip of waist. She felt both threatened and cherished as tantalizing fingertips stroked over her with layer upon layer of burning sensations even while completely stripping her of the cloth hampering his access to silky skin.

Pulling little more than a breath away from his tender prey, Comlan's gaze burned with emerald flames that seared while slowly studying the delicious sight of her lush body pillowed on thick ebony hair. He visually caressed the warm cream and deep rose flesh of this woman openly yielding herself to him.

But still Comlan held back for the sake of lightly rubbing his mouth across the full bounty filling a large cupped hand to overflowing. Nuzzling Amy's breasts slowly, he cherished her softness until she trembled under flashes of wildfire. Only after a soft whimper escaped his sweet prey—earning the slight, satisfied smile of a predator intoxicated by the sound—did the whisper-light brush of his mouth across the peak yield what she innocently sought.

Amy tugged Comlan closer still, senses unmercifully teased, wanting more, and arching against his mouth while another sweet moan slipped from her tight throat. Wandering through desire's dense smoke, she writhed against him in shattering intimacy and reveled in the dark fires of wicked sensations.

Visions of the inevitable culmination impatiently beckoned, leaving Comlan aware that the end of his control was perilously near. Never more grateful for his amazing powers, in the blink of an eye he was rid of unwelcome clothing. After eliminating any need for a distracting pause, he was free to carry his temptress so deeply into passion's blaze that the unavoidable flash of pain would be lost amidst a maelstrom of flames. He pulled Amy into the hungry cradle of his arms, savoring the feel of her generous curves melding to his body while he again stroked exquisite torment slowly over her aching flesh.

Shaking under sparks of wild pleasure, Amy twisted against Comlan's powerful form, driven to incite in him a measure of the unmanageable need he'd roused in her. As she sensuously moved against him, Comlan surrendered to a fever of unquenchable desire. He urged Amy back and rose above her to rest on his elbows, enabling him to gaze down into eyes gone black with wanting while slowly joining their bodies in the most intimate of embraces.

Amy's instant of pain passed unnoticed in a fire-storm of pleasures near too great to be borne. Over-whelmed by blazing sensations, she instinctively twined silken limbs about him in welcome and clung desperately to this burning source of delicious torment.

Slowly, gently, Comlan began to rhythmically rock his naive temptress higher, ever higher on a whirlwind of flame. Then, when the once reserved colleen far beyond logic whispered her love for him, the last bonds of Comlan's control were incinerated. The rhythm grew wilder and wilder as he desperately swept the one he'd lose too soon up into the very center of passion's relentless tempest.

Feverishly crying out as the spinning blaze of incredible sensations burst, Amy abruptly dropped from fiery heights down an impossibly steep, strangely thrilling precipice. And all the while a glittering shower of sparks rippled through every nerve in her body.

Stunned by unbelievable pleasures she'd never suspected existed, moments later Amy drifted on billowing clouds of contentment. They carried her into a light sleep blessed with tender dreams of the fantasy lover whose powerful and very real chest supported her cheek.

Satisfaction was intense but made bittersweet by the unpleasant tang of reality, as Comlan tightly closed his eyes against despairing truth. Although he loved Amy as surely as she loved him, it was a futile emotion destined to bring naught but the melancholy ache of loss. Amy could be excused for being unaware of the pain she'd dared in attempting to bridge the wide gulf between their worlds, but he assuredly had both the experience and years to know better.

The only comfort Comlan could see for the future lay in the fact that at least Amy's lifetime of empty loneliness would be limited to decades—infinitely shorter than the centuries he'd endure.

Chapter 14

~

*T*he sun had traveled beyond its journey's half-way mark when a feathery touch trailed from chin down an elegant throat to trespass in the sensitive valley between luscious breasts and gently nudge Amy toward wakefulness. Black lashes fluttered as the sleeper reluctantly roused, slowly becoming aware of the firm pillow beneath her cheek—warm and furred!

Amy abruptly sat up. At the sudden action a strong hand unintentionally pulled the lock of ebony hair wielded to summon her from potent dreams. Despite the welcome fires and wicked pleasures recently shared, the woman raised to prim virtue was shocked to discover herself in a man's company totally bare . . . worse, publicly exposed on a hilltop for any idle wanderer to see.

Snatching up her discarded dress, Amy wrapped herself in its cranberry folds and, horribly self-conscious, huddled like an awkward fowl at roost. She'd no doubt the hue burning smooth cheeks was as bright as her makeshift garb. And it was distressingly true that the crimson tide was unlikely to soon ebb when even carefully lowered eyes couldn't block a frightening, exciting awareness of the magnificent male body too near and as indecently naked as her own.

"Don't worry." Comfortably lounging on a soft carpet of grass, Comlan lifted up on one elbow to gaze at his skittish love with a smile wry and yet so tender it could've melted a stone heart.

Unfortunately, by refusing to look his way the frowning Amy failed to see either Comlan's devastating expression or the emotion it betrayed. Instead she was perversely annoyed by his attempted reassurance. What an easy thing for him to say. This fantasy figure could probably disappear—leaving her to seem a brazen trollop—in the same brief twinkling of an eye in which he'd appeared this morning in Daffy's cottage.

Deep laughter rolled like velvet thunder from the fairy ring as Comlan sat up, powerful muscles flexing. Daffy's darlin' Amy was becoming remarkably adept at the kind of mercurial mood shifts rare in humans but admired in his realm. To spare his bashful colleen's belated modesty he casually draped the otherwise unnecessary jacket across his lap even as he spoke with lingering amusement.

"Were the whole village to climb this peak and troop through Lissan's ring of flowers, we still wouldn't be seen."

Comlan paused, giving Amy the opportunity to question his unambiguous reference to the use of magic—as she'd done more than once before.

Amy remained mute and he continued.

"Have you realized yet that it was by Daffy's design that we met?"

Though lending unmerited attention to green blades crushed earlier by their intimate embrace, the corners of berry-sweet lips lifted as Amy nodded. "I suspected as much. She was so clearly disappointed after I chose not to confess our encounter that first afternoon that it seemed likely even then."

"But do you know why?" Mocking humor lent a curious tilt to Comlan's question.

Amy bit her lip to strangle a gasp stillborn. Did he? Had her great-aunt's teasing grins and blatant satisfaction at the sight of them together made her futile matchmaking hopes as apparent to him as to her?

Comlan recognized the inaccurate assumption in Amy's flustered state. No, perhaps not inaccurate but only a part of the whole and not the intended subject of his query. He immediately spoke to clarify matters.

"As the end of Daffy's long life draws nigh," Comlan began, slipping into a cadence of speech more comfortable to him, "her fortune's secure hideaway must be made known to someone from your world."

The formality of these grim words demanded Amy's complete attention. Her wish to deny the bleak specter of death deepened gray eyes to charcoal, but she admitted its inevitability.

"Daffy chose you," Comlan solemnly announced. "And her decision made our meeting necessary."

Amy bit her lip even harder against this news

that she'd completely misunderstood the manner of help her great-aunt needed. And, likely influenced by her own doomed wishes, she'd wrongly interpreted the older woman's reason for planning her meeting with the king of the Tuatha De Danann.

Comlan found himself host yet again to emotions unsettling even to one with his mercurial nature. Aching to protect the vulnerable yet courageous Amy from potential grief, he was sorely tempted to risk shattering important rules for the sake of granting her the gift of happiness. But, Comlan sternly reminded himself, meddling in human affairs was more likely to bring trouble than peace. It was that truism espoused by Gran Aine, his great-grandmother and the previous ruler of the Faerie Realm, which held him back.

For the good of them both, Comlan knew he must see his mission soon accomplished. And then he could prevent deepening the anguish of an inevitable parting by hastening back to his own realm before further treasured but bittersweet memories were added to the store already hoarded safely away.

"Because your great-aunt's wealth has little value in my realm, it rests safe with me." Comlan reached out to gently release a small hand's desperate hold on dark red cloth and rubbed comfort across its back with his thumb. The action succeeded only in sending Amy's cloudy gaze skittering farther away.

"When Daffy is gone," Comlan quietly added, holding Amy's fingers warmly in his much larger hand, "you need but to ask and I will deliver all or any part of the whole to you."

This disclosure of the unexpected role she was intended to play broke Amy's determined preoccupation with the lovely yet curiously whimsical mix of flowers forming the fragrant ring encircling them.

"Is this the action you said I and only I could take for Daffy's sake?"

"Almost." Comlan's potent, mocking smile returned and intensified when Amy scowled her disapproval of his inadequate answer.

"My great-aunt told me last night that if I asked you a question, you'd give me an honest answer." Amy looked squarely into Comlan's eyes. "Because I've asked and you haven't, I think you must take pleasure in trying to disconcert me."

"Ahh . . ." Comlan's voice dropped into a chill tone revealing nothing of his satisfaction with her amazing perception. His cryptic answer hadn't been issued because he enjoyed her confusion but rather it was an impulsive test of her ability to deal with his true nature. And Amy had recognized, although slightly misinterpreted, the purpose behind his intentionally contrary actions. "I've been exposed."

His stunningly handsome face had gone utterly blank at the very moment when Amy expected either anger or laughter. Nonetheless, she refused to be so easily diverted from her path and continued staring back at him with an intensity equal to his unblinking gaze.

Impressed by her courage, Comlan rewarded it with an additional morsel of information.

"Informing you is the first step toward ensuring that Daffy's wishes are respected now and after she has slipped away . . . by *natural* causes."

"And the next step is . . .?" A thick mass of black hair cascaded over an unintentionally bared shoulder as Amy tilted her head with this question she refused to allow remain unanswered.

"The next step is the one *only* you can perform." Comlan steadily met a somber, dove-gray gaze. "On returning to London, you must locate a reputable solicitor and arrange an appointment with him for both you and your great-aunt to keep."

"London?" Amy was amazed. "Daffy can't have agreed to this. Not when she hasn't returned there even once since her marriage a good many years ago."

"Can it be that you underestimate Daffy's tenacious will?" Comlan flashed a sardonic smile. "Or her obstinate determination to prevail against all odds."

"Oh, no!" Amy firmly denied. "No, I'd never be so foolish as that."

Comlan merely grinned wider and Amy, assuming it a further quirk of his illogical nature, continued with hardly a missed beat. "But what use a solicitor?"

"When the pair of you meet with him," Comlan promptly responded, "an irrevocable trust can be legally prepared and signed."

Amy frowned, reluctant to confess ignorance of such matters.

To atone for the inadequate answers earlier provided, Comlan immediately explained. "Daffy, as bequeather, and you, as heir, must sign a document clearly listing your great-aunt's wishes for the disposal of her estate. Only the two of you, *together*, can change its terms. No later will produced during Daffy's lifetime can supplant it and after her death its provisions cannot be contested by anyone."

Pondering the implications of this action and pleased by its promise of safety for Daffy, a slow smile warmed Amy's mouth. It widened as Comlan went on to succinctly outline this plan's expected conclusion and specify the goal to be won.

"Once that document has been signed and the tale of its making—but not the heir's name—spread far and wide, further shenanigans can profit no one."

It was true. Relieved that her logic hadn't been dulled by the rapid pace and alarming slant of recent events, Amy clearly saw the plan's excellent design. With Daffy's treasure literally hidden in a realm few humans would ever see and legally protected by the trust, her great-aunt would be safe. Yes, indeed, it was an admirable plan and one providing that although Comlan might not value analytical judgments, he was a master strategist and doubtless able to outreason any human she had or likely would ever meet.

Gazing into the warm admiration in cloud-soft eyes, Comlan was struck by an urgent need to repeat a warning earlier given but likely dismissed.

"Until that trust is signed and guarded by human laws, please tread cautiously around your friend Orville Bennett."

Blinking rapidly, Amy was once again shocked by her companion's abrupt twist on a topic.

"My parents are determined that I marry him." Amy slowly shook her head. "I think he's a pompous fool and mean to do all I can to thwart his intentions but . . ."

Golden brows met in a fierce scowl. Comlan knew quite well the power human parents wielded over their daughters' choice of future mate. In most cases he found it amusing but not when it threatened Amy's happiness.

Without sane forethought Amy moved closer, intending to smooth away that deep furrow. But Comlan caught the gentle fingers reaching toward him and buried his lips in her palm while the feel of his big, powerful body did exciting things to her senses. She was suddenly aware that here was another, likely final, chance to share a few intimate moments in her impossible love's arms. She ought to retreat into the cold world of sensible logic. But would she? No, she emphatically would not!

When Comlan glanced up, Amy gazed directly into eyes that promptly flashed with dangerous green flames. And in the depths of their fire she saw visions of flesh against flesh that roused wildly thrilling memories of shocking sensations.

Comlan lowered a mouth hard and warm to drink the intoxicating berry wine of hers with restrained ferocity. Once had been wrong. Twice would be madness. And yet not even his exceptional powers could prevent him from again claiming this incredible woman who with only human wiles had effortlessly pierced the armor protecting his heart for more time than mortal minds could easily grasp.

Amy yielded eagerly to Comlan's demanding kiss, and as strong arms pulled her close, turning her full into his embrace, her body instinctively welcoming the power of his. In silent praise her hands smoothed over his broad chest, exploring its erotic combination of hard muscle and abrasive hair, and measured the width of his shoulders.

Urged back against nature's soft bed by gentle hands, Amy felt herself sinking again into passion's fiery lake. She felt only his slow, burning caresses while mulberry cloth was dragged free to be once more discarded, unnecessary, unwanted.

From above, emerald eyes took visual possession of the pale cream and tender rose of her sweet body. Interlocking his fingers with hers, he held her hands immobile above her head while hovering a tormenting whisper away and ravishing her mouth. Touching only at joined hands and lips, he deepened the kiss with devastating slowness until she writhed in an agony of need.

As if to touch at any point would be to lose control too soon, Comlan pulled back but green flames scorched over the exquisite creature's lush curves until a moan welled up from her depths and she arched in wordless invitation.

Driven by a craving stronger than his will, Comlan bent to her body and put his open mouth over her breast. Gasping beneath the shocking pleasure of a sweet suction, slender fingers reached up to tangle in golden strands and pull him even nearer. Amy was certain that never again in her life would she experience a shattering pleasure more intense until he moved to settle his whole long length atop her—hard chest against soft breasts, hip to hip, thigh to thigh.

Their bodies merged again into delicious intimacy, twining, surging in the burning rhythm of passion. The tempo grew wilder and wilder until at last, bound tightly together in desperate abandon, an explosion of near unbearable tension seemed to split the earth below and open a sea of sweet satisfaction.

When Amy awoke in Comlan's embrace a second time, she savored the experience, wanting to recall every detail, every sensation of their love play to cradle near as solace through all the lonely years to come.

Comlan hadn't fallen asleep again. Instead, he'd cherished this precious woman in his embrace while she slept. But during the time since Amy began floating up from the mists of sleep, he had almost come to regret the acuteness of senses making him too aware that she expected a forlorn future of unhappiness. Plainly she was seeing the same bleak, lonely destiny he'd been examining too closely since satisfaction lulled her into dreams. Knowing the vision wouldn't improve with prolonged viewing, he took measures to divert her attention.

"If we want to keep Daffy from suspecting all that's happened between us here, we'd better make our way quickly down to her cottage."

Amy pulled just far enough back to cast Comlan a glance of exaggerated scorn for the ridiculous suggestion that the older woman might somehow fail to guess as much anyway.

Comlan's laughter soared as he gently moved Amy aside and sat up. "Ah, but no matter what pictures Daffy's hopes have painted, if we neither confess nor betray our actions, she'll never know for certain."

So, as she'd initially thought, he did know what her great-aunt had schemed to inspire. A cranberry blur dropping from above landed in Amy's lap. Comlan had risen and retrieved their clothing.

As Amy tugged on the disgustingly rumpled dress, she glanced sidelong to find Comlan already dressed—and looking remarkably fresh in unwrinkled garb.

"Tch." Amy copied the sound of mild disgust she'd heard so often at home. "I see your powers have mundane uses as well."

Comlan's white smile flashed. The narrowed gray eyes minutely examining his immaculate appearance made the source of Amy's complaint obvious. But it was what she said next that made it possible for him to act.

"You look as unmussed as if we'd merely taken a sedate stroll through Hyde Park while I look as if I'd been doing"—Amy flushed but courageously finished—"exactly what I have been doing."

"I wish"—Amy reached up, making a futile attempt to tame black hair into some semblance of normality without a comb—"I had your talent and could do the same."

The next instant Amy's hand rested on a neatly coiffed head. Glancing down, she fought the momentary disorientation of amazement. Her old gown had been restored to a far better condition than it had seen in years. Refusing to question the miracle, she met Comlan's grin with one of her own.

In the space of a single instant more, Amy realized

that they were now standing a single step from the back border of Daffy's rear gardens. Determined not to let her bemusement show again, she put her hand into the waiting crook of Comlan's arm and let him lead her around the cottage to its front entry.

Her abruptly scowling escort's sudden halt threatened to revive Amy's confusion.

"The window hasn't been repaired." It was clear by the irritation in Comlan's voice that he'd expected the broken pane would be whole again.

Wanting to soothe his annoyance, Amy calmly reasoned. "Even in London glaziers can't be expected to work so quickly."

"Glaziers, no." Late afternoon sunlight glowed on golden hair as a sardonically smiling Comlan shook his head. "But my people?"

Comlan's prolonged appraisal of her appearance summoned a rosy blush to Amy's cheeks. How could she be so foolish? Clearly he or his could restore the window in no more than a heartbeat.

While Amy silently berated her silly error, Comlan led her to the cottage's front door. As he swung thick planks open, it squeaked, and the sound earned an immediate reaction.

"Amy-girl? That you?" Daffy's voice betrayed a rare strain in her control and a hint of exasperation, as well. "We've company."

"Yes, it's me," Amy responded, promptly moving the few steps between entry and parlor.

"Ah, I see you found Lord Comlan." Daffy spoke quickly, anxious to let the couple just entering know what excuse she'd given her guests for Amy's absence. "I hope this means you've accepted my invitation to dinner, Comlan."

Restraining his broad grin with difficulty, Comlan gave a gracious nod first to Daffy and then to her visitors, Patience and Paddy O'Leary.

"And, of course, as I said before"—Daffy turned to the O'Learys—"you are welcome to join us."

"Thank you, but no." A plainly put out Patience rose. "We only stayed this long to ensure that you not be left alone, Daffy dear."

With the last statement, Patience sent Amy an accusing glare.

"Come, Paddy, we've work of our own to see done before the sun sets."

Chapter 15

~

$\mathcal{A}$s dusk settled over an Irish cottage, a like
gloom filled its interior. Two sheets of paper,
carefully unfolded and aligned on a dark tabletop
held the unwavering attention of three people. The
first paper had been found tucked into one of the
many books filling a large oak case in the parlor.
The second had been curled into a long unused but
treasured drinking horn hung on that room's wall
by a satin ribbon attached to the vessel's gold-
rimmed mouth on one end and to the golden cap
on the tip of the other.

"They both say the same thing." Daffy ended a
long, morose silence by pointing out the wry jest in
this absurd fact and then added another. "And both
are utterly unnecessary as the true document states
much the same."

Amy was uncomfortable with the prospect of her
gain at the cost of Daffy's life and promptly hurried
the discussion forward. "Also, though different peo-

ple planted these false wills, each was determined to ensure the same end."

"Personal gain." Daffy nodded. "But whose? Only you profit. Or, indirectly, your family."

"Yes, Amy inherits." Comlan was growing impatient with their laggardly mortal pace. Fortunately, as the issue at hand involved only facts that could be easily divined by human reasoning and would surely be recognized (eventually), he was free to immediately direct their attention to the obvious danger. "But her future husband will be the one to control its usage."

"I know what you think," Amy responded to the mocking glint in emerald eyes pointedly watching her. "But I still can't agree. Orville is a wealthy man with no reason to take mad risks to increase it."

"Few humans ever feel they have so much that they wouldn't welcome more," Comlan wryly argued. The next instant his amusement disappeared but the intensity of his gaze did not waver. "Remember the false faces I warned you to guard against?"

Preoccupied with questions of who and why, Daffy gave scant attention to Comlan's words. Instead she responded to her grandniece's claim, providing additional support for that position. "Without a desperate need for riches, no *English* noble would go to such lengths for a simple cottage and wild *Irish* lands. Most certainly not one as snobbish and proud as Amy assures me this Orville is."

"Besides," Daffy quietly mused, "that man isn't Amy's only suitor." While visions of her birdlike friend tending a weak hatchling floated through her mind, she added, "Patience nurtures barmy dreams of a match between her beloved grandson and my grandniece."

Amy was shocked. Not by either Patience's hopes or the too obvious intentions of the vain Paddy but by her great-aunt's discernment.

"Tch, tch." Daffy shook her head in faint reproach. "That you believed me unconscious of my ambitious friend's scheme suggests you've a poor opinion of my intelligence."

"Oh, no. I am very well aware of your agile wits and shrewd understanding." Amy reached across the table to clasp age-thin hands and earnestly explain. "But knowing your fondness for Patience, I wouldn't expect you to take her never hidden goal seriously. I didn't, not until I spent a deal too much time in her company on our hasty journey here."

While the two women continued their discussion of possible perpetrators only to uncover a dearth of alternate possibilities, Comlan watched with growing frustration. His opinion wasn't asked and without a direct question he couldn't give it. Amy might—*might*—be forgiven that lack. But, really, it was too bad of Daffy. She'd known for years the importance of asking, yet made the same mistake.

Having already done too much in reminding Amy of false faces, Comlan dared offer no further unsolicited clues. To prevent falling under that temptation, he vanished.

* * *

"Thought it a great jest, they did—at my expense," Paddy raged, stomping from one side of his granny's kitchen to the other while describing yet again the scene of his ridicule.

Patience applied the sentiment of her name while watching as her frustrated grandson's mask of lazy cheer was reduced to useless ashes by the fires of fierce anger.

"The whole bleedin' lot of them took glee in tellin' me tha' the only abode ta Daffy's north is the ruins me namesake allus swore ta be the Tuatha De Danann's splendid palace."

Hope that if left to work his way through resentment of the likely unintended insult, Paddy would eventually be restored to calm, proved futile. Patience realized that her grandson was only working himself into an even less manageable temper and knew she must intervene.

"But—" Patience tried to slow the spinning storm of Paddy's anger with a sensible question. "Did ye ask *specifically* about a Doncaully family seat?"

"Oh, aye. 'Course I did!" In his frustration Paddy nearly lashed out physically. "And what did I earn for me trouble? They laughed the harder."

His clenched fist smashed down on the tabletop, shaking its planks and slopping tea over the side of his granny's cup. "Seems 'tis tha' verra thing old Patrick was forever blatherin' about while spinnin' wild tales of fairy raths and magic."

Never one to cringe, despite a dithery facade, Patience calmly inquired, "Then what shall we do?"

His granny's unshaken serenity began to slowly smooth the ragged edge of Paddy's anger. And though he wouldn't admit its fire misdirected, his voice was quieter as he responded.

" 'Tis a bad and sorry state we be in, me ole girl. If I don't find that wretched man's house, can't rightly sneak in and put an end ta his interferin' ways!"

"Never liked your plan," Patience softly confessed. "It'd be certain ta see us in gaol."

Paddy's black brows scowled but his granny continued. "Sure, and don't ye see that no' findin' the Doncaully home is an omen, a warnin' to fall back on our first design."

Dissatisfied with his granny's too soft, too weak scheme, Paddy paused in his restless pacing while his fierce scowl deepened.

"There need be no killin'." Patience sent her too easily riled grandson a stern glance. "Jist steal the colleen away and no' bring her back till vows ha' been exchanged and the match consummated."

"Steal Amethyst away? How?" Paddy at last sat down at the table opposite a determined woman. He'd done it once already only to have the mysterious Doncaully sweep her safely away.

"Faith be! Do you mean ta tell me tha' after the ease with which ye stole into the colleen's fine London home ye'd balk at the challenge of slipping into Daffy's old cottage?" Patience's question held both disbelief and irritation. "Surely tain't so. No' now when her parlor's shattered window is proof enow tha' others covet our prize?"

"But," Paddy stubbornly argued, "even if I capture her, who'll do the deed? We've already left one reverend waitin' uselessly."

Patience immediately responded without the

slightest question. "Tha' sotted reprobate, Reverend Scheely, who vainly waited on the coast will gladly see the rite performed—for the same handsome fee."

A hint of moisture filled the night air, signaling coming rain. But it wasn't the hint of changing weather that held Paddy motionless. Concealed by darkness, he waited in a stand of trees just to one side of where Daffy's front walkway ended. He'd seize the opportunity—which ever one presented itself first.

Whether it meant killing the apparently homeless lord, the elderly woman who'd already lived too long or simply abducting a possibly reluctant bride, he wasn't particular. Not so long as his feat won the prize.

A sliver of light pierced the gloom as a sturdy door opened. In that same moment a pistol was raised. The firearm was heavy and old, but the man holding the weapon had long experience in using it for bringing down prey—small animals to supplement the dinner table's meager offerings and occasionally the larger, two-legged variety for monetary spoils. However, experience with the time-consuming process of reloading also underscored the importance of seeing his single shot succeed.

Two women stepped beyond the threshold with a golden-haired man. Paddy was annoyed when Daffy, doubtless by long ingrained habit, pulled the door shut, limiting him to the dull glow of a cloudy night sky. Then when the younger female, whom he daren't harm, stood as unintentional shield between him and the mysterious lord, their hostess became the most promising target.

Daffy's warm voice carried across still air. "I'm so glad you returned, Comlan. We feared you felt insulted and abandoned us for all time."

A loud crack suddenly shattered the country-side's peace even as an invisible force shoved Daffy harshly back against the closed door.

The strong-willed victim, though pale and flustered, clutched her cane like a weapon and glared into the night. Amy rushed to cradle her great-aunt's fragile figure a single moment before Comlan wrapped his infinitely stronger arms about them both.

Pushing the door open, Comlan urged the women back into the cottage. As he did so neither he nor Amy could help but see the bullet imbedded in the thick oak door.

Amy glanced over the neat, white braid coiled atop Daffy's head to silently question Comlan. No, she chided herself. It could hardly be a question. Rather, it merely requested confirmation of an amazing fact revealed by the bullet's position directly behind where Daffy had been standing. Clearly, it must have passed through the shaken yet uninjured woman. How? By the same magic that had seen Comlan survive an assailant's blade in Hyde Park?

A ruefully smiling Comlan nodded, an action that seemed to draw and trap light within the golden strands of his hair.

Comlan helped an unusually weak Daffy up narrow steps before retreating to wait in the parlor while Amy aided a waiting Maedra to settle her great-aunt in bed for the night.

Standing with broad back to the miraculously restored window, he spoke softly the instant Amy stepped into a room dimly illuminated by the flickering light of a single oil lamp. "I have something for you."

Preoccupied with constantly repeating memories of the recent assault, Amy's delicate brows arched in surprise. Comlan's announcement seemed woefully inappropriate. But then, hadn't he warned her during their first encounter that predictability had no value to his kind. The thought of that warning put a slight upward curve on berry-bright lips. Whatever else might be true, it appeared certain that life in his realm was never boring . . . unlike the strict rules governing her daily routine. An image of the staid future mapped out for her even before birth loomed but she chased it away with a bright if impossible fantasy of life at her love's side and in his magical land.

Amy suddenly laughed and her unexpected action was a delight that shocked a stunning smile from Comlan. However, it abruptly disappeared as he solemnly said, "I blame myself for our serious wrong."

Fearing Comlan regretted their lovemaking, Amy would've spoken had he not immediately continued.

"And I repent the danger to you that I cannot cure."

This statement perplexed Amy.

"Having taken your innocence, I know how naive you are but surely you realize that the time we spend in Lissan's circle of flowers could bear fruit?"

When Amy's face instantly flamed, Comlan saw that it had never occurred to her.

"That you gave no thought to such a price is understandable. You lack experience while I ..." He shook his head and confessed a failing whose rarity she was unlikely to understand. "Though in my realm babies cannot be conceived without prior intent, I knew the dangerous possibilities in your world ... but my control is perilously weak whenever you are near."

Her companion's admission of so strong a response to her was something Amy would treasure for the rest of her life. And she didn't want him to regret a possible child, not when she would welcome a baby and adore it the more for being a part of him.

"If blessed with a child"—Amy steadily met Comlan's green gaze and spoke with undeniable sincerity—"I'd love and care for it always."

"But your family—"

"No matter," Amy firmly interrupted. "I'd gladly escape with my wee one here to Ireland where I'm certain Daffy would greet us both with open arms."

Yet again Comlan was host to an unfamiliar experience at Amy's hand. She'd caught him utterly unprepared and uncertain how to react. Off kilter, he fell back on the promise of this conversation's first words.

Marylyle Rogers

"Then my gift may be of even more value than I dreamed when arranging for its creation."

Amy blinked. She'd completely forgotten the words Comlan had spoken when she first descended from Daffy's bedroom.

"If you remember the tale of the gold horned unicorn that can never be caught nor harmed"— Comlan reached inside his jacket and pulled out a small bag of supple leather—"you may appreciate this amulet."

Amy's eyes first darkened with curiosity and then widened as he upended and gently shook the bag until a broach of great beauty fell into his palm.

"This pretty piece is imbued with diverse powers able to provide you with a protective spell equal to the one you saw render a bullet harmless." With his free hand Comlan gently untangled Amy's nervously entwined fingers, allowing him to lay the amulet into her cradled palms.

Amy studied Comlan's gift with awe. An exquisitely carved, ivory unicorn reared inside an onyx circle while its golden horn gleamed. But not even her admiration of the amulet was stronger than the power of a steady, emerald gaze and she glanced up.

"Do you have an amulet, too?" No longer bothering to hide her fascination, she visually caressed this fantasy figure come to life . . . her devastating lover. "Is that how you remained unscathed when attacked the day our Queen opened her Grand Exposition?"

With a wry smile Comlan promptly shook his head. It was that instant when Amy acknowledged a realization arrived at slowly, steadily. Over time she'd begun looking beyond surface mockery for glimpses of the deeper, rarely revealed emotions below.

Having earlier been annoyed by her failure to ask direct questions, he welcomed this one. And yet, he yielded to his contrary nature long enough to briefly tease. "There's no need."

Amy grimaced in sham disgust for his surely inadequate response.

"Truly, the answer you seek is that simple." Comlan atoned for his gentle jest by providing a complete explanation. "No mortal weapon, whether wielded by human or fairy hand, can wreak more than temporary harm upon any member of the Tuatha De Danann."

Far beyond doubts, Amy nodded her acceptance of his statement as simple truth before glancing back down at the charmed broach.

"Did you say my lovely amulet is imbued with more than a single power?"

"Yes and no." Comlan wasn't certain that Amy was ready for more but she'd asked a solemn question and deserved an honest answer.

The darkening of green eyes to a serious, forest hue was enough to convince Amy that these words represented more than a further demonstration of contrary moods.

Pleased that Amy hadn't instantly questioned his statement, Comlan continued. "The strands of many spells are woven tightly together to form a single protective blanket."

His winsome colleen remained silent but her

steady gaze and somber expression proved an effective demand for further explanations.

"If you keep it with you always, you'll be able to summon my aid against any threat."

Amy's brows drew together in a slight frown. Did he mean that their relationship need not end . . . so long as *she* did the calling? As a properly raised debutante she found that a disconcerting notion . . . and yet . . .

"For all the pleasure my kind takes in the unexpected, we are also an honorable race," Comlan flatly stated, after recognizing the direction of Amy's thoughts. The idea that she might believe him capable of such discreditable intentions was dismal and annoying—particularly after their recent talk of babies. "I'll be able to hear your call only when serious peril looms."

Amy's face burned. The speed with which she'd shifted from satisfaction with her growing ability to see through Comlan's careful facade to unworthy suspicion of his motives was deplorable!

"After all you've done to keep the oath given a mortal and his wife, your honor could never be questioned." Standing a brief distance from Comlan, Amy gazed up with shamed regret filling serious gray eyes. "And I can only beg you to forgive my momentary but utterly unworthy doubts."

"I would be wrong to fault you for so small a misstep when, in truth, you've come closer to understanding my nature than any human ever has." Her sincerity earned a more complete response than could safely be given and his voice was strained as he added, "Closer even than a good many of my own people."

Indeed, Comlan inwardly confessed, with Amy he shared a rapport more intimate—on more than a physical level—than with any being he had ever known. But he dare not confess that fact to her after he'd already said and *done* far too much.

Amy's blush glowed brighter but now with pleasure. The suggestion that her incredible fantasy hero felt an affinity with her was wonderful though futile.

The warmth on Amy's winsome face was more temptation than Comlan could easily bare—not with burning memories of all that had passed between them in the fairy ring so fresh. (He refused to deepen his gloom by admitting they were unlikely to ever fade.) To distract himself and Amy, he let frost cover his words as he formally continued with what else she needed to know for putting his gift to its intended use.

"When danger threatens, lay your palm flat over the amulet, close your eyes, and concentrate while *silently* calling my name again and again and again. . . ."

Against the chill of his voice, wistfulness clouded Amy's eyes and lingered until the crystal brightness of unspoken love laid bare broke through—a tender, dangerous enticement.

"Do you understand?" Comlan softly asked even as he fell to temptation by stroking over ebony hair from crown to shoulder. "Will you remember?"

Certain she'd never forget a single word her unbelievable lover had ever said to her, Amy nodded while mindlessly leaning toward his warmth and strength.

"Then listen well." He reluctantly held her at arm's length, cursing himself for wrongs already committed and determined to prevent such a further lapse of his strong willpower as only this beguiling colleen could cause. "As with all dealings between your world and mine, there are rules and limits that must be observed."

Amulet carefully cradled between her hands and pressed against her heart, Amy concentrated on listening intently despite the pain of his rejection.

"If you're in motion when you call, I won't be able to locate you." His flat statements lacked natural inflection of any kind. "Nor can I hear if your palm fails to completely cover the amulet."

Amy's attention fell to a scrutiny of the pretty piece, waiting in the expectation of more rules and restrictions. None were forthcoming and she glanced up to discover herself alone.

Hyde Park daily drew crowds anxious to view the Crystal Palace and its treasures. Even today's scattered clouds and intermittent rains had failed to lessen the flow which make it the perfect site for a secret meeting.

"He's gone orf to Ireland," Macraedy defensively whined. "Can't strike an end to a man what won't stay put."

"Hmm." Orville was not placated. "So, you've failed me—*again*."

" 'Tis no failure, jist a delay what weren't my

fault." Macraedy squared his beefy shoulders with false bravado but nervously twisted the cloth cap in his hands. "I only wanted to know if yer wants me to follow him ta that blighted land . . . what with Miss Danton already there."

"Why are you discussing my sister's whereabouts with this rough-looking lout?" Garnet demanded. Attention caught by the sound of his sister's name on an uncultured tongue, he'd initially been shocked to find its source was a filthy oaf sporting a ragged eye patch but no less so by the identity of his companion.

As Orville spun to face the younger gentleman, the "rough-looking lout" hastily faded into the anonymous crowd.

"Ah, so nice to see you, old bean." Orville thought it best to simply ignore Garnet's question. He hid annoyance with both the interruption preventing him from issuing instructions to Macraedy and the foul quirk of fate allowing this one man out of the hundreds in Hyde Park to stumble across his path at so inopportune a moment.

"How is your great-aunt Daphenia?" Orville politely inquired. "Recovering, I trust."

"Daffy is not ill."

"But your mother said . . ." With mock amazement, Orville let the statement trail off on the higher note of a silent question.

Garnet's lips compressed into a tight line.

Sounding aggrieved, Orville said, "And here I thought Amethyst would return to London as soon as the dear woman's health improved."

"My father left today to bring Amy home," Garnet responded without thought and regretted it a moment later.

"Marvelous." Lord Comlan might be there, but Amethyst was coming home. Orville greeted this news of his intended wife's return with a smug satisfaction that left her brother horribly uncomfortable. "Then doubtless I'll see her at the Duchess of Worthington's ball at the weekend."

"Stay away from Amy."

"Now, now." Orville slowly shook his head with a ruefulness belied by the unpleasant gleam of delight in his eyes. "Remember, the sharp edge of the weapon you hold over me can be just as effectively turned on you."

Black brows scowled.

"Be calm, my friend," Orville advised with apparent concern. "As I've assured you before, we've a delicate relationship able to guarantee the security of us both—at a price. You leave that sword safely sheathed in exchange for the wherewithal to build your pretty little wife her own home while I also leave it untouched in return for your support of my courtship of Amethyst."

Already enduring growing shame over his dishonest report on this man's produce and products, Garnet realized that this contract with the pompous devil would exact the greatest penalty. It would force him to helplessly watch as his youngest sister was permanently trapped in a despicable marriage.

As it had with increasing regularity in recent days, again in Garnet's mind rose the perversely beckoning vision of a confession made and price paid that cleansed his soul and rescued Amy. An honorable man at heart, the stress had grown so intense that now it was only the fearful threat of the loving trust on Lovey's face melting into disillusionment and disgust that held him back.

And this, Garnet acknowledged while turning to stride away from the self-satisfied toad, was the shape of a nasty gaol he'd built for himself, one unknowingly guarded by the two women he most loved and one from which he could never escape.

Chapter 16

~

"*A*my, we're going home—now." Weary and badly out of sorts, a stern-faced Lord Farley Danton, Viscount Wyfirth, stood in the doorway of his aunt's parlor.

Amy's eyes widened with the unpleasant shock of her father's arrival. Only moments before she'd been chatting amicably with her great-aunt and waiting with growing anticipation for Comlan's appearance.

"Your mother is frantic," Lord Farley raged. He'd not soon forgive his errant daughter for forcing on him this preposterous jaunt to Ireland.

Amy gazed warily at her father's broad figure, and to calm flustered nerves studied how the spattering of raindrops across his thick shoulders gleamed under the faint light falling through a restored window.

"And I shouldn't wonder," the viscount roared on, "but that Orville has begun to worry if madness runs through our family bloodlines." With the latter he glared unwaveringly at Daphenia. When both she and his daughter burst into laughter, he was nearly convinced that it was true himself.

Heavy face fairly glowing with testy color, he demanded, "Come, Amethyst!"

Amy obediently rose and yet tried to reason with the man plainly in an unreasonable mood. "Father, there was a purpose for my journey."

"Humph . . ." he growled. "None that can excuse inconsiderate, foolish, dangerous actions threatening to be the ruin of your reputation and deliver a mortal blow to all your mother's dreams."

Now there, Amy acknowledged, was the crux of the matter—her mother's dreams. Against their fragile assault she had no defense.

"At least . . ." she quietly begged a small concession from her father, "let me fetch my cape and satchel."

"Now, Farley," Daffy spoke for the first time since her nephew's arrival. "For gracious sake, this bleak day is half-done. Stay here until morning when, hopefully, the dawn will be blessed with less nasty weather."

"Thank you, no." The crisp edge to Lord Farley's words ensured that no one would mistake them for honest appreciation. "I have rooms reserved at an inn in Liverpool. Amy and I will spend the night there, the better to reach Wyfirth House by tomorrow's end."

Once in the quaint little bedroom at the top of Daffy's cottage, Amy packed her satchel with as much haste and scant care as she had while Paddy waited in London. Glancing through the bedroom's tiny window, she saw her father's hired coach tied to a tree barely more than a sapling at one side of the cobbled walkway.

Amy wanted to linger in hopes that Comlan would appear but daren't risk further angering her father. Closing the satchel and brushing fingertips over the amulet pinned to the chemise beneath her bodice, she took a final look around the small room, wishing it were possible to stay. Once back in London, even if Comlan returned (and she prayed he would), they'd be allowed few private moments and never another opportunity for intimacy.

Feet making soft thudding sounds, Amy slowly descended the narrow stairway to meet her impatient father in the cottage's entry.

"Now you remember, Amy-girl," Daffy whispered as she gave her grandniece a farewell hug. "I am perfectly safe in my snug little home."

Amy nodded and whispered back, "I'll see you in London soon." Despite this planned reunion, part of Comlan's scheme for Daffy's safety, unshed tears sparkled—first for the distress of this separation and second for the prospect of a permanent one underscored by Comlan's talk of the brevity of human lives and Daffy's in particular.

"We must leave." Lord Farley was impatient with overly emotional women delaying the departure. "I don't want to miss our ship to Liverpool."

Daffy remained in her open doorway until the coach completely disappeared from sight. Only then did she return to a parlor seeming even emptier now that Amy's sweet presence was gone. She retrieved a fat needlework bag from behind the couch and settled in her favorite chair to resume her knitting.

The blanket Daffy was working on for the local rector's charity had truly begun to take shape by the time a soft rapping summoned her attention. She glanced up and smiled to see a welcome sight.

"I'm sorry it's taken me so long to come," Comlan gently apologized—an action rarely necessary in his own sphere. "When I'm away for any great length of time, even simple matters become snarled and demand a deal of trouble to see them untangled."

"I will always understand," Daffy assured him. "But I fear it's made you too late to find Amy here."

"What?" Dark gold brows scowled.

"My nephew Farley, the Viscount of Wyfirth, arrived earlier and hustled his daughter away with almost as much haste as you are able to move."

"Hah!" The mere fact that Comlan gave the expected response was proof enough of how deeply affected he was by this news. "I hadn't thought Lord Wyfirth the sort of man to willingly undertake a journey made arduous by a nightlong train ride."

"And that he isn't," Daffy agreed. "Which is why he's already reserved rooms at a Liverpool inn."

Comlan slowly nodded. This information was inadequate yet possibly enough if Amy had reason to call on her amulet's powers.

Amy rolled over. This bed was too narrow and the blanket too thin. Both perfectly good reasons, she assured herself, to explain why she couldn't sleep.

But her tireless conscience wouldn't let that false-hood stand unchallenged.

Though they'd been together a single day past, already Amy badly missed Comlan. She hated to think how much more painful the ache would grow each day endured without him. *Time heals all wounds,* she'd heard it said. But not for a single moment did Amy believe it would be true of loneliness for her fantasy king.

Was it Comlan's contrary nature or her own that made it so? While pondering that question, sweet memories returned and soon lulled Amy into dreams.

Even the crowded Woolvester Inn settled into silence as night hours advanced. The clock in a distant church tower struck three times and faded away before a dark shadow slipped across the rented room's floor.

A wad of cloth being stuffed into her mouth awakened Amy. Choking, she worked her tongue trying to thrust the obstruction out. An attempt to sit up was met by a pair of wiry arms flipping her over to lie facedown. She was harshly shoved against the bed and firmly held there while the muffling gag was fastened in place with a length of cloth. Next her arms were roughly jerked behind and tied against her spine.

"Fear not, sweet bride," a familiar voice whispered. "Next time I have you in a bed, I'll handle you with far greater care."

Amy wanted to demand what Paddy thought he was doing, what insanity drove him to assault a woman in her bedchamber while her father rested in the next room and was not a heavy sleeper. But, of course, she couldn't. She couldn't speak but she could growl ... and *loudly did*. Apparently to no avail since the only response was a harsher hold when jerked to her feet and the bed's lone, thin blanket was wrapped around her inadequately clad body.

Slung over Paddy's shoulder like a sack of grain, Amy could see only the back of his heels while he rapidly carried her down one narrow flight of back stairs and then out through a ramshackle door—plainly the servants' entrance.

Bundled into a rented coach of much lower quality than the one her father had hired, Amy stubbornly averted her face from her abductor. Surely Paddy couldn't dream she'd willingly say the words that would make her his wife! Besides, no banns had been called. And, although a woman's consent might be dismissed, her father's approval was required.

Grateful that her unwanted companion soon dozed in his corner, Amy let her forehead dip forward to rest against a cracked window frame while gloomy suspicions rose. Though it was not seemly for debutantes to be taught the laws of marriage, Amy suspected there were always methods to dodge such restraints. Would some dishonorable minister betray his calling by performing the ceremony? She hadn't a doubt. Oh, depressing thought!

Don't be a pigeonheart! Amy heatedly berated herself for the momentary surrender to gloom. *Fight for your freedom! Escape!*

Heartened by the fervor of this self-advice, Amy took time to closely examine the coach's shabby interior—torn seats, missing windowpanes, door handle replaced with a wire and piece of twine.

Door handle? Amy studied it more closely and her eyes began to sparkle. Even without the use of her hands, there was hope. The next time this vehicle slowed, as it did on every corner, she would fall free. Of course, she'd still be bound and gagged . . . but first things first and that was freedom.

So much time passed while they rolled onward in a straight line that Amy began to despair. Fortunately, she didn't relax her readiness. At the sound of the coachman softly calling to his horses, Amy tensed. And when the coach both slowed and rocked, thankfully in her direction, she threw her body against the flimsy door. Not only did the latch break open but the barrier split down the middle, allowing her to tumble out.

Amy landed hard against the lane's hard-packed surface but quickly rolled until she felt the rough vegetation that grew on its verge. It was difficult to stand without the use of her hands but she accomplished the feat before the coachman could calm and halt horses spooked by the cracking door.

"Amy!" Paddy screamed, half out of a coach window missing its pane. "Stop!"

Rudely awakened, a testy Dooley blinked against the unwelcome light held by a friend's hand.

Comlan announced, "There are advantages in being able to move through the human world unseen."

Annoyed, Dooley didn't doubt this was a true fact but why had he been awakened to hear it? In the next instant he grimaced. He certainly ought to be accustomed to the Tuatha De's disconcerting habits . . . however, he'd also learned that they usually had some oblique purpose.

"Ta shake me bed like tha', ye must have a purpose." Dooley peered through narrowed eyes. "Learned somethin' o' import, have ye?"

"It's what I didn't see that worries me." The wavering glow of his single candle's flame gave a curious cast to Comlan's sardonic smile. "At a Liverpool inn Lord Wyfirth sleeps undisturbed in one room while Amy's satchel and shed clothing reside in the next."

Raising up in his bed to rest on one elbow, Dooley gave the other man a speaking glance that demanded a sensible explanation. It came in a precious few, succinct words.

"Amy's bed is empty."

"Smart and full of pepper, is she. Likely fled to escape her da and all them infernal rules," grouched Dooley, looking an odd sight with bright hair twisted in a multitude of impossible directions.

"Yes, she is both of those things." Comlan solemnly nodded. "Which makes it the more improbable that she'd flee in only nightclothes and a blanket."

Dooley unwillingly admitted that Comlan had him there. Sitting fully upright with difficulty, he awkwardly swung his legs over the side of the bed. The prospect of the pretty, dark colleen being abused was no more agreeable to him than to his master.

"So what is it that I can do to help?"

"Go to the Wyfirth town house." Comlan's wry smile was a warning his companion uncomfortably recognized. "Speak with Amy's maid."

Dooley's brows arched and then dropped as sharply into a scowl. "Beastie?"

Comlan's white grin flashed. In the several centuries of human time that he'd known Dooley, rarely had Comlan seen the merry man quail as he undeniably did now. Was it, perhaps, because in this instance Dooley's opponent taunted with a tender challenge?

"Why me and not you?" Dooley irritably queried.

"If I, as the Lord of Doncaully, were to call at Wyfirth House at this most unconventional time of night, Lady Wyfirth would be called to greet me. And she would no doubt be terrified, fearful of what I might have to say since such an intrusion would only occur under the direst of circumstances."

"Ah, well, at least you *are* a lord and they'll be openin' the door to you." As Dooley slowly shook his head, spikes of red hair trembled. "For the likes o' me they won't."

"Not the front door," Comlan agreed. "But the servants' door in the back is answered at odd hours, and even now the boot boys will be about their work in a tiny room just inside."

"That's as may be." Not easily mollified, Dooley argued. "But Beastie is no' like ta answer me call."

"She will if you send one of the boot boys to her door with this note."

Dooley scowled suspiciously at the folded paper Comlan extended to him. "What's it say?"

"That her 'lambie' is in danger." Emerald eyes gazed steadily at the questioner. "And that she needs the aid of a chaperone to see her reputation untainted while her body is safely delivered from the threat."

Reluctantly accepting the logic and likely success of his friend's message, Dooley nodded and yet probed deeper. "And then what?"

"Then . . ." Mockery sparkled in green eyes although Comlan's face remained serious while he gave the answer his cohort wanted to hear. "I'll whisk you both to Liverpool and we'll find the lost colleen."

Whisk? Dooley grinned. That was the term Comlan used to describe his uncanny ability to see a body moved even long distances in a heartbeat. And he'd like to hear the skeptical Beastie explain how anything short of fairy powers could transport her so far, so quickly. That prospect did more to speed Dooley on his way than any other argument could've done.

Chapter 17

~

Running as fast as she could through the loose dirt of a freshly tilled field, bare feet sinking into its furrows, Amy struggled to reach a line of trees faintly seen on this near moonless night.

But Paddy could run faster than Amy and with unrestrained hands was more easily able to keep his balance despite the earth's uncertain surface. He had nearly caught up with the figure looking like a ghost dashing through the dark in a flimsy nightrail, when she took a misstep and fell—hard.

Knocked breathless, Amy couldn't move for several minutes. And by the time she could, it was too late. Paddy picked her up and set her on her feet before brushing away loose dirt with a gentleness she found more ominous than the roughness he'd employed in her capture.

The next instant Paddy swept Amy off bare feet to carry her back to the waiting coach. She'd have found this action more frightening still if it hadn't also reminded her of the source of certain rescue pinned inside her night attire but forgotten until in Paddy's lifting of her, it raked across sensitive skin.

"Tch, tch." Beattie fell back on her favorite response to any and all things inexplicable—silently. Out here in the country during the darkest hours of night, even the slightest noise sounded like the loud chime of a discordant bell.

Still, if ever there were circumstances to justify her irritated, skeptical comment, this night's did. She'd been disconcerted at the outset by a boot boy waking her to deliver a written plea for the aid of her company in preserving her lambie's reputation, particularly since the message gave no hint of what or who threatened Amy. More unbelievable than the summons had been the discovery that she was expected to join *two* mad Irishmen on a mission to rescue Amy from an abductor. But the most extraordinary, most incredible of the night's events had come when she stood one moment in Lord Comlan's drawing room and the next found herself here between dusty lane and hedgerow.

And all this for what reason? A heavily overcast sky hid the moon but even so Beattie recognized the rustic nature of her surroundings. Who knew where this deserted site was located? She didn't and scowled. However, that was far less important than the also unanswered question of why they were here beside an empty road, with no Amy in sight.

While Beattie stewed and Dooley dozed atop a thick clump of vegetation, Comlan silently gazed into the night. His thoughts, too, were with Amy but he looked beyond her current predicament to another challenge far more complex. Inwardly he searched for a resolution granting the ultimate paradox—a happy ending for both the king of the Faerie Realm and his dark *human* colleen.

Under intense concentration distant shadows seemed to take form and berate him for failing to see an obvious answer.

The night seemed endless—but not long enough. Amy would've sighed but for the annoying gag drying her mouth as effectively as a blotter absorbing ink.

Rolling over an unusually rough stretch of road the decrepit coach lurched, jostling Amy against Paddy. She groaned, not for the bone-jarring bumps but in frustration. These reviving jolts were most unwelcome to someone impatiently waiting for her companion to drift into at least a light slumber. Paddy straightened and repositioned himself to gaze through a paneless window while Amy glared through the one opposite.

Their journey had begun with Paddy sitting in the seat across from Amy but following her unsuccessful attempt to flee, he'd moved to sit beside her. His body was a block between her and the gaping hole where the door she'd shattered had once been, leaving her to more thoroughly feel a prisoner.

A faint glimmer of hope beckoned her toward the beacon at its source. When thrust back into the coach at the end of her failed flight, Amy had made a discovery. Her escape, run, fall and recapture had resulted in at least one positive consequence. Her bonds were looser—only slightly but possibly enough. Unfortunately, so long as her abductor watched, she could hardly struggle free without drawing the kind of attention that would smother her hopes.

The instinct to nibble her bottom lip thwarted by intruding cloth, Amy admitted an even less pleasant reality. As useful as unfettered hands would be, winning liberty would still be difficult for a woman alone, dressed in her sleep attire, and only heaven knew where in a night-dark countryside.

The beacon of hope was near and yet too far away—pinned inside among the many folds of a cotton nightrail while Amy's hands were tied behind. This fact left her depressingly aware that opportunities for escape were reduced by every turn of the coach's wheels. She had to try *something*, had to risk bold measures no matter how improbable.

Staring blindly through the window, expression unchanged, Amy tried to limit the movement of her arms while nimble fingers released one and then another of the already loosened knots binding her hands together. Grateful that night's dim light would hide the flush of victory on her cheeks, she next held a cuff tightly while slowly pulling up the arm inside its thankfully loose sleeve.

Once the freed right arm lay curled across a bare midriff, Amy began surreptitiously moving its hand in search of the onyx circle so tantalizingly near. When fingertips at last found their goal, Amy restrained an urge to immediately wrench it free. Instead, she tamped down small flames of anxiety and impatience while taking care in unfastening its hold on white cloth. The amulet slipped loose, and she gently cushioned its fall.

Remembering Comlan's admonition to be sure her palm completely covered the amulet, Amy laid the precious broach atop one thigh and carefully laid her hand over the whole. His additional warning about the difficulty of locating her while moving hadn't been forgotten. But she had no choice. Might the desperateness of her situation compensate for their pace? At least she must earnestly try.

"Comlan ... Comlan ... Comlan ..." Silently, over and over, Amy repeated the call, praying her fantasy king would hear. . . .

Three figures lingered, motionlessly waiting beside a country lane until the rural-quiet was invaded by the sound of an approaching vehicle. While a horrified Beattie watched, Lord Comlan irrationally stepped into the roadway's center as a sorry excuse for a coach—one door missing—slowly rounded the sweeping corner some little distance away.

"Halt!" Hair glowing brightly despite the cloudy night, Comlan issued an implacable, single-word command.

The coachman's response was to send a whip curling and cracking over the back of his horses, callously urging powerful animals to run the interloper down.

Beattie couldn't stifle a shriek and the coachman gasped when, rather than moving aside, the reckless man strode forward with hands raised palm-out.

Despite the coachman's zealous efforts to drive

his horses forward, they slowed to a halt one pace from the again motionless Comlan.

"Leave the reins on the seat and climb down."

The panicked coachman instantly obeyed with every shred of haste his considerable girth permitted. He was terrified. After all he'd seen the speaker exert control over horses supposedly under his command, great beasts whose strength he'd attempted to use in crushing this man.

Dooley promptly climbed up to replace the coachman and in taking control of the horses released Comlan to set his beloved colleen free.

But no sooner had Comlan turned to do so than the one they'd come to rescue threw herself headlong into his unprepared yet welcoming arms.

"It worked!" Amy gazed up at her golden savior, heavy masses of ebony curls tumbling down and around her shoulders in sharp contrast to her white nightgown. "It really worked!"

"Of course." Comlan knew Amy referred to the amulet's powers, and dazzling silver lights flared in green eyes to match the crystal joy in a gray gaze.

"But the coach was always in motion . . . never still." Amy softly confessed this wrong, hoping it wouldn't chill the warmth of his attention.

A smile of piercing sweetness was Comlan's answer to words that held a far deeper meaning than their speaker could possibly know. This was no place for explanations but when next they were alone he would tell her how bridging the gap caused by a broken rule revealed a closer bond than he'd thought possible between Tuatha De and human.

With steady scrutiny of the prize came recognition

of a serious lack. Comlan had expected to find Amy wearing nightclothes but wrapped in the missing blanket. However, she'd apparently abandoned her blanket in the carriage. Promptly stripping off his jacket, he settled it about Amy's slender shoulders. Her nightgown, though hardly immodest, had never been intended for public view. Garbed only in it she was a lovely, seductive vision he appreciated but one he hated any other man to see . . . least of all the devious Paddy who had held her captive too long.

Paddy! Ominous emerald flames lost none of their power for flashing from temper-narrowed eyes. Comlan was upset with himself for permitting anything—or anyone—to divert him from even a secondary goal. Dealing with the devious Paddy was a lesser goal but one that had to be accomplished. Fortunately, from his viewpoint, it was at this moment that Amy's maid chose to assert her influence by acting the chaperone she'd been asked to play.

Beattie brushed Comlan's hands aside to adjust the jacket more closely about her lambie the better to conceal luscious curves. At last she saw justification for her participation in this mission. Were any member of the Quality to catch even the briefest glimpse of Amy alone at night, dressed in bedgown, and in the company of bachelors, her reputation would quickly be in tattered shreds. Only the presence of a chaperone *might* rescue Amy from such a dreadful fate.

Far too cognizant of the Lord of Doncaully's nearness to her lambie, Beattie was relieved when the man moved to peer into the coach through the gaping hole left by a missing door.

"Ah, you're still here?" Comlan murmured, lips slowly curling upward with no hint of real humor. "I thank you for saving me the effort of hunting you down."

Paddy cringed which lent a deadly sharp edge to Comlan's mocking smile and that, in turn, frightened the red-haired man all the more. But what the Irish lord did next completely disconcerted him.

"Be gone now," Comlan ordered. "And yet be assured that I'll know where you are."

"I would if I could." Paddy's dark eyes were cold despite the burning scorn in his voice. "Tha' little hellion's got the punch of a coal miner and the kick of a mule."

Comlan's smile warmed with gentle sardonic amusement. "I agree, Miss Danton possesses a fine measure of unexpected talents. So, get out of the coach *now* before I set her on you again."

"I can't," Paddy wailed, forcing a facade of wounded dignity over the ugly truth of his anger. "Purposefully kicked in me most tender area, she did. Shoved me aside jist ta reach ye."

"Shall I help you step down?" The frigid tone of Comlan's sensible response contained a clear threat which inspired a miraculous recovery and saw Amy's erstwhile captor instantly scrambling out and onto the lane with no hint of grace.

Paddy mutely glared, annoyed with himself for yielding to this mysterious stranger who had clearly lied about an ancestral home.

"Begone with you," Comlan ordered the fuming

Paddy who instead widened his stance, signaling a determination to stand firm.

In this match of wills the latter had no chance of defeating his golden opponent. And yet before Paddy was shamed by being forced into turning helplessly away, the vexed coachman interrupted.

"Wot the bleedin' hell!" exploded the man evicted from his post although he most resembled a small mountain and looked to be nearly as immovable. After surrendering by climbing down so easily, he'd been ashamed of his craven action and had lingered, unwilling to abandon the vehicle and horses which were his livelihood. "That rotter gots to pay t'other half of me fare when I sets him down where he says."

Mocking grin flashing, Comlan turned to face the coachman whose vast size made him conspicuous even though standing slightly behind Beattie and her charge.

The challenger's bravado faltered in the face of a confident smile more ominous than scowls on the faces of a whole army of men.

"I'll see your expenses better than twice paid for taking my friends to London," Comlan steadily informed the churlish owner of the necessary vehicle and horses.

The coachman gazed at the speaker suspiciously. Didn't the nob know how long a journey that entailed? Perhaps it was a ploy to lure him to a site more favorable for robbery? Like as not that was so. There was something peculiar about this too handsome, too golden man. For instance, how'd he gotten out here in the nowhere with neither coach nor horse? Aye, this man was plainly some kind of footpad who preyed on honest, hard workers and took their earnings.

Amused by the rough character's unspoken concerns, Comlan said, "I trust the new door will be acceptable."

New door? Either this blighter was mad or harbored a nasty sense of humor! Nonetheless, the coachman glanced back toward the portal broken in the woman's desperate attempt to flee and found his door restored. Nay, not *his* door. This one was sturdy, new, and out of place on the battered carriage . . . yet welcome.

"How?" Apprehensive of odd matters he couldn't explain, the coachman's brief question shook.

"No matter." Emerald eyes glittered while Comlan waved one hand as if brushing useless crumbs aside. "If you go never questioning the speed with which your vehicle travels, at journey's end the rest of your coach will be the match of that door."

Knowing Dooley would be pleased by this oblique promise of unnatural haste, Comlan took note of the opposite response welling up in both the coachman and Beattie. Their expressions betrayed discomfort with strange powers clearly at work. However, with his experience of humankind, Comlan was certain the coachman was too greedy to further question a promised gift while the opinionated Beatrice was unlikely to admit having seen any of the inexplicable deeds occurring in past hours.

At that moment Comlan realized Paddy had obeyed his order to begone. His cynical smile tilted further awry. Doubtless that untrustworthy human's departure had been motivated by his terror for the source of incredible events just seen—and rightly so.

After the hulking coachman arduously hoisted himself up onto the driver's perch again, Dooley handed the reins back to him and clamored down with all the agility that the other lacked. An unexpectedly mild Beattie allowed the Irish lord's manservant to help her into the coach's less than comfortable interior without comment. And her often acidic tongue remained silent as he climbed in behind her.

As the coach rolled out of sight, Amy gazed trustingly up into her intently watching companion's face with a question in dove gray eyes. While the others were off to London, how and to what destination would they go?

Amy blushed when, in answer, emerald mockery both gentled and deepened. The first part of her wordless question was unworthy even of a child fresh from the nursery. After seeing Comlan appear and disappear in the space of a heartbeat; after being transported from fairy ring to cottage garden in an instant, how could she question the method of travel? But still, acknowledgment of that simple fact did nothing to reveal their destination. Before she could put the query into words, Comlan spoke.

"Remember, once you're back in London, find a solicitor for Daffy." Despite stern words, when Amy glanced up it was to be enveloped in a green gaze of uncommon warmth. "It's a task made the more important by our discovery of the two forged wills."

"I'll do it as soon as I possibly can." Amy immediately nodded agreement to both the matters already discussed and the promise earlier given, anxious to earn her fantasy king's approval. "But how shall I get you word of the appointment?"

"Send Beattie with the message."

Amy grimaced. Beattie was unlikely to take kindly any order involving a further encounter with Dooley.

"You're wrong," Comlan quietly said, face gone amazingly solemn. "Our *servants* have begun building a rapport that only concern for your great-aunt has kept you from noticing."

His beloved colleen looked so skeptical that Comlan abandoned the subject and bent to divert her attention with a kiss quick but of devastating power.

Willingly yielding to a potent fire she feared becoming as necessary to her as breath, Amy fanned the flame higher with the experience he'd given her.

Comlan abruptly lifted his head. "Your lips are chapped."

Though initially startled—unpleasantly—in a few seconds time Amy recognized this as an example of the Tuatha De's contrary nature and likely another test of her ability to cope with his unexpected reactions.

"The gag was tight," Amy patiently explained, determined not to betray surprise even while unable to keep herself from helplessly studying the incredibly handsome face so near she could see individual eyelashes. Despite cold certainty that such dreams were doomed, she wanted to prove herself unshaken by the odd mood shifts of his kind, wanted far more to remain forever in her devastating lover's embrace.

"Gag?" Bronze brows crashed together. "Paddy gagged you?"

"Indeed, yes." Amy grinned, taking her cue from the unique blend of notes joined in the curious harmony of Comlan's nature. Besides, she was pleased by his obvious distress over this further indignity having been inflicted on her. "Had to or I'd have screamed the inn down. Tried to anyway."

Delighted with the dark beauty's response, Comlan's head abruptly fell back and deep velvet laughter rolled through the night air an instant before he wrapped Amy in his arms. The next moment he released her in the corridor just outside her rented room in the Woolvester Inn.

While her father slept in the next room, utterly unaware of danger met and overcome, Amy quietly pushed that sturdy barrier open and took a single step inside. A softly tangled cloud of dusky curls framed her winsome face as she cast an enticing, come-hither look over one shoulder.

Emerald eyes flared with desire but Comlan reluctantly shook his head and his hair was gilded by the faint predawn light falling through a small window at one end of the hall. He earnestly wished it were his right to accompany Amy into the bedchamber and carry her with him again into the shimmering brilliance of passion's fires.

He couldn't. Not yet and possibly never but, by the amazingly clear solution he'd glimpsed earlier this night, he might be able. . . .

* * *

" 'Tis an apology I owe you," Dooley solemnly announced before a merry grin broke through and nearly lit the dilapidated coach's gloomy interior. "With your vinegary tongue 'tis a right tartar you are . . . but now I've seen ye've also the courage of a tartar."

Beatrice was flustered. She wasn't accustomed to receiving compliments and peered suspiciously at its unabashed source. No mistake, it was a compliment and from this least expected quarter—the mad Irishman who'd so often taunted her. And since he'd apologized to her, Beattie felt she ought to prove herself gracious first by making a confession and then by repenting both belittling words and determination to disbelieve what had seemed far-fetched claims.

"I misled you the day we met."

Dooley's brows arched in exaggerated surprise.

Meeting his gaze unflinching, Beattie said, "I allowed it to seem that I'd a husband when in truth I've never been married."

"But . . ." Now Dooley honestly was confused. "Why then do they call ye *Mrs.* Milford?"

"It's an honorary title of respect."

"I see," Dooley promptly said although he didn't.

Determined to see the intended task through, Beattie added, "And I fear I've been a mite too rigid in my ways," Beattie allowed. "I see now that I ought to have seriously considered all you've tried to tell me about the Tuatha De Danann."

"Ah, ha!" Dooley chortled. "Then ye do believe?"

Beattie stiffened, unprepared to take quite so bold a leap.

"Now, Beastie." Dooley squeezed one of her plump hands without thought. "I swears every last scrap I've told ye 'tis true. Why if ye could see half the wonders I've seen . . ." Slight shrug wordlessly indicating the magnitude of his experience, he gazed heavenward or at least to the tattered ceiling of their compartment.

For the first time, instead of sending Dooley an incredulous sneer, Beattie gave her companion a look encouraging him to share more.

The rest of their magically abbreviated journey passed with the two in deep conversation and amazing harmony.

Chapter 18

~

*T*he first morning after her return to London, while the other ladies of Wyfirth House remained abed Amy rose early, donned a comfortable lavender morning dress and started down the winding staircase. Halfway between upper landing and elegant entry she sank down on one broad, highly polished step to peer through the handrail.

Partially concealed by the ornate banister, Amy waited to see her father leave for Parliament after finishing his breakfast. She sat by necessity motionless, quiet . . . and unable to block the flow of unpleasant memories. Only hours earlier Amy stood in stiff silence, a prodigal daughter justly called to bear her mother's lengthy rebukes and even longer sermon on proper behavior.

And now, like then, Amy smiled. A response that had fanned the fires of Lady Cornelia's displeasure. And though the contrariness of it would likely have pleased Comlan, she hadn't smiled for that reason. No, her flashing grin came with recognition that her mother's ire was but a small price, willingly paid for the pleasures in time spent with the incredible man she loved.

The sound of an opening door jolted Amy's attention back to the present. She watched as her father strode from the informal dining room to the entry hall.

An excellent butler, Bingley soundlessly appeared from nowhere to hold the entry door wide for his master's departure.

"Bingley." Lord Wyfirth paused in its frame. "Assure Lady Wyfirth that I will try to return in time to escort her to the Flovershams' ball this evening. But if I haven't appeared when the time for departure arrives, she must allow Garnet to escort her and Amy, as well as Louvisa, to the ball."

Amy nearly yelped when, as Bingley gave a well-practiced, emotionless nod, his eyes met hers. But the butler betrayed her presence by neither flicker of eye nor momentary change of expression, giving Amy further reason to be grateful for his sterling training and long experience.

"And also assure my wife ..." Completely oblivious, the viscount continued his instructions. ". . . That I'll only fail to be here if too many important issues arose during my unfortunate absence. If that proves the case, I may be required to remain in the City and will spend the night at my club."

After the door closed on her father's back, Amy stood and gave a sweet smile to the motionless butler as she descended sweeping stairs.

"Thank you, Bingley." Amy didn't elaborate. There was no need. They were both aware that had the youngest daughter of the house, decades beyond the nursery, been discovered peering like a curious child through the handrail it would've become the latest tasty dish for gossip's feast. And, no matter how nonsensical the act—or perhaps because of its seeming lack of purpose—it would've caused a minor domestic scandal. Having just returned from one rather more serious, Amy was anxious not to be the subject of another, particularly as it would surely increase the difficulty in keeping an important promise.

"Perhaps next time, if there is another," Bingley soberly suggested, "you'll allow me to tap on your door after Lord Wyfirth's departure?" It was only during this, her fourth Season that Miss Amethyst had begun shaking off her mother's chains. Wordlessly applauding these efforts, he would gladly support her cause.

"I appreciate your suggestion." Amy truly was grateful although she hoped that this one morning spent in her father's study would see her goal secured. "And if the need arises, I shall call on you."

"Very good, Miss Amethyst."

Amy hadn't confided her intended destination, but Bingley moved to open the study door—earning from her a cheery grin that put a twinkle in his eyes.

Once Amy was seated at her father's vast mahogany desk with study door closed for privacy, she began methodically flipping through papers, seeking mention of a reputable solicitor. Instead she found something more startling to her than even Comlan's inexplicable ability to instantly move from one place to another.

"Amy, what are you doing here?" Shock tangled with strain to lift Garnet's voice a full octave.

Holding one of many damning sheets in her hand, Amy instantly responded, "Garnet, what have *you* done?"

"Give me those documents." He made the desperate demand while striding from open door to desk edge.

"I would gladly consign them to the devil," Amy heatedly responded, though not even anger could hide the misery in her tone. She had found the cause of her brother's stress, the reason he couldn't eat or sleep.

"But," Amy continued in an anguished tone twined with compassion, "even so extreme an action couldn't wash away the stain in what I've just read."

Raking a hand through thick dark hair while sinking into one of two nicely padded leather chairs facing the desk, Garnet sought to shake his logical little sister with an abrupt change of focus.

"What are *you* doing here?"

Amy, accustomed to Comlan's contrary ways, was no longer so easily disconcerted and without hesitation gave an honest answer. "I came looking for the name of a solicitor."

"Why?" Garnet sharply demanded, frustrated by this rare failure of his skill at diverting attention, annoyed by the loss of sufficient time to devise a plausible explanation for the wrong he'd committed. "Are you planning to bring suit against someone?"

Amy shook her head, biting her lip to prevent the escape of words she'd likely regret.

"Then for what purpose do you want a solicitor?" Garnet firmly asked again.

"For a friend in need of sound legal advice." Amy was growing impatient with challenges to her intentions which, if not completely innocent, considering their secretive nature, assuredly had a more positive purpose and end than what she'd read of her brother's recent actions.

Garnet was not happy with this succinct response but saw that by forcing more he was likely to see his little sister dig in her heels and stubbornly refuse to say a single word more on any subject.

"The family solicitor is Aaron Bidgwell from the firm of Bidgwell, Bidgwell and Parson." He gave the information sought without insisting she confess its purpose, in hopes that she would be as generous by allowing him to keep his own secrets. "They're a staid group but utterly reliable in all legal and confidential matters."

"Thank you, Garnet," Amy said quietly before neatly turning the tables on him by returning to the subject of her unpleasant discovery. Not only had her brother falsified test results on Orville's behalf but then he'd gone on to blackmail the pompous man she daily grew to dislike more and yet could never coldly cheat.

"Why were your reports among Father's papers?" Remembering her father's fascination with the issue of adulteration, Amy was suddenly struck by an even more distressing possibility. "Surely he's not a part of your schemes?"

Recognizing his sister's fear that dwindling capital might've driven even their father to wrongdoing,

Garnet felt even more despicable for being the source of a shadow threatening to besmirch Lord Farley's pristine reputation. "I left them here for Father to find."

Amy's brows arched. "Why?"

"Though as his heir I hadn't the courage to confess my wrong face-to-face, I hoped that after reviewing what you've seen, Father would help me find a way free of the tangled mess I've made of my life."

"But why, Garnet?" Seeing painful remorse turn his eyes nearly black, Amy's heart went out to the brother she'd loved and admired all of her life. "Why when I know you to be an honest and honorable man?"

Garnet's mouth curled not up but down. "I made a foolish decision, followed by a series of terrible mistakes. After accepting Orville's bribe to *correct* the reports on his holdings, hiding a plethora of dangerous practices, it was too easy to demand further payments for keeping the truth hidden."

"But why?" Amy quietly asked again. "We Dantons are not a wealthy lot yet hardly destitute."

Garnet's answering smile was sincere but forlorn. "My Lovey dreams of being mistress in her own home, and I wanted to grant her that happiness, wanted to see her established as lady of the kind of house she deserves." Again he raked a hand roughly through his hair. "Now I fear I've succeeded only in raising the prospect of us both becoming social pariahs. And worse, I've put my precious Lovey in danger of being made an outcast from all she enjoys."

"Garnet," Lovey softly called from the doorway

he'd left ajar. Leaning against its frame, she had watched unobserved and listened since almost the first words exchanged between brother and sister. The relief in hearing enough to be certain Garnet had no regret for their union was so powerful that she would gladly forgive him any crime.

An anguished groan escaped Garnet's tight throat. He hadn't wanted his Lovey to ever know about the shameful wrong he'd committed.

"So long as you love me"—proudly moving to kneel at her husband's knee, Lovey assured him—"I'll never care where we live nor will I ever need any companion other than you."

With the last words, Lovey brushed tender lips across the back of a strong hand that immediately joined with another to lift her into his lap.

Realizing her presence was decidedly unnecessary and doubtless unwanted, Amy quietly rose. She moved quickly toward the open door, trying to ignore the hollow ache taunting her with the bleak truth that by giving her heart to the king of the Tuatha De Danann she'd surrendered any hope for a lifetime of sharing such gentle comforts. But still she refused to regret her doomed love.

Quietly closing the door behind herself, Amy forced attention back to the mission ahead. She had the name she'd come looking for . . . and a great deal too much besides.

Only two days later, with Beattie at her side, Amy tried to be unobtrusive while waiting on a cobbled sidewalk in the heart of the City. It was a nearly impossible goal considering the tide of conservatively dressed businessmen rushing past two lone females on every side. Gray eyes repeatedly tried to peek from beneath demurely lowered lashes for a first glimpse of anticipated arrivals.

"Are you sure Lord Comlan received my message?" Amy asked her maid again as she repeatedly had before.

Beattie heaved a deep, long-suffering sigh. "I gave your note to Dooley. Then I personally watched as Dooley placed it into Lord Comlan's own hand."

Amy absently noted the gentleness with which Beattie mentioned Dooley, the man earlier referred to with considerably more colorful descriptions. Again she peeked up and down busy sidewalks and across crowded streets—in vain. Though wanting to stomp her feet like a child, Amy curtailed her frustration to a mere nibbling of lips to berry-brightness.

"Sorry we're later than planned." The deep voice came from behind and just above Amy.

Dark head whipping about so fast the action nearly unseated a stylish bonnet, Amy was again startled by an arrival whose suddenness she knew to expect but suspected she never would.

"What happened?"

" 'Tis my fault, Amy-girl," grimaced Daffy, dressed in black as the widow she'd been for decades and looking even smaller and more frail amid hustling businessmen and massive buildings. "Forced by circumstances to return to this city that never welcomed me, I dithered in my preparations like a slow-witted child—misplaced my bonnet, my cape and nearly myself. . . ."

Amy gave her uneasy great-aunt an affectionate hug. "I doubt we're too late for our appointment with Mr. Bidgwell but we'd best lose no more time."

While Beattie waited in the outer office, an earnest young clerk escorted Daffy, her grandniece and Lord Comlan into the rooms of a Mr. Bidgwell clearly the elder of the firm's two. What little hair remained on an otherwise shiny head was a white near as bright as his obsequious smile while he welcomed the black-clad woman nervously clutching her cane.

"Mrs. Kilmarny, I'm pleased you've chosen our firm. But then you know, of course, that my father was your father's solicitor."

Daffy knew no such thing but graciously nodded as the solicitor, elderly yet still young enough to be her son, politely led her to one of the comfortable chairs facing his impressive desk.

While Amy and Comlan settled in seats matching Daffy's, Mr. Bidgwell took his place behind the desk. Gazing across its wide, gleaming expanse, he asked, "Now what can Bidgwell, Bidgwell and Parsons do for you?"

"I wish to establish an irrevocable trust."

"A wise choice." Mr. Bidgwell, Senior, ponderously nodded. Then, wrongly assuming this aged woman garbed in an antique style to be a befuddled eccentric, he made the mistake of speaking to her in a tone normally reserved for small children and fools. "But you do realize, I hope, that such complex matters often require days of preparation."

"No." Daffy thumped her cane and straightened while the piercing glitter in her eyes quickly showed

Mr. Bidgwell the error of his reasoning. "I don't believe that will be necessary. You see, it's really quite simple. I leave all I possess to my grandniece, Miss Amethyst Danton."

As Great-aunt Daphenia formally motioned toward her, Amy gave the foolish solicitor a cool nod.

"Now surely," Daffy sternly said, "that can't require so much of your time that to see it done we need linger here—in *your* office—for more than an hour."

Horrified by this serious blunder after years of experience in exercising tact, Mr. Bidgwell gladly went to extreme lengths to see his new client's every wish promptly and thoroughly fulfilled.

"What? Marry them both? Now I know you're both daft!"

A gray gaze snapping with ice crystals darted between the elderly woman Amy had thought too wise for such ridiculous logic and the stunning man who held her heart, it now seemed, with too little care. How could she see that issue any other way when Comlan had just suggested she should marry another man? No, not another man . . . *two* other men!

They were politely seated amid the subdued elegance of Comlan's parlor where shades of cream, taupe and deep forest green had been blended with exquisite masculine taste. Their conversation had begun along perfectly normal lines. But, in Amy's opinion, it had rapidly taken a shape, peculiar and most unsettling.

Once their visit to the solicitor's office was done, Amy had been constrained to keep a promise by taking Beattie and rushing off to join her mother and Lovey at an early afternoon tea party. Escape from the stifling atmosphere of that event had been impossible until she feigned a headache, the excuse her mother used so often she could hardly fail to support her daughter's claim. But, of course, rather than returning to Wyfirth House, Amy had come directly here to meet Daffy at Comlan's leased home . . . an action which after their conversation left her questioning not only their sanity but her wisdom.

Unaware of the depths to which her grandniece's misgivings had fallen, Daffy's dry chuckle seemed to float on the velvet wave of Comlan's laughter. The sound so thoroughly increased Amy's irritation with the pair that she impetuously leaped up and strode toward the door with every intention of abandoning their company.

Repenting the jest in which Amy clearly found no humor, Comlan intercepted his dark colleen and swept her stiff body into his arms to cradle her close while Daffy fought to stifle giggles and explain.

"Now, Amy-girl, tame your wild spirit." Daffy could hardly believe she was cautioning her grandniece to restrain the spirit she'd been urging her to free for years. "Comlan would not see you marry another man. And even if you were to repeat the vows, false rites can never end in a union honest and true."

Despite her lover's will-weakening nearness, Amy scowled. These two made no sense. Oh, yes, her loving heart wished Comlan would truly regret her marriage to another but in her mind the cool logic she'd begun to think gone forever reasserted itself with a crisp, chill denial of the mere possibility.

"The person presiding over the ceremony we've suggested wouldn't be a minister." Wanting to alleviate Amy's lingering confusion, Comlan offered further facts about the plan he and Daffy had devised while Amy sipped tea and exchanged idle chat at the afternoon social event. "The two men will wed not you but each other."

As each deep word vibrated from the broad chest beneath her ear, Amy frowned again. This time not in irritation but with the concentration she gave an earnest attempt to sort through tidbits of information delivered in hopelessly random order.

"Don't know who we'll recruit to play the minister," Daffy mused an instant before mischievous gleams began dancing in her eyes. "But just imagine the mortified expression on Paddy's face once that vain lothario finds himself 'wed' to another man! Too bad Patience will miss her grandson's great performance."

Amy barely heard Daffy's voice but nodded while in her mind details once hazy began resolving into a clear pattern. The final image lit a spark of amusement that warmed her lips with a slight smile which one heartbeat later burst into a grin.

Now this was precisely the type of wry scheme Amy realized she ought to have expected of a being with Comlan's sardonic wit. Yes, a plot built as much of humor as vengeance. Moreover, beneath the promise of humor and at least as pleasing, she saw the possibility of additional benefits—particularly one able to free Garnet and Lovey of the hovering clouds threatening them with ruin.

Aye, Amy silently mimicked an Irish brogue, 'twas a grand thing. She heartily approved and glanced up at Comlan. The intensity of the immediate bond between her crystal eyes and his emerald gaze made words utterly unnecessary.

Chapter 19

~

The weak light of a sickle moon cast its silvery glow over the park's rain-damp vegetation. From the concealing gloom behind a towering hedge, Amy peered at the lone figure waiting with a motionless patience she'd always found amazing. Bingley sported a false beard and was soberly dressed in a frock coat, top hat—and clergyman's reverse shirt collar.

Intent on her view of this small glade long a site of lovers' trysts, Amy jumped when Comlan squeezed her shoulder to direct her attention toward the indistinct figure of a new arrival. He was fairly short and swathed in a voluminous cloak and a layer of shadowy veiling while his uneasiness was clear in the many furtive glances cast over one shoulder.

Nodding, Amy glanced left and returned Comlan's wry smile with a pleased grin she next shifted to the right and shared with Daffy, this strange event's third designer.

It was working. The plan so convoluted that logically it should fail had crossed its first hurdle. No, Amy corrected herself, its second hurdle since the first had been overcoming considerable difficulty to assemble an audience of carefully chosen witnesses.

Amy could single out their darker shadows only because she knew where to look. Garnet and Lovey crouched behind the dense shape of a topiary bear while her reluctant parents stood in stiff discomfort beneath the drooping branches of the weeping willow bent over a stream lazily flowing parallel to the selected site. Beattie and Dooley, now amazingly together by choice, had settled in relative comfort and obscurity on a lap-rug covered stone bench that was nearly surrounded by neatly trimmed yew bushes.

While Amy took stock of invited viewers, another figure slipped into the scene. This one was also heavily veiled and cloaked from shoulder to toe. She was amused to see the single white rose in one gloved hand—a romantic gesture though likely the bloom had been stolen from elsewhere in the park.

Amy was amazed by the foolishness of the two who'd allowed themselves to be lured into the park by her suggestion of secret wedding rites—secret yet *binding*. And yet here, facing the disguised Bingley with his open Bible, stood their cloaked figures. Amy's smile brightened. This bit of trickery was hers. She had foreseen the unpleasant consequences likely to follow premature recognition of any participant. And when meeting individually with her two suitors, she'd urged each to arrive with identities thoroughly concealed, ostensibly to confound possible uninvited guests. Even now she could hardly believe that neither had questioned obvious discrepancies in height and weight. But then she did understand the weaknesses she'd played on to draw them here during the darkest hours of night.

Paddy's was the tall figure. His vanity had allowed him to believe her protestations of regret for refusing the advances of such a handsome and charming man. And, too, he'd easily accepted her mournful explanation that because her father, the viscount, would never accept an Irish commoner for son-in-law, their only hope was a clandestine wedding.

As for the shorter, rounder Orville . . . his pride of position and wealth had been his downfall. Having always believed that the surely desperate graduate of so many debutante balls would be grateful for the attention of such a fine gentleman as himself, he hadn't been surprised by her proposal. He was only, as he'd said, "charmed by her delightful eccentricity." However, unbeknownst to him, she knew all about his unsavory business with Garnet and by that was aware of the true reason for his anxiety to marry her as soon as possible—before guilt drove her brother to confess and see them both destroyed.

A single muffled voice could be faintly heard, and it scattered Amy's memories of the morning's individual conversations with the unwitting pair of the grooms. But that indistinct sound droned on and on until Amy began to wonder if she'd made the right choice in appointing Bingley to perform as minister. That silent doubt seemed to act as catalyst since by its end Bingley had carefully closed the Bible—an action signaling others to be taken.

"Congratulations." Comlan gently propelled both Amy and Daffy forward. "Yes, *gentlemen*, congratulations on your nuptials . . . truly a memorable event."

Comlan's mocking words earned their targets' immediate attention.

"But I fear you may be a wee bit disappointed by the mate with whom you've exchanged vows. As you see"—Comlan wrapped his arm firmly around Amy's shoulders—"the intended bride is here at *my* side."

"Wot the bleedin' hell!" Color flooded Paddy's face as temper drove him forward with fists at the ready.

Amy flinched but Comlan remained motionless, his only visible response the ominous flaring of perilous flames in emerald eyes.

Paddy threw a vicious punch and groaned in pain when, a breath short of the goal, it landed against what he'd swear was a wall of solid stone. Cradling a crushed fist, he stared up into an unsmiling face and recognized a truth that sighed out on another moan, "Tuatha De."

Comlan gave an infinitesimal nod.

Amy gasped. She was surprised by this admission of his nature even though beyond herself and Daffy only Paddy could hear or would understand.

But while Comlan's action startled Amy, it earned Daffy's brightest grin. That would teach Patience and her grandson the folly of feigning friendship and belief while privately mocking her Patrick's tales of the Faerie Realm.

"And, boy-o," a grinning Dooley called from the

stone bench still shared with Beattie, "I own I'd be pleased to carry the good news of your nuptials throughout the home county."

The dark color earlier staining Paddy's face drained completely away. This tale of an alliance with another man was a threat to his prized reputation as a ladycharmer. Many others less successful in amorous pursuits would gleefully welcome the story, and no claim he made of trickery would weaken their sniggering ridicule . . . he'd be the butt of everyone's derision.

"Ah, now," Dooley nearly chortled in delight. "I may or I mayn't. It rightly depends on you. . . ."

Picking up where his friend left off, Comlan spoke in a quiet voice more threatening than ever any snarl. "Go home, Paddy. Stay there and never risk my displeasure again. For I promise that if there is a next time, I'll be considerably less restrained in my defense of all people and things dear to me."

Paddy cast aside the heavy veil, a token of his shame, and disappeared as quickly as he had on the night he'd been ejected from a dilapidated coach.

At the moment when Paddy's temper exploded, the second deluded suitor had gladly used the diversion to try and slip away unnoticed. That feat was difficult for one of his girth . . . and unsuccessful.

"Orville," Lord Wyfirth had demanded, stepping into the fleeing man's path. "Why this strange charade when you already had the approval of Amy's parents?"

"Because—" Garnet interrupted, moving to within a pace of the frustrated man thus effectively trapped, "Orville is on the verge of a disgrace likely to see you rescind your approval before he can wed Amy, thus securing Great-aunt Daphenia's wealth for himself."

"No, it can't be." Lord Farley's eyes skeptically narrowed. "Orville is a respectable man who has nothing disgraceful that needs hiding."

"Ah, but, Father," Garnet reasoned, "you would likely say that of me while, in truth, Orville and I share in the same wrong—a shame to us both."

"We're ruined." Lady Wyfirth, having moved to her husband's side, sagged against him under the sudden prospect of being toppled from the pinnacle of social standing she'd made her life's work. "Simply ruined."

"Not necessarily." Comlan had escorted both Amy and Daffy to stand directly behind Garnet who immediately spun around to face him. Although emerald eyes focused on Amy's brother, Comlan still spoke to her mother. "There's excellent reason to believe that if your son returns to Mr. Bennett's warehouses and retests, the results will match those he's already recorded."

"But how can you—" Utterly unprepared for this suggestion, Garnet frowned.

"Garnet, do it for me?" Amy pleaded, gray eyes earnest. "Trust Comlan's suggestion and retest. After all, what more harm could it do?"

"Yes." Lovey stepped free of the topiary bear's shadows to join her husband and add her soft voice to the appeal. "Please, Garnet."

Garnet would've done it for Amy . . . eventually. But for his Lovey's sake he would start in the morning.

"If by some miracle of fate the tests are clean . . ." Garnet turned a chill gaze to the erstwhile cohort now foe. "Then, Orville, let me assure you that I'll never again do business of any sort with you."

"Oh, really?" Orville's vicious sneer stabbed at the younger man. "But you *owe* me a substantial debt and I must insist that you repay the whole."

"Or what?" Garnet laughed, spirits lifted by growing hope that he'd been led to a path through the dark tunnel he'd dug for himself. Surely by following it he would find his way into the sunlight beyond. "Will you take me to court so we both can explain to the magistrate all the details of how our dispute came about?"

"Oh, I say—" Though Lord Farley had only the sketchiest suspicion of what wrongs lay at the heart of their contention, he recognized Garnet's honest regret and spoke out in support of his son. "I hardly think Mr. Bennett would care to have his lofty reputation tainted by too close an acquaintanceship with the courts."

Watching this exchange and greatly heartened by its promise of a happy resolution, Amy nestled more closely against the man who'd wrapped his strong arm about her shoulders.

"Daffy is safe and after this you are, too." Like a rumble of gentle thunder, Comlan whispered in Amy's ear, "And so now we must talk."

In stark contrast to the pleasure of an instant before, Amy's heart sank. Clearly, the moment she dreaded had arrived; the moment her fantasy king intended a return to his own realm.

Comlan felt Amy's distress as keenly as if it

were his own. He gently pulled his dark colleen to stand in front of him and then lowered his mouth to again whisper into her ear. "Let me whisk you to our private haven, whisk you to Lissan's fairy ring where we will have uninterrupted time together?"

Turning the head resting against a broad shoulder to glance up at him, Amy gladly sank into emerald fires. She would revel in every moment together stolen from a forlorn future and hoard them all securely against the loneliness to come.

The sweetness of Amy's smile was answer enough for Comlan and in the blink of an eye they stood together in his sister's magical ring of flowers.

Alone with her love, thrilled and yet terrified that this would truly be the last time, Amy nibbled her bottom lip and stared determinedly down at the lush grass about their feet. Then, as if her eyes had been opened by a flash of heavenly light, Amy realized that the prospect of an unhappy existence was hers to change. She'd known it all along but the habit of cool logic had blinded her to simple truths. Comlan would never ask her to make the sacrifice of leaving her world to live in his . . . but of her own free will she could.

Comlan had arranged these private moments to ease the way for a conversation he realized was likely to be the most important of his life. After turning Amy to face him, he gently tilted a small chin upward with one forefinger. He gazed down into gray eyes gone dark but glistening with the crystal sheen of tears she clearly refused to let fall and opened his mouth to speak. And yet before he could, she did.

Knowing she must make her brave proposal now or live forever with painful regrets and desolate questions of what might have been, Amy began while tears escaped beneath dark lashes resting on pale cheeks. "Bonds of honor held your sister's husband, Killian, in his king's court rather than yours but—" Heart pounding so hard she thought it might choke her, Amy risked a mortifying embarrassment and the pain of final rejection. "No such restraints hold me back."

Admiring her courageous speech and its message, Comlan was torn between a selfish desire on one side to hear longed for words of love and on the other a need to immediately ease her distress.

"I love you too much to watch you leave me." Amy paused to take another deep breath. It was difficult to give her heartfelt plea to this seemingly emotionless man until she glanced up to be overwhelmed by fathomless emerald pools of deep feeling.

Amy rushed to finish her plea in fear that something might steal the words from her lips. "I beg your permission to accompany you back to that mystical castle on yonder hill."

Deeming her daring speech well-rewarded by Comlan's devastating smile, Amy fell to its potent powers and nearly missed the first precious words of Comlan's response.

"You are a treasure more rare and valuable than any contained in my realm." Emerald eyes studied

Amy so long and so thoroughly that she swayed nearer in willing surrender to the green fires within their depths. "And if we were there, I would cherish you as the precious gift you are."

Despite his enticing gaze and honeyed tone, to Amy this sounded like the beginning of a gentle but completely unexpected rejection and tears again began sliding slowly down pale cheeks.

"No, my darling." Comlan's lips tilted in a crooked smile of piercing sweetness as he wrapped her in his embrace. "I'm not refusing your priceless gift, not when I could no more bear a permanent separation from the one I love than you wish to live apart from me."

Comlan's lips brushed across the silky, black hair atop her head before adding, "On several occasions you've demonstrated an ability to adjust to the peculiarities of my nature. And by that ability, that willingness I believe you would give up your own world for me."

"I would," Amy earnestly assured Comlan, tightening her arms around him.

"And I love you for it." Comlan rained brief kisses over her brow, eyes and cheeks. "But I've found a way for us both to have the futures we seek ... while sharing them with each other."

"How?" Though loath to question so desirable an end, in these words Amy clearly heard the kind of contradiction so valuable to his kind.

Comlan saw on Amy's expressive face a struggle between hope and disbelief. Yielding immediately to a gentle concern he might once have belittled as more human than fairy, he tried to lessen her turmoil by explaining.

"My Gran Aine, the ruler of the Tuatha from whom I inherited, along with all those who came before were so accustomed to looking for the peculiar, the contrary or simply hidden that they failed to recognize the obvious."

Amy could easily believe this might be true, particularly as she'd been guilty of much the same error. But still she frowned. Comlan hadn't revealed the most important fact, the one freeing them to be together. He hadn't told her *what* his forbearers had failed to see.

"It's simple." Comlan's smile contained the myriad of pleasures anticipated in their shared future. "You already know the life spans of those in my realm are a great deal longer than any among humankind. Indeed, to us the length of a mortal life is almost negligible."

Amy's slight frown deepened. What was it about a human's apparently inferior lifetime that would make an alliance between the two of them possible? The only fact she clearly saw was discouraging. If Comlan was still in the prime of life, despite its incredible length, how would he deal with a mate who would show the ravages of age so much faster?

"Sit with me." Comlan had noted Amy's expression. Was she already regretting her offered sacrifice?

Though yielding to the gentle tug of Comlan's hand and settling beside him on nature's green carpet, Amy nervously wrapped her arms about updrawn knees.

Comlan reached out to release ebony hair from tidy restraints while quietly speaking. "I will live the length of your mortal lifetime in this world with you."

Amy gasped and looked up, shocked, delighted and alarmed. How could she possibly hold the interest of her fantasy hero for even the length of a single human life? And then what came after for him? Surely Comlan would return to being king of the Tuatha De Danann? If not, she couldn't allow him to relinquish so much for her.

Comlan saw a myriad of fleeting emotions cross Amy's face and tried to relieve the one most basic— confusion. "I'll live with you here so long as you give me a vow in return."

Amy was curious about the nature of this vow but having already made the decision to surrender everything for his sake, she refused to appear uncertain by asking questions whose answers wouldn't make a ha'porth of difference to her choice.

"Whatever you ask, I'll gladly give to you," Amy softly responded, an assurance for which, once again, Comlan's devastatingly slow smile was reward enough.

"I ask you to swear on all you hold most dear . . ." Comlan's expression became as solemn as his request. ". . . That when the end to your mortal life looms near, you will give yourself into my hands."

"Then, as now, I'll always be yours." With the

words Amy gave Comlan a whimsical smile of such intense warmth it near melted him.

Thrilled by the open love on her face, Comlan's eyes exploded with green flames as he pulled her willing body into his arms.

"I knew you couldn't be truly happy at the expense of anguish brought to loved ones by an inexplicable disappearance." He spoke against the cream satin of her throat. "And yet, I can never again be happy without the dark colleen I love."

The body yielding moments before went still as Amy responded. "No more than I could be happy if your tarrying in my world prevents you from returning to your home and responsibilities." She struggled to lean a handsbreadth back and see his expression. "So, please, tell me if remaining with me will cost all that you hold dear?"

"Waste no moment worrying on that matter." With a reassuringly broad smile, he nuzzled her ear. "It will all come right in the end."

Amy would've asked for an explanation had his mouth not taken hers and driven every sane thought from her mind.

Comlan gladly welcomed Amy's surrender and stroked his hand down a slender back, urging her even closer. Amy loved the feel of his big, hard body against hers. She savored the warm maleness of him as his lips drew back to test the texture of hers, teasing them open again to welcome the hungry depth of a kiss that went on and on. And all the while her dainty hands worked their seductive magic on him until his breathing grew harsh, quick, and his arms trembled about her.

Within the fairy circle and invisible to unlikely human wanderers beyond its borders, Comlan eased Amy back to lie on the soft cushion of grass. Lazy, sensuous eyes of green flame brushed over Amy's passion-rosed face as he slowly drew the clothes from her willing body and rid himself of his own. He then lowered himself into invitingly raised arms, and joined together they flew into a blaze stoked by mutual love proclaimed to an incredible firestorm of immediate delight and promise of future joys.

After long moments that seemed to stretch without end, Comlan rolled to his back and drew Amy into the shelter of his arms. Smoothing the tangled silk of dusky hair and stroking gentle ease over his trembling colleen, he marveled at the realities of this human lover who so far surpassed all others he'd known before.

Savoring the feel of crisp curls and hard muscle beneath her cheek, Amy nestled closer to the heat she knew could so easily blaze into a wild inferno of sweet pleasures.

"Amy-love," Comlan whispered after shifting Amy to lie on the grass and rising up on an elbow to nuzzle the ear beneath a thick swathe of black silk.

Amy remained so perfectly still it was clear she merely pretended to sleep.

"Wake up, Amy-love," Comlan called again, nibbling the creamy flesh of a bare shoulder. "We've been gone too long, and I fear your father will call me out for besmirching his daughter's good name."

Amy's lips compressed tightly, obviously to quell a grin.

Seeing her poorly restrained amusement, Comlan added, "And I really hate considering to what manner of retribution I've left myself vulnerable when it comes to the ire of your good mother—a fire-breathing dragon in another life, I've no doubt."

A bubble of laughter escaped, forcing Amy to abandon the game. Not, she conceded, a serious loss when much more enjoyable play was so near. Reaching up to run the fingers of one hand through thick golden strands, she belatedly provided a defense, of sorts, for her parents.

"The announcement of my upcoming marriage to Lord Comlan of Doncaully—the Season's most sought-after bachelor—will excuse our tardiness, even our absence. And you'll be welcomed into the bosom of my family with every possible sign of good cheer."

Comlan cast Amy a dubious glance which she promptly allayed.

"Oh, yes." Amy solemnly nodded. "They'd have welcomed any marginally appropriate suitor (hence, Orville) to relieve them of the embarrassing burden of an unwed daughter rapidly sinking into spinsterhood."

"You? A prune-faced, passionless spinster?" Comlan's skeptical expression deepened. "Couldn't happen."

"Indeed, it could. Indeed, I'd have preferred that

independent state to marrying someone like Orville." Clear crystal gray eyes steadily met emerald. "And, like Daffy before me, I would gladly have exchanged Society's tight bonds for the peaceful countryside."

"Ah, but Daffy wasn't alone in the peaceful countryside," Comlan reminded Amy. "She had Patrick."

"Patrick ..." The name reminded Amy of another, small puzzle waiting to be solved. "Please tell me how you first encountered him. Daffy says that the story is not hers to tell but that you might share it with me."

Golden hair glowed as Comlan tilted his head to one side and began a tale oft repeated in both the human world and his Faerie Realm.

"Far into his cups one summer evening, Patrick staggered into the ruins you were drawing the day we met. It doesn't happen often and rarely enough that it seldom interferes with our plans. But Patrick was different. Patrick boldly shouted out his demand that as a true believer he must be allowed to see us."

Comlan paused to send his listener a meaningful glance that Amy wished herself able to understand.

"I sat with Patrick that night and many nights more before he proved himself trustworthy enough to be invited into our midst." He nodded in answer to Amy's unspoken question. "Yes, into my castle where he joined in our amusements."

"But if it took so long for Patrick, *a true believer*,

to be accepted, how is it that a skeptic like me was taken there at our first meeting?"

Bronze brows lifted into exaggerated arches but mockery gleamed in the green eyes below, and Amy nearly bit her tongue to belatedly silence the foolish question.

"Daffy." She answered her own query.

Elaborating on her simple statement, Comlan said, "Daffy, Patrick and the drinking horn on her cottage wall."

"Drinking horn." Amy gave him a speaking look that made it clear she believed this strange addition another example of the delight he took in confusing her with convoluted puzzles.

Comlan nodded. "Over the years the jolly Patrick told his tales far and wide—some true and some not—until too many scoffed. Wanting something to prove his adventures real, one night he slipped away with a drinking horn from my hall."

"He stole something from you?" Amy was horrified.

"Oh, now I don't think he'd ever have said his action was that." Ruefully grinning, Comlan softened her statement. "Nay, Patrick would've insisted he'd merely borrowed my drinking horn for a time. However, when he took that vessel, he unknowingly carried away its powers, too."

"Powers?"

"Aye." Comlan's wry smile returned. "Fill it once and it'll never run dry."

Amy couldn't help but grin. "From all I've heard of Patrick, that must've greatly pleased him."

"Indeed, but it was the drinking horn's ability to summon me that he most delighted in."

"A *drinking* horn summons you?" Amy blinked in surprise.

"When the golden tip end is removed and the horn blown, it issues a clarion call I alone can hear—but, like your amulet, it is effective only under the direst of circumstances."

"Are you saying that Daffy used the horn to summon you and arrange a meeting with me. If so, what dire circumstances prevailed? Couldn't Maedra have more easily carried Daffy's request to you?"

"Daffy senses her end drawing near, circumstances sufficiently dire for her call to be heard." Comlan solemnly met Amy's gaze. "Yes, Maedra could've given me Daffy's message but I wouldn't be required to answer. Nor, more importantly, would I have been required to grant Daffy's wish."

"So, after being summoned by the drinking horn you had no choice but to meet me?"

"Yes—but no as well."

Again Amy recognized a paradox so favored by his kind and patiently waited.

"At Daffy's request I agreed to meet her grand-niece *if* she entered Lissan's fairy ring. You did. And, though you claimed you didn't, like Patrick, you saw me because you do *believe*. If you hadn't, you wouldn't have been able to see me in my natural state, and then not even Daffy's wish could have compelled me to escort you to my home."

Before Amy could stew herself into a froth, worrying that Comlan felt trapped by her great-aunt's shenanigans, he swept such unworthy fears aside.

"Think how fortunate we are and what endless joys we would have missed had you truly not believed in fairies?"

Beneath her devastating lover's gentle smile, Amy laughed . . . until he bent his head to seal their commitment by fitting his mouth to hers with exquisite care.

Chapter 20

$\mathcal{T}$he sky was a cloudless azure and only the gentlest of breezes blew on the summer day when Lord Comlan of Doncaully married Miss Amethyst Danton in the most elegant and well attended event of the Season. The newlyweds greeted every guest during the lengthy reception that followed. And they couldn't depart until after congratulatory kisses were given by every relative from Amy's youngest niece to the great-aunt dressed for the first time in many years in a warmer shade than black.

And yet it was the felicitations of another new-wedded couple that brought the brightest grin to Amy's lips. Though initially surprised, she was pleased that Dooley had chosen to remain in the human world and live out a mortal lifetime with his tartar-tongued but remarkably sweet Beattie.

As an open landau pulled away from the crowd of well-wishers spilling from lawns into the street, the bride and groom waved. However, this was but

the first of two rites planned for today and the only
one familiar to Amy.

Nervous about what lay ahead, once their vehicle
had moved beyond the wedding guests' view, Amy
thought to hold nerves at bay with small talk. She
turned to her wonderful new husband with a small
question.

"While we chatted with Lord Palmerston after
the wedding breakfast, I realized that I've never
asked you how it is that the king of the Tuatha De
Danann is so well acquainted with a British lord?"

Comlan grinned but didn't speak.

"Come now, satisfy my curiosity." Under his
silence, her initial niggling curiosity intensified.
"You don't have a home in Ireland. So how did you
meet? How did you become friends?"

"I certainly do have an Irish home!" Comlan
returned with mock fervor while ignoring her questions.

Amy teasingly batted at him. "Not a *human* home
where *humans* can visit."

"I do now—just for you." Again Comlan
promptly responded.

Her groom was purposefully avoiding her questions, and Amy's curiosity soared as she gravely
announced, "I've been reliably informed that you
must answer direct questions."

Comlan's loving grin tilted awry. "Only if the
information is mine to give."

Amy's head tilted and she gazed at him skeptically.

"Truly." His handsome face went solemn. "As
with Daffy and the story of her Patrick's first

encounter with the Faerie Realm, there are some tales that are not mine to share."

"I see." Amy slowly nodded. "I won't ask again."

His *human* wife's willingness to abide by the rules of his land reaffirmed Comlan's confidence in the rightness of their union.

A very few minutes later the landau pulled into the gloomy stable behind Comlan's rented London home. He didn't help his bride down. Instead, he pulled her close into the circle of his arms.

An instant later the couple stood in the silken garb of a distant past and only a brief step from the drawbridge leading to the Tuatha De Danann's incredible Irish castle.

A cheering crowd waited beyond the door at the far end of the wooden bridge. Amy drew a deep, reviving breath before laying her fingertips atop Comlan's upraised forearm and walking forward at his side.

As on her last visit, once inside the luxurious hall where laughter filled the air, Amy was swept into a merriment even cheerier for being a celebration.

Amy was amazed at how little time passed before Comlan's subjects began forming in a double ring. While they waited in an uncanny silence, Comlan placed a crown of fragrant blooms upon ebony hair and led her to the center of the two circles where a very old woman garbed in scarlet stood motionless. When the couple were in place she tied Amethyst's dainty hand to Comlan's much larger ones with silken ribbons. They were next given a finely chased goblet of gold from which to offer each other the finest ambrosia.

Marylyle Rogers

Taking a final sip of the heady brew, Amy realized that everyone had returned to their prior amusements.

"Contrary in all things?" Amy grinned up at the devastating man who now was unbelievably hers by the rites of two worlds.

"It's nearly the only unchanging principal in this realm," Comlan agreed.

The bride and groom soon joined the ongoing feast. As Comlan had already assured her that she no longer need fear eating or drinking in his realm, Amy savored incredible dishes and sipped elixirs unlike anything she'd ever tasted. In very little time she felt as overstuffed as a Christmas goose.

"Come." Comlan took her hand as he rose. "I have one duty to fulfill before we leave all of yours and all of mine behind and escape to our private paradise."

Comlan led Amy through the crowd to a far corner of the hall where a man, equally green-eyed and golden, stood waiting.

"Gair, this is my bride, Amethyst."

Considering the similar coloring of these two men, Amy wasn't truly surprised to see that Gair's wry smile was very nearly a replica of Comlan's and even less surprised to hear what next Comlan said.

"Amy, this is my younger brother, Gair, who will rule in my stead while I'm gone."

"And don't worry, little sister." Gair grinned. "I don't covet my brother's position and would refuse to hold it for any great span of time."

296

Amy's attention shifted to Comlan as he bent to lift a previously unnoticed staff of fine wood intricately inlaid with precious metals and studded with gems.

Steadily holding that item upright in one hand, Comlan turned to face his hall. Several firm taps of the staff against a stone floor echoed loudly. The chamber went instantly quiet. When every subject's eyes were focused on their king, the jewels on the symbol of his position began to glow as brightly as small suns.

"I entrust this staff to my brother, Gair, and with it I entrust my realm to his care." Comlan's gaze slowly moved from face to face. "While I am gone give him the respect and allegiance you've so long given to me."

Comlan waited for a soft rumble of voices to fade before adding, "I'll be away for but the span of a single human life and on my return will expect to hear that all continued as if I were present."

Abruptly thrusting the staff into his brother's hand, Comlan swept Amy into his embrace. An instant later they were gazing from a large window across a verdant valley dotted with sheep and blessed with fields of vibrant wildflowers.

With love unhidden, Comlan turned to his bride and in a voice like velvet thunder said, "I promised both paradise and a *human* abode . . . and here we are."

Amy laced her arms about him and stared up with equal emotion. "My dream in Lissan's ring of flowers began with the words *Once Upon a Time* and now my fairy tale has come true!" With all her might Amy hugged the powerful body of her fantasy hero come to life.

"And your dreams are doubly effective for your fairy tale also brought happiness and love to one who foolishly thought that during his very long life he'd tasted every experience from the bitter to the sweet." Comlan paused while Amy rose up on tiptoe to steal a brief kiss. "With you every hour is new and filled with more joy than I ever dreamed could be."

In delightful retribution for her theft, Comlan gave Amy a lingering kiss before pulling back to murmur, "I no longer grieve for Lissan's choice. If she was as happy with Killian as I am with you, she made the right decision. A few days of such happiness as this is more valuable than an eternity without."

Amy's smile grew in brilliance. Here was proof that she needn't fear Comlan would come to resent her for what he'd left behind. And when the groom took his bride's hand to lead her to their massive bronze bed, she welcomed its promise of a continuing firestorm of sweet love and devastating pleasure.

Epilogue

~

May 1, 1900

If at dawn that May Day morn anyone had gone exploring through the green and gentle hills of Ireland, they might have glimpsed an astonishing sight.

Up a slope, surely too challenging, climbed a white-haired gentleman with the firm stride of a much younger man. He cradled an elderly woman close, effortlessly carrying her to the hilltop. And all the while they were followed by a startlingly beautiful woman like some golden fairy maid from the mystic past.

No human voice disturbed the pastel peace as the much younger figure embraced the aged couple. After the older female pinned a broach on her bodice, the blond woman stepped well back. It was then that the man lowered his burden's feet to the ground just inside the ring of glorious flowers encircling an ancient oak.

With the endless gentleness of a loving heart, Comlan held his Amy close against his side and began guiding her unsteady, halting steps on the first of several trips around the fairy ring ... and a journey back through time.

Years fell away with each completed circuit until Comlan gazed again at the young, dark beauty he'd first encountered on this very site so many years before. With an elated smile as bright as his again golden hair, he dropped atop a grassy carpet.

Intoxicated by this magical experience, a laughing Amy happily tumbled into the fairy ring with the returning king of the Tuatha De Danann.

During all the years spent in Amy's world, through the joys and sorrows of mortal life, Comlan had remained her steady, loving support. But never had he revealed what was to come after. Nor had Amy ever asked to know what price the vow she'd given would demand for the happy human lifetime shared.

"We're young again!" Amy grinned.

"You are." Comlan wryly nodded but added, "I have remained the same—although to blend into your world I've donned a guise of slowly advancing age."

A slight frown marred Amy's smooth forehead as a bolt of comprehension struck. "We've returned to the day we met. ..."

Comlan grinned, always pleased by his wife's sharp mind and intuition.

That quick mind immediately leaped to those who with Comlan shared Amy's heart. "What," she anxiously asked, "does this mean for our family?"

"Our two sons and three daughters are successful, satisfied in their world, ready to accept the passing of their parents—and physically healthy." With this answer Comlan motioned toward the figure of a blond beauty looking into the fairy ring, dazed.

Relieved that her youngest daughter remained unchanged, Amy gazed into emerald eyes. "Lissan can't see us now, can she?"

After the tiny shake of a golden head, she asked another question. "Because the fairy ring's concealing powers shield us or . . .?"

"By walking counterclockwise around my sister's circle of flowers with me, you became what I have always been." Comlan took Amy's dainty hand and kissed its palm before lifting his mouth to brush across the soft, luscious curve of her lips.

Amy welcomed his tantalizing caress with a fathomless love that had deepened daily, monthly, yearly. Comlan had kept his promise that "all would come right in the end." He'd given her a human lifetime of happiness and now she'd join the returning king of the Tuatha de Danann to share a nearly endless future in his bright realm.

But first they stole another private hour of fiery pleasures and sweet delights in the fairy ring of fragrant blossom.

IF YOU ENJOYED *ONCE UPON A TIME*, READ
ON FOR AN EXCERPT OF MARYLYLE ROGERS'
ENCHANTING NEW ROMANCE, *HAPPILY EVER
AFTER*:

Prologue

May 1, 1900

A slight breeze teased the mass of golden curls
and skirts of a white-gowned woman gazing
up an Irish hillside. Lissan's attention rested on
beloved parents nearing its crest and bathed in
dawn's bright pastels. Her father, remarkably fit for
all his years, climbed a few paces ahead and carried
her fragile mother with no sign of strain.

Clearly the time she and her older siblings—two
brothers and two sisters—had been told to expect
had arrived. On their twentieth birthdays each had
been called by their parents into the study for a
private talk during which a solemn promise was
extracted. When their mother's failing health made
it clear that her end was near, her children and
grandchildren were to bid their last good-byes. Lord
Comlan of Doncaully was then to be left in peace
to carry his wife into the Irish hills unchallenged.

Each child had given a solemn oath to neither
follow nor question their father's action. The four

older siblings, all married and with families of their own, had curiously discussed this odd command but none questioned the wishes of a father both loved and respected. However, Lissan took pride in an independent nature and her curiosity was not so easily quelled.

A few days earlier when his frail wife sank into an unmistakable decline while visiting a cherished retreat, the small Irish home known as Daffy's Cottage, Lord Comlan had summoned their children to her bedside. And none of them had been surprised when during the dark hours of the previous night their father announced his intent. Though her brothers and sisters accepted this decision with deep sorrow, a decade younger than the next older child, Lissan had begged that she be permitted to accompany her parents at least so far as the first hill's summit. A frowning Lord Comlan had agreed only after his gravely ill Amy added her whispered plea.

When her parents halted at the brow of that first hill, Lissan thought they'd paused to wish her a last farewell before sending her off to keep a promise by returning to the family waiting in the quaint, ivy-covered cottage below.

"This can't be the last time I see you, not yet, not now. . . ." Lissan huskily whispered as she wrapped her arms about both her father and the woman in his arms. She bent to press a kiss against her mother's papery cheek.

"But it is either *now* or never," Lord Comlan firmly stated before brushing his lips across the golden silk of his youngest daughter's hair.

Lissan's arms dropped and she started to retreat

but the delicate hand of Lady Amethyst restrained her.

Green eyes clouding against the prospect of a last farewell, Lissan glanced down to see fragile fingers affixing a beautiful broach to the tucked and daintily embroidered white dimity of her bodice.

"Wear my amulet always and it will protect you."

"But, Mama—" Lissan started to protest this giving of her mother's most treasured piece of jewelry—an exquisitely carved, ivory unicorn, gold-horned and rearing inside an onyx circle.

"Hush now, my baby, my fairy-child," Lady Amethyst gently rebuked. "Do as your mama says this one last time."

Firmly nibbling lips to block useless pleas, Lissan stepped back yet froze a short distance away, watching and waiting for her father to continue the foretold journey through Irish hills.

The sight of small white teeth biting at a full lower lip put a sad half-smile on Comlan's mouth. She bore his own youngest sister's name along with his fair coloring and emerald eyes, but this daughter was very much her beloved mother's child.

Lissan was surprised when, rather than continuing the journey, her father stepped into the ring of beautiful flowers encircling an ancient oak and paused.

Her name came from this site known since the distant past as Lissan's Fairy Ring. It was her favorite place in all the world, and she had long thought that fact the likely reason her mother always called her a fairy-child.

As a youngster Lissan had begged again and

again to be told the magical tale of a dainty fairy damsel who'd fallen in love with a mortal warrior. Then, to share his life in the human world had shed her mystical powers and thus created this circle of perfect blossoms. During the magical days of childhood Lissan had often wished that fairies were real and fantasized about the wondrous adventures she would have if only she were one. Then, inevitably, she grew up. . . .

Lissan was horrified at having allowed foolish memories to claim her thoughts while a serious and sorrowful event loomed. Guilt joined sorrow as she closely watched her white-haired father lower his frail burden's feet to the ground. Then, holding the delicate woman close to his side, he started to walk counterclockwise around the ring of flowers. With each pace forward the woman's steps became firmer while an aura of ever brighter light wrapped about them. Lissan's eyes widened as with each completed circuit years seemed to drop away from the luminous couple.

Abruptly, the glowing pair fell into the circle's center—and disappeared completely!

Where were they? Lissan started forward but stopped. Clearly this was exactly what they'd warned their children was to come. But *how* had they done it? What did it mean? Worse yet, how could she possibly return to the small cottage and explain to her waiting siblings that their parents hadn't died but miraculously grown young again? And then vanished.

Bewildered, Lissan sank to ground padded by thick grasses. She had long since outgrown fairy tales and didn't believe in magic. But if what she'd just seen wasn't magic, then what . . .? And how could she explain the impossible? The truth certainly wouldn't satisfy her scientifically minded oldest brother, Garnet, nor David, the younger who was a well-respected clergyman. As for Opal and Pearl, the two sisters preoccupied with finding her a husband to see her as happily wed as they were, well—Lissan grimaced, green eyes darkened to a forest hue gazing morosely into the fairy ring.

They'd think that grief had weakened her hold on sanity and driven their little sister back into her childhood's wild tales of fairy magic. No, she couldn't rationally expect them to accept the truth for truth. But neither would she lie and say their father had simply carried his gravely ill wife ever farther into the hills. But if not that, then what?

Perhaps, Lissan's eyes narrowed. Just perhaps she would discover a rational explanation by following her parents' path? Folly, utter folly. But still—

Yielding to the impetuous spirit that had so horrified old Beattie but always earned a secret smile from her father, Lissan rose with innate grace. She unhesitatingly moved to the very point at which her father had lowered her mother's feet and began retracing their footsteps.

Before completing a first circuit Lissan wished she'd counted how many times her parents had gone around the circle before falling into its center, but by the time she'd made the second lap it no longer mattered. As if unseen hands were pushing from behind, she stumbled onward at an ever increasing pace until, feeling caught by centrifugal force, she was swept along at a terrifying speed. Panicking, she summoned every shred of strength and threw herself free.

Lissan landed on her back—hard! Even the ground's thick green padding was no protection. Her head bounced but her eyes stayed open ... and widened against the flash of a double-bladed broadsword slashing straight down with deadly force!

Chapter 1

~

*R*ory O'Connor silently led his band of warriors through the ebbing shadows of night and up a heavily wooded hillside. They had tracked O'Brien's bloodthirsty raiders from the burned-out shell of an aging farmer's cottage and meant to wreak vengeance upon the vile curs.

Despite his men's desire to see the deed immediately done, Rory had convinced them of the wisdom in banking the fires of anger the better to see greater punishment inflicted with smallest cost. At his direction, they'd circled around their foes to wait in wooded shadows surrounding an ancient fairy ring in the glade at the hill's summit.

With deceptive calm Rory stood motionless, broad back resting against a strong tree trunk while awaiting the most propitious moment to strike back. As castellan for one among a ring of fortresses belonging to his uncle, King Turlough of Connacht, he was honor bound to defend it and all its holdings against forces commanded by the too proud king of Munster.

King Muirchertach of Munster had long claimed the high-kingship of all Ireland but Turlough, ever rising in power, presented a danger to that ambition. Intending to weaken his threat, men from Munster harried the borders of Connacht by terrorizing inhabitants, burning farms, and stealing precious livestock.

A snapped twig, a muffled voice earned Rory's immediate attention. He leaned forward, peering through thick leaves and down the slope to where men climbed toward the fairy ring single file. The rising sun painted a morning sky with its brilliant shades, an appropriate backdrop for the violence erupting at Rory's signal.

Warriors with raised swords closed in on the summit's newcomers from all sides. Gasps of surprise ending in harsh curses accompanied the fierce clash of blade meeting blade. But through the skirmish's uncounted passage of time initial taunts and blasphemous oaths settled into either grunts of exertion or groans of pain.

Caught in a prolonged and brutal fight with the strong leader of Munster's raiders, Rory lightly whirled to avoid the downward slash of the other's broadsword . . . and froze as it sliced through a beautiful golden woman inexplicably tumbling at their feet.

Lissan glimpsed blood on the terrifying blade lifting from its deadly attack. That ominous sight shook her from a state of shock and into horrified recognition of peril all around. In this glade gone eerily quiet, she was surrounded by men dressed as warriors from a distant past and apparently terrorstruck to stone although armed with broadswords, spears and daggers.

Too startled for deep fear or sensible thought, Lissan automatically pushed her skirts demurely down while struggling to sit up. She knew exactly where she'd fallen and yet this long familiar scene had changed. The ancient oak suddenly seemed half as old while dense forest and thick undergrowth covered ground where there'd never been more than lush grasses and a sprinkling of trees.

"The White Witch—"

Lissan's emerald eyes instantly flew up to the source of these gasped words, the stocky man still standing above while clutching a blade stained with blood as red as his hair. His epithet was echoed by many fearful voices even as their speakers whirled and fled into woodland shadows.

Thoroughly disconcerted by these extremely odd doings and unaccountably strange surroundings, Lissan struggled to restore some measure of calm and make rational plans. She ought to return to her family waiting in the cottage below ... but with everything so changed she didn't truthfully know what path would lead her there.

A deep voice like rough velvet intruded. "Are you unharmed?"

Further befuddled to discover herself not so alone as she'd believed, Lissan instantly responded. "Indeed, yes. Although my fall will leave bruises, it's only my pride that truly suffers."

As the words left her mouth, Lissan glanced up

to meet a penetrating blue gaze so dark as to seem all of black. It belonged to the huge figure towering above—taller than any man she knew save her father and brothers. With a powerful frame and night black hair, this stranger was stunningly handsome.

While the maiden with sun-gilded hair gaped at him, Rory studied her so long and so well that a wild blush rosed her cheeks. She was strangely dressed in a gown of amazingly fine cloth such as he'd never seen before. But, despite courageously uptilted chin, it was clearly apprehension that widened emerald eyes of amazing clarity. Surely the White Witch couldn't, wouldn't be afraid of him?

"Once well struck—" Rory calmly probed for a more satisfying response. "O'Brien's blade rarely fails to mortally harm its target."

Cheeks rosy an instant earlier went pale. The broadsword! Sweet Heaven! It had well and truly struck her, as proven by the blood on its blade. But how could that be? She glanced down to a midriff so completely untouched that even the delicate cloth of her morning gown was whole and unbloodied. No wonder her attacker and the other men had fled in fear.

"Can you account for your deliverance?"

Lissan blinked at the man plainly growing impatient with her. Unfortunately Lissan could no more account for this miracle than she could solve the puzzle of the abrupt changes in her surroundings or her parents disappearance.

Believing that the golden maid's silence was a

refusal to respond to his oblique demand for an explanation, Rory flatly asked, "*Who* are you?"

"Lissan." She was pleased that this question, at least, had a simple answer.

"Like the fairy responsible for those forever-blooming flowers?" The sunlight gleaming over Rory's black hair as he nodded toward a circle of blossoms was the antithesis of his dark frown. As one who scoffed at superstitious tales and foolish portents, he was uncomfortable with these constant hints of otherworldly magic, particularly after this woman's extraordinary arrival.

Lissan's attention flew to the fairy ring she could nearly swear had been trampled by fighting men but now looked fresh and untouched—just as she was, despite the broadsword's blow.

"Yes." As she nodded, golden tresses tumbled over slender shoulders. "I was named for the fairy in that tale."

Rory's frown deepened. "And from whence do you hail?"

"My home is in London." Uncomfortable beneath a masculine disapproval rarely encountered, Lissan smiled winsomely at the man so unaccountably displeased by her answers.

Rory was more thoroughly and, he was certain, justifiably annoyed with this beauty who blandly confessed what she must know he'd view as a crime even while boldly enticing him to forego his own honor.

"I assume, then—" Ice coated Rory's words. "—That you were sent by King Henry."

Lissan rightly heard this statement for the accusation it was. These words, however, merely added another layer of confusion. After all, Queen Victoria had ruled the British Empire for several decades and there hadn't been a royal Henry in a very, very long time.

As a first step toward solving this daunting riddle, though fearing the answer, Lissan quietly asked, "What year is this?"

Disgust for this blatant and foolish attempt to cloud dangerous issues further deepened Rory's voice as he growled, "The year of our Lord, 1115."

Drawing a deep breath and gazing forlornly down at the hands tightly clasped in her lap, Lissan sighed, "I have no home in this world."

Happily Ever After—
**Marylyle Rogers' next romance
from St. Martin's Paperbacks!**

It only takes a second filled with the scream of twisting metal and shattering glass—and Chris Copestakes' young life is ending before it really began.

Then, against all odds, Chris wakes up in the hospital and discovers she's been given a second chance. But there's a catch. She's been returned to earth in the body of another woman—Hallie DiBarto, the selfish and beautiful socialite wife of a wealthy California resort-owner.

Suddenly, Chris is thrust into a world of prestige and secrets. As she struggles to hide her identity and make a new life for herself, she learns the terrible truth about Hallie DiBarto. And when she finds herself falling for Jamie DiBarto—a man both husband and stranger—she discovers that miracles really *can* happen.

ON THE WAY TO HEAVEN

TINA WAINSCOTT

ON THE WAY TO HEAVEN
Tina Wainscott
_____ 95417-4 $4.99 U.S./$5.99 CAN.